To LUKE FROM AUNTY LEIGH

PRAISE FOR *SIDEKICKED*

"As riveting a rendition of superdom as even Superman's creator, Jerry Siegel, could have pulled off."
—*NEW YORK TIMES BOOK REVIEW*

"From memorable characters to a complex yet accessible plot, this is a superhero story that any comics fan will enjoy."
—*PUBLISHERS WEEKLY* (STARRED REVIEW)

"The perfect training manual for superheroes everywhere. And that means all of us." —*KIRKUS REVIEWS*

"A seriously thrilling plot with a conclusion that satisfies without resorting to easy answers makes this novel a strong selection for comics kids." —*THE BULLETIN OF THE CENTER FOR CHILDREN'S BOOKS*

"The clever humor, coupled with some thoughtful exploration into the nature of friendship, courage, and heroism, makes this a solid addition to the field of superhero novels." —*SCHOOL LIBRARY JOURNAL*

"*Sidekicked* is a super book! Okay, maybe it can't leap tall buildings in a single bound, but it will make you wish you could turn pages faster than a speeding bullet just to find out what's going to happen next. Whether you see yourself as a hero, a sidekick, or just an OC (ordinary citizen), you'll find a lot to love in this funny, suspenseful book!" —MARGARET PETERSON HADDIX, AUTHOR OF THE SHADOW CHILDREN SERIES

W9-BOB-387

JOHN DAVID ANDERSON

KICKED

WALDEN POND PRESS
An Imprint of HarperCollinsPublishers

Walden Pond Press is an imprint of HarperCollins Publishers.
Walden Pond Press and the skipping stone logo are trademarks and
registered trademarks of Walden Media, LLC.

Sidekicked

www.harpercollinschildrens.com

Library of Congress Cataloging-in-Publication Data
Anderson, John David, 1975–
    Sidekicked / John David Anderson. — First edition.
        pages   cm
    Summary: Thirteen-year-old superhero sidekick-in-training Drew
"The Sensationalist" Bean must overcome his not-so-superpowers and
become the hero everyone needs when a supervillain, The Dealer, returns
to Justicia.
    ISBN 978-0-06-213315-1
    [1. Superheroes—Fiction. 2. Adventure and adventurers—Fiction.
3.   Identity—Fiction. 4.   Self-confidence—Fiction. 5.   Ability—
Fiction. 6. Middle schools—Fiction. 7. Schools—Fiction. 8. Humorous
stories.] I. Title.
PZ7.A53678Sid   2013   2012025495
[Fic]—dc23   CIP
                                                              AC

Typography by Erin Fitzsimmons
15 16 17 18   OPM   10 9 8 7 6 5 4 3
❖
First paperback edition, 2014

To my parents, Wes and Shiela Anderson,
who never leave me hanging

Captain Marvelous sighed.

The Nullifier loomed over him, arms crisscrossed in a pretzel of triumph. The supervillain held the detonator in one hand, his thumb hovering over the oversized red button. His black armor leeched the light from the streetlamps, and his mask hid his undoubtedly twisted grin. All around echoed the heavy percussion of gunfire as the minions of the Void confronted the Legion of Justice in a battle that had raged for hours.

It was pretty much epic.

Battles like this only came around once every decade or so. Most of a Super's time was spent stopping bank robberies, starring in commercials, and changing the spark plugs on the fill-in-the-blank-mobile. Seldom were a Super's powers truly tested.

Then again, seldom did a villain like the Nullifier get his hands on enough explosives to take out the entire city. In the comics, this would have been a five-part special.

And for a while it looked like a happy ending. The Legion of Justice had managed to locate and disarm four of the Nullifier's bombs and crush twelve dozen Zilchbots, all before evening rush hour. But their heroics were ultimately for naught. Kid Caliber and the Diamond Dame were trapped in the Nulzone, Mr. Malleable was stretched to the limit nearly two miles away, and the Mantis had fallen prey to a posse of armored mechanical minions.

And Captain Marvelous, the leader of the Legion of Justice for nearly two decades, the cover boy for superhero fanzines everywhere, had been beaten for the first time in his thirty-year career. There were still six bombs planted around the city, and the Nullifier was simply one drawn-out speech away from ending it all.

Captain Marvelous lay helpless on the cold pavement, his own superpowers sapped by the Nullifier's coup de grâce—the marvelantium-infused laser that had leveled the Legion's leader with one blast. Marvelantium was the Captain's only known weakness; there was nothing the Captain could do but squirm. The big yellow M on his chest was obscured by the explosive charge the Nullifier had strapped there, and his arms and legs were bound with simple duct tape—more than enough to hold him in his weakened state. With his ruby-red cape wrapped half around him like a shroud, the Captain could only watch as his nemesis quivered with glee.

"You wewe foowish to think you could beat me."

The Nullifier's words were muffled through his mask, but the Captain had heard enough of these final speeches to get the gist. The villain would lead with a taunt or insult. Next would come a series of revelations designed to induce feelings of shock and chagrin in the Super, followed by some grandiose claim to power, something along the lines of "Soon I will take over the world!" Or Manhattan. Or the top bunk. Depending on the rank of the criminal.

Most of the time Captain Marvelous took these speeches as opportunities to gather his strength for his final heroic maneuver—a pile driver or a simple bone-crunching punch. This time, however, he really *had* been foolish and nearsighted. He couldn't beat the Nullifier—not without his powers. He couldn't even wiggle around enough in the tape to scratch his butt. Which meant that, for the first time in decades as a Super, he would have to listen to this stupid speech from beginning to end.

And then, apparently, he would blow up.

The Nullifier cackled. "It was *I* who intercepted the armored convoy and stole the top-secret sample of marvelantium. *I* who sent you that text message that you thought was from that redhead at the bookstore, which led you to your doom, *I* who crippled your precious Legion. And soon I will rule the *galaxy*!"

The Nullifier cocked his head to the side, perhaps rethinking his ambition. But it felt right. He had bombs. He had laser-toting robots. Things were on fire. So for emphasis he added, "I will be the greatest supervillain the world has ever known!" Then he laughed again, because, as near as the Captain could tell, insane supervillains always laughed at nothing funny at all.

Captain Marvelous grunted. Even *that* took effort with the weight of the explosives on his chest. He knew he had to say something. If he could just keep the Nullifier talking, he might stall the city's destruction, though what he would do with the bought time was beyond him.

"You'll never succeed, Nullifier!" Captain Marvelous said through clenched teeth.

"Really?" The archvillain held up the detonator and wiggled it. "Which one of us has ten pounds of C-4 strapped to his chest, hmm?"

The Captain looked at the gray stuff settled above his rib cage, like a mound of Play-Doh with all the colors mixed together. There were a few wires and a little red light and a little green light. The little green light was on. Even if he still had his super strength, he wasn't sure he could withstand the force of the explosion.

The Nullifier took five steps back. His titanium armor would protect him from the force of the blast, of course, but there was no point getting bits of Marvelous all over it.

"O Captain, my Captain, I'm afraid your days are done."

Captain Marvelous clenched every muscle he had. He hated

poetry. Almost as much as he hated exploding. The leader of the Legion of Justice closed his eyes.

The Nullifier pressed the big red button.

At least he would have, if the detonator had still been in his hand.

Instead, the supervillain turned to see another man looming over him, five fingers wrapped around the detonator, the other five wrapped into a fist. The stranger was at least a foot taller than the Nullifier. He wore torn blue jeans and a tight black T-shirt underneath a leather jacket that barely seemed to contain him. He had no weapons, no capes, no armor. There were no letters, emblems, or sponsors on his chest. His only distinguishing feature was the sunglasses he wore, despite the fact that the sun had long ago set on the presumably doomed city.

The Nullifier shrugged his shoulders and reached out with one armor-clad fist to take back his remote, but the stranger slammed his fist into the villain's metal mask. A normal human would have broken every finger and not even made a dent, but this stranger's punch crumpled the helmet like aluminum foil, crunching the Nullifier's nose and causing the villain to spin halfway around before collapsing to his knees.

The Nullifier was out cold.

The mysterious new Super crushed the detonator in one hand the way someone much less extraordinary would crumble crackers over a bowl of chili. Then he bent over Captain Marvelous and tore the bomb from his chest, lifting the surprised Super to his feet.

"Who *are* you?" the Captain asked, brushing himself off.

It was a question the Captain himself had answered at least a few dozen times before. But he had never asked it.

The stranger looked up heroically into the sky.

"You can call me . . . the Titan."

Four hours later, in a hospital room nearly seven hundred miles away, an infant coughed the last bit of fluid out of his lungs. The whole world assaulted him. The heartbeats of humans and machines, the smell of plastic and antiseptic and bodily fluids, the cool rush of air and the instant heat of the lamp, the intricately engraved tips of fingers poking and prodding him. If he could open his eyes and focus, he would see every pore in his mother's skin as she held him against her and the crystalline reflection of his own red and wrinkled face in the single tear that lingered near her eye.

On that day a hero was born.

PART ONE

IN WHICH I
ALMOST DIE

JUST HANGING AROUND

It's Tuesday.

It's Tuesday and I'm in costume, but just barely. That is to say that I have my mask and outfit on, so nobody knows who I am. Or almost nobody, at least. Which pretty much sums up my life as a whole.

It's Tuesday, which means it was sloppy joe day in the cafeteria, which is bad enough, but that's not the worst thing that can happen to you.

It's Tuesday—middle of September, only about a month into the new school year—and I'm hovering over the Justicia community pool, which only two weeks ago was still filled with a dozen drowning bugs and the farewell tinkle from the last toddler to be dragged screaming out of it.

Today it is filled with acid.

Seriously. Acid.

There are only so many things you can fill a swimming pool with that will kill someone and make a dramatic spectacle in the process. I don't see any alligators or piranhas. Sharks are good, but you have to have saltwater. Spikes work if they are positioned properly and a suitable force is applied. But ask any supervillain, and they will tell you that acid will always do in a pinch. Besides, I can identify over three hundred chemicals by smell alone.

Note that this is far from a typical Tuesday for me. Most days I'd be at home, zombied out in front of my computer or asleep on top of my math book, my cheek in a puddle of drool, $x + y$ marks the spot. Of course, I also understand acid-filled swimming pools are potential job hazards, but that doesn't make me any happier about it.

So today is Tuesday and I'm suspended by my wrists above a pool of acid, feet dangling below me in my gray, faded Pumas, my bandanna hiding my identity from the nose up but doing nothing to conceal my frown. The number of yards I am away from death can be counted on one hand.

And all I can seem to think about is how much homework I've got. Act One of *Julius Caesar* to finish for tomorrow and a big math test on Thursday. Not to mention I have an outline due to Mr. Broadside on the military tactics of Hannibal in the Second Punic War as part of a history presentation I have to give, and all I know about *that* guy is he rode an elephant through the Alps. I guess for some people a horse just isn't good enough.

10

My only consolation is that I'm not alone. Jenna is dangling beside me, long legs stretching well below mine, her silver spandex uniform clinging to her like aluminum foil, both of us suspended, just waiting to be rescued. She's not Jenna right now, of course; she's the Silver Lynx, sidekick to one of the most powerful Supers in Justicia, maybe even the world. But to me she will always be Jenna.

"I don't think gym teachers should be *allowed* to be health teachers unless they have a gnat fart's inkling of what they are *talking* about."

That's Jenna. She is one of those girls who talk just as much with her hands as her mouth, which means between the three of them you don't get a word in. But she's a little restricted by the thick steel cuffs around her wrists, so right now she is just wiggling her fingers. Vigorously.

"I mean, the man doesn't know the difference between a femur and a tumor. He thinks iPods cause cancer and he still calls Coke soda pop."

Jenna's long blond hair is a little matted, and there's a dark red spot below her ribs where she was stung resisting capture, but otherwise she seems nonchalant. As if dangling above a pool full of acid is just part of her after-school regimen—right in between gymnastics and dinner with the fam, though she seldom eats dinner with her parents. They work two jobs apiece and are usually not around, and even when they are, they aren't. I try to mimic her coolness, but she knows I'm faking it.

Besides, I have more to be concerned about than she does. After all, *her* Super is probably only a few blocks away. Somersaulting over taxicabs or leaping from rooftop to rooftop. Mine probably doesn't even know I'm here. It's because of this, I suspect, that she is trying to distract me with her rant about our new health teacher.

"It's middle school health. It isn't rocket science," she says.

Jenna would know. She knows a few things about rocket science.

My fingers are falling asleep. The handcuffs are tight, and the way the steel cable is wound around them makes them bite into my skin even deeper, cutting off circulation. I'm a little dizzy. I take a look at the winch and hoist we are connected to, and then at the motor that is lowering us at the rate of about an inch every three seconds: a slow and deliberate pace designed to cause maximum suspense, I suppose. If I try really hard, I can actually hear the metallic click of the individual gears meshing together, but I am blocking most of this out. It is simply too excruciating.

That's my approach to most of life most of the time: to ignore it. I have to in order to stay sane. Until something like this happens, and I realize what I've gotten myself into.

I take a look at the pool of acid below me. Hydrochloric, I think. I've got pretty good senses—some of the best in the world, in fact. That's what got me into this in the first place, that led me to Mr. Masters. To H.E.R.O., training to be a sidekick. To become the Sensationalist.

12

And to dangling here.

I happen to be pretty good at chemistry, so I know that hydrochloric acid isn't the absolute worst thing you could be dipped into to death. After all, our stomachs are full of it, and in a diluted form, it was probably used to keep this same pool clean. But there's a difference between an ounce of hydrochloric acid and a swimming pool of it. Plus the murky stuff below me is bubbling and seeping a noxious green fog. All signs that the acid is probably mixed with something else, something even more horrifying. I drop another inch and conclude that supervillains have *way* too much time on their hands.

"I mean, why do I have to listen to him when I can just read the stupid book myself? You *know* I don't have time for all of this."

Whether Jenna is talking about health class or dangling here, waiting to be rescued, I'm not sure. She's in all advanced classes, not to mention gymnastics *and* track, and then there's this *other* thing that we're both a part of. How she manages to balance it all without completely freaking out is beyond me.

I can hear grunts and pops about three blocks away, and something like an *urrf*, which means *somebody* is on the way. Below me and to the right, there is a line of police cars keeping their distance, their uniformed contents spread out behind them like ants circling dropped candy. Their revolvers are drawn, but they won't fire. They're just here as backdrop. The fire department is here too, as are the EMTs, but there isn't much they can do either. They know the rules. This is clearly beyond their scope, and these guys are out of their league. They're basically here for crowd control. Besides, have you ever seen an EMT jump into a pool of acid to rescue two costumed teenagers? Do you even *know* what those guys get paid?

Then there are the bad guys. I guess I haven't mentioned them yet. After all, somebody had to capture us and secure us to this cable. A whole hive of somebodies, in fact. Scattered here and there across the gray sky, men in fuzzy yellow-and-black suits with mechanical vibrating wings. Seriously. Mechanical wings. And harpoon guns. They actually have harpoon guns. Like the kind from the movie *Jaws*. I wonder how they even managed to find that many harpoon guns in a town that is at least five hundred miles from the ocean. Jenna says they probably got them from Walmart.

They are the drones, those fuzzy, flying guys circling around us. The ones who ambushed us, who brought us here and chained us up. Though, as the name suggests, even they are only acting on orders. They aren't shooting at the cops, and the cops aren't shooting at them. Everyone knows his place.

The OCs—that's ordinary citizens, for those of you who happen to be one—look appropriately doe-eyed, with hands clasped over their doughnut-shaped mouths, waiting. You'd think they would be running. Ducking for cover. Crawling under cars. And many have. But the ones I'm looking at now are the believers. The devotees. The sky watchers. The ones who still possess an all-abiding faith in their heroes to show up and save the day.

Of course they aren't the ones on the hook.

I hear explosions from somewhere behind me, but I can't make out too much over the thumping of my own heartbeat. I try not to think about the words *acid*, *dissolve*, *flesh-eating,* or *sloppy joe.* We lower another inch. My feet are less than five yards away from doom now. I can hear buzzing all around me. I look down.

I can't believe I left my utility belt at school. Again. Not that I could reach anything on it. It's just a comfort thing. Like forgetting your watch or not putting on underwear. Without my utility belt, I am basically harmless. With it, I am at least somewhat potentially threatening.

I twist around. Still no sign of him.

Jenna is still talking, still not the least bit concerned, it seems. She has moved off health class and is now complaining about the cost of shoes. Jenna's always short on cash. Most of the time I spring for the french fries after school. I feel for her, but now doesn't seem to be the best time to worry about new shoes when the ones we are wearing are about to be liquefied with our feet still in them.

I crane my neck and scan the clouds for some glimpse of the man responsible for our impending demise, the one controlling the drones, the demented scientist with his own pair of mechanical wings and a shoulder-mounted rocket launcher who orchestrated our capture. He calls himself the Killer Bee. No joke. I have no idea what his deal is—though anyone who dresses up like a bumblebee and carries around a missile launcher is obviously several eggs short of a carton. Mr. Masters says that more often than not, today's supervillain is just some kid who was beat up too many times in middle school and decides the best form of therapy is world annihilation—and the freak in the bee suit seems to fit the bill.

Of course here *I* am, in my second year of middle school, nearly straight As, still wearing tighty-whities, incrementally descending to my death. I'm thirteen, I have a zit on my left eyebrow that hurts every time I blink, I've been beaten up four times (not in costume), and I haven't kissed a girl yet. Unless you count Suzie Walsh, which I don't, because it was three years ago, the bottle clearly got kicked, and the whole thing lasted, maybe, a nanosecond. Still, it does make you wonder how I'm going to turn out.

The Killer Bee is nowhere to be found, no doubt waiting to pick on someone his own size. Three drones buzz past us, harpoons in hand, and I'm guessing I won't be around to watch anyways.

Then, in the distance, I see her—long before anyone else can. Energy beams dancing in her eyes, samurai sword in hand, her wavy red perm holding up remarkably well in the humidity. Her white body suit looks glued to her. She runs toward us, nimbly hurdling the obstacle course of parked cars clogging the street, launching herself at the first wing of drones that spots her.

My jaw drops just watching her. The Fox. By far the hottest, coolest Super to grace the cover of the *Justicia Daily Trumpet*—which is saying something when you think about how Venus looked back in the glory days. But the Fox ups the cool factor by hundreds. Only a year into her career and already considered the best there is at what she does. The kind of Super eight-year-old girls dream of being and twelve-year old boys just dream of.

Our hero.

Or at least Jenna's hero. I'm not her sidekick, so I'm not *technically* her responsibility, though I am keeping my fingers crossed. Or I would if I could feel them anymore.

The Fox dispatches the first wave of drones without even breaking stride. Slices her way through the onslaught as a half dozen more swoop down from the clouds. I can hear the split of the wind with each swing of her sword. I can see the aura of energy radiating from her pores. Watching her in action, I kind of forget that I am only a few feet from a really unpleasant death. Then the crank turns and I drop another inch and it all comes rushing back to me.

Eleven feet and counting. I look around frantically.

As if reading my mind, Jenna says, "Don't worry. He'll show."

And I just give her a dirty look. For all of her talents—extraordinary athleticism, super strength, lightning-fast reflexes, gorgeous green eyes—Jenna's not a great liar. We both know the odds aren't really in my favor. But even after all of this, even with everything I've been through in the past year, I have to give him the benefit of the doubt. Have to trust that he knows what he's doing. It's part of the Code.

"He's got two more feet," I tell Jenna, who flashes a glance that is somehow sympathetic *and* condescending, as if to say, "Okay, and then what?"

I don't know and then what. I haven't figured out *how* I would save myself. Unlike Jenna, I don't have extraordinary physical abilities. Unlike my friend Nikki, I can't just phase through solid objects. I can't shoot lightning or breathe fire. I'm not even double-jointed. In fact, at this point, I would trade my powers for those of just about anyone I know.

"Just hang in there," Jenna says. I really think she is trying to be funny.

The Fox is battling right outside the pool's entrance now, moving quickly. The crowd gathered behind the yellow caution tape is cheering like it's the Super Bowl. Sometimes I wonder if they even care who wins, so long as they get a show. The last four drones surround the Fox, thrusting their harpoons. I figure she'll just pound her fist into the ground and create a shock wave to bowl them over. Or maybe she will spin around super fast, creating a whirlwind that will knock them back on their fuzzy little butts. But instead she just does this thing with her eyes, where they roll back in her head and little bolts of red energy start arcing back and forth between them. It's really pretty intense, and it's just the kind of thing Supers do when they want you to know that they are totally cranked off. I've seen that same look on my mother's face, even though she's not a Super, and I know what it means.

The drones are smarter than their name suggests, and they take the Fox's electric eyeball arcing act as their cue to retreat, flying up, up, and away.

While I keep going down. Eight feet.

He's not going to show.

Even now. It's one thing not to make it to training. Or to neglect to take me out on the weekends. But now? Here? When I'm really in danger?

The Fox looks up at the two of us dangling like minnows, and I know what she is thinking. She is thinking that it's a trap. That the moment she tries to save us, the Killer Bee will come out of nowhere and blindside her. And she's probably right. Otherwise, what's the point in even capturing us?

But I really don't care. Because, frankly, I just want her to rescue me so that I can go home, put bags of frozen peas on my wrists, and forget that this day even happened.

Seven feet. I think the crank is going faster. Jenna looks at me expectantly. I look back at my toes. I happen to like my toes. I really don't want to see them dissolved.

And then my ears are suddenly filled with a high-pitched buzzing, much stronger than that of the drones, and I know that the villain is above us. I crane my neck to see him, the Killer Bee, hurtling our way, his multifaceted goggles reflecting a hundred versions of my own freaked-out face, his rocket launcher perched on his shoulder. Before I even have time to take a breath, he fires a stinger missile at the only Super who bothered to show up today.

I see Jenna twist around sharply in her cuffs and start swinging. The Fox leaps, sword in hand, those little electric bolts still crackling around her eyes. Thanks to Jenna's motions, now *I'm* rocking back and forth. My stomach lurches. I can smell the smoke of the missile as it zips by me, and I suddenly see the next second of my life play out before me before it even happens, just in time to do absolutely nothing about it.

Jenna gives one last giant swing of her legs. I see a blur of white, the glinty gleam of a razor-sharp sword coming toward me. I hear a snap. The cable breaks, and I am plummeting to certain death.

Except I'm not really *plummeting.* I'm actually kind of *somersaulting,* with Jenna's arms and legs wrapped around me like a papoose, clearing the edge of the pool . . . in fact, clearing the entire fence around the pool, and landing in the grass by the parking lot.

I hit and skid. The grass is soft, at least, though I can't say the same for the dirt underneath it. I watch the world spin for a moment. If this were a Sunday morning comic, there would be bluebirds circling my head. Jenna untangles her limbs from mine and immediately springs to her feet, combat ready, but it takes me a moment to clear my senses, acute as they are, and realize what has happened. The smoke in the sky tells me the missile missed its mark, harmlessly exploding in the air above us.

And standing on top of the crane, a hundred feet up, the Fox has the Killer Bee by his antennae, both of his mechanical wings severed by two more swift strikes of her sword. I see her whisper something to him, but even with my powers I can't make it out in all the commotion. All around us, the crowd is hooting and hollering. Chanting her name. *"Fox. Fox. Fox. Fox."* As if she's the only one who matters.

And here I am, still flat on my back, staring up at the sky, still handcuffed and a little bruised, but unmistakably alive. Having been saved by the wrong hero.

Andrew Macon Bean.

The Sensationalist.

A sidekick without a Super.

SPLIT PERSONALITY

I am home less than an hour later. All part of the act.

Though I am irritated, and exhausted from my afternoon at the pool, I haven't sustained any real bodily harm save for a few bruises and the bright red circles around my wrists. Besides, it's more important that I be home at a decent hour so that I can put on a good face for my parents. The longer you have to be somebody else, the harder it is to convince everyone you are you.

My house is the last one on the block—the one with the peeling brown trim, the stunted evergreens, and the seldom-used swing set. It's dinnertime on Stanley Street. I can smell the garlic and basil before I even open the door. I can actually smell it from halfway down the block. That's how I know it's lasagna night at Casa de la Bean. If I concentrate, I can tell you what everyone's having for dinner. The Hungs ordered pizza.

The Randals are grilling out—barbecue chicken and roast vegetables. The Shaumbergs are celebrating something. I can smell the smoke from burned-out candles and the buttercream frosting on the cake. The Powell kid is having strawberry Pop-Tarts for dinner. Again.

Oh, and Mrs. Polanski hasn't scooped the litter box in a while and Li'l Mittens is just finishing some business, so I stop concentrating and hold my nose.

When I walk through the door, my dad's nailed to the TV set, fixated on the story of a wacko in a bee getup who kidnapped and nearly killed two supposed sidekicks and his thrilling defeat by the city's most celebrated star. There's footage of the two sidekicks dangling from the crane. Even with my extraordinary eyesight I can't make out the features of my own face onscreen—there's just too much going on. I watch, breathless, as Jenna swings back and forth, gaining momentum. I see the Fox leap, deflecting the missile with an energy blast from her fingertips and severing the chain that holds me and Jenna with her sword. The camera traces our less-than-graceful fall, and by the time it jerks back up, the Fox has the Bee in her grip. The cameraman didn't catch Jenna and me slinking away or manage to get a good look at our faces.

I watch for a moment from the entryway, easily seeing and hearing the television from three rooms away, careful not to draw attention to myself. The news reporter is gushing about the Fox. "Remarkable," she says over and over again.

23

"Another day saved by Justicia's newest Super."

"And *that's* why we need to move," I hear my dad say. "To a town with fewer freaks."

"You mean the guy dressed up like a bumblebee, or the one shooting lightning from her eyes?" my mother asks from the kitchen.

I close the front door with a little emphasis. My mother turns to greet me with a smile that is meant to only half mask the worry in her eyes. For a moment I think I'm done for, that my cover is broken. That somehow she has seen something, something in the frown of the boy on TV, something in the slump of my shoulders, something that only a mother would notice. My other life would finally be exposed, and I would have to come clean and tell them everything.

How I am sworn to protect ordinary citizens like her from the evils that threaten them.

How I spend three days a week training to fight crime.

How I sometimes mix nitroglycerin in the bathroom sink.

And it isn't an entirely dreadful feeling, this idea of opening up to them, telling them everything. There would be consequences, of course, but we could endure them together, as a family.

But her sad smile is just general maternal transference. *Some*where *some* mother has a teenage son who is dressing up in costumes and being suspended above vats of bubbling acid by men with artificial wings and military-grade weaponry. She's just glad it isn't hers.

"Hi, honey, where have you been?" She kisses me on the cheek.

"I was working on a chemistry project," I say, using the excuse that has been assigned to me this week in case of such an emergency.

"Yeah, Mr. Masters called and said you would be coming home late," my dad says, eyes still suctioned to the television, watching as the Fox waves to the cameras before taking a flying leap over the pool house and disappearing. "You can call us yourself, you know. After all, that's why we pay for that cell phone you insist on having."

"Sorry, Dad," I say, failing to mention that I left the cell phone at school, along with my utility belt—actually *attached* to my belt, right beside my cryogenic grenades and concentrated sleeping gas.

"Did you hear what happened this time?" Mom asks, pointing to the TV that's now showing cops rounding up a half dozen injured drones and piling them into an armored truck.

"Yeah. Crazy stuff," I say, trying to sound impressed. I keep my hands in my jacket even as she hugs me. It may be a little suspicious that I don't hug her back, but it's better than showing off my raw, red wrists.

"I just don't know why anyone would *do* such a thing," she says.

"And where does somebody get that much acid?" my father adds.

I shrug. "Like you said, they're all crazy, every last one of them," I say. "What's for dinner?"

My mother smiles, knowing I already know. I smile back at all the things she still has no clue about.

"We could move to Albuquerque," Dad says. "Surely this kind of nonsense doesn't happen in Albuquerque."

I don't say anything, though I'm pretty sure Albuquerque has its own problems, though it probably doesn't attract the criminal element quite the way Justicia does. Something about this city just draws the bad guys like flies to a Dumpster. Mr. Masters calls it job security.

"I'm just going to go wash up," I say, and slink up the stairs, listening to my father whisper to himself that the Fox is easy to look at, though.

Back in my room, I pull my mask from my backpack and take it to the bathroom to wash it out. There are few things worse than having to put a sweaty, snotty piece of spandex on over your face. I rinse it carefully and set it over the vent beneath my bed to dry; then I peel off my shoes and change into a pair of sweats. I slip on a Highview Middle School sweatshirt to help hide the cuff marks, just in case, and look around the room for my homework.

The place is a disaster—a landfill, my mother would say, though it is mostly by design. Like most thirteen-year-old boys, I have a few things that I don't want my parents to discover—heavy-duty steel cable, highly volatile chemicals, thermal imaging goggles, fuse-head electric blasting caps, that sort of thing—all carefully concealed. I've found that if you keep enough other junk lying around, the sheer effort to clean it all up is too much for any parent, and they don't even bother to touch the stuff you keep in the top of your closet or underneath your bed. There are a few posters on the wall, a couple of junior academic decathlon medals, and a dozen books strewn about. I sift through the piles to find *Julius Caesar* and then promptly drop it into another pile of schoolbooks representing the night's to-do list. Finally I turn on my computer to see if I have any messages. There's just one. From Jenna.

Give me a buzzzzz later.

I try to think of something clever to say back, but I'm not in the mood.

I walk to my parents' bathroom to raid my mother's medicine chest for something to put on my wrists. My only discovery is some lotion that claims to come from rain forests and smells like melons. Scented lotions have a tendency to give me migraines, so I just turn on the cold water and soak. If I concentrate, I can block out the slow burn and focus on the sweet sting of the cold. It has taken me *years* of therapy to learn to control my power this much—to focus my overly keen senses and weed out all the extra input. I close my eyes and listen closely for a moment. I hear the sound of the TV and my dad scratching his armpit. My mother is chopping onions for a salad. Next door, Mrs. Polanski is singing Justin Bieber in the bathtub.

I open my eyes and get a good look at the boy in the mirror, who watches me back, mimicking my squinted expression.

27

Shaggy brown hair, skater style. Dull bluish-gray eyes. Mostly straight teeth. Blackheads checkerboarding my nose. The rumor of stubble on my chin. "You again," I say to myself.

When you're a teenager, everybody is waiting for you to be something or somebody else—your friends, your parents, your teachers. Sometimes you lose track. Are you the shy kid in the back of the room who apologizes for even *accidentally* touching Susan Childress's arm, or the guy making bombs in the backyard? Are you the helpless nerd with the backpack on hoping you don't get the snot beat out of you by the school bully, or the helpless nerd with the mask on, hoping you don't get the snot beat out of you by the town's crazy new super-villain?

Or maybe you're just the helpless nerd staring at the other helpless nerd in the mirror, talking to yourself, wondering which of you needs more help.

The bread is burning, though my mother doesn't know it yet. She calls up that dinner's ready, which is my cue to put my mask back on and pretend to be the kid who stayed after school to finish his science project. The honor-roll kid who the bumper sticker on their Corolla brags about. The kid they don't have to worry about.

Not the one who needs saving.

I head downstairs to eat.

HOW I GOT OUT OF
GYM CLASS

Jenna was right. Mr. Booner really is a terrible health teacher. He doesn't know the names of any of the parts of the brain, instead simply calling them "the front part," "the left part," and "the right part," and "that bumpy thing in back." He insists that the bigger your forehead, the smarter you are. He uses Shakespeare and Ben Franklin as evidence. That his own hair has receded probably factors into his argument.

Apparently he is a cool gym teacher, though, pretty much letting the fat kids sit in the corner during dodgeball and counting every pull-up you do double if your arms are like Twizzlers, which mine are.

I wouldn't know, of course, because I never go to gym. That would be fourth period on Mondays, Wednesdays, and Fridays, which happens to conflict with my participation in our school's *highly* selective environmental club, otherwise known as the Highview Environmental Revitalization Organization.

Our job is to keep the trash off the streets.

I'm not kidding. That's what our T-shirts say: H.E.R.O. WE KEEP THE TRASH OFF THE STREETS. There is a picture of a teenager dressed in a cape and tights, slam-dunking a crushed tin can into a recycling bin. Our club's faculty sponsor designed them. I guess the thought was that nobody would put two and two together because it was simply *too* obvious. Sometimes it's the thing that's right in front of you that you keep looking over.

There are only six of us in the program, the only one of its kind in Justicia, maybe the only one of its kind in the world; at least the only one *I* know about. It's basically a training program for would-be sidekicks, who then become would-be Supers. Kids with powers who hope to use them someday to fight the forces of evil, save damsels, help the meek inherit the earth, that sort of thing. Saving the environment is just a cover, though we do spend a few days each year planting trees and planning recycling drives to keep up appearances. Nobody ever questions the time we spend together—you can't say that cleaning up the environment is a waste. Besides, our program director can be very convincing when he wants to be.

His name is Mr. Masters, and in addition to being the head of H.E.R.O., he is also the eighth-grade science teacher. A tall, clean-shaven, square-headed man who looks a little like a bald Lurch from *The Addams Family*, he has a forehead that would make Mr. Booner proud. Mr. Masters always wears horn-rimmed glasses and patterned sweater vests over long-sleeved solid-color shirts, and he keeps a tarnished old rail conductor's watch on a chain tucked into his right pocket.

Like the rest of us in H.E.R.O., Mr. Masters isn't exactly *normal*. That watch is the thing. *His* thing. The key to his power. No one besides him is ever allowed to touch that watch, and most people who are around when Mr. Masters checks to see what time it is find themselves feeling a little lost, wondering what they have been doing for the past minute or so. Sometimes it can even make you forget what you were thinking or doing long before that. *That's* the kind of watch it is. The time-stopping, memory-befuddling kind.

Both his father and his father's father used that watch to various ends, not all of them noble. His great-grandfather, Michael Masters, first found the watch during a hunting expedition in Kenya. It saved him from being gored by a rhinoceros—at least, that's the story. His grandfather, Roger Masters, used it when fighting the Nazis, often catching unsuspecting German soldiers off guard, leaving them wondering where their rifle had gone and why there was a grenade in their lap.

Mr. Masters's father, on the other hand, used it to steal—wallets, cars, artwork, you name it. He was one of the few men to be kicked out of every casino in Las Vegas. He would have left his son a stolen fortune had he not squandered it all.

Instead, he left him a watch that can stop time, though only

31

for a minute before having to reset.

That watch represents the extent of Mr. Masters's powers. No weapons. No laser vision. Not even a costume, really. The sweater vests are just a fashion statement. Still, he is highly connected in the superhero network, a former agent in the Department of Homeland Security's Supernormal Activities Department. H.E.R.O. is his baby. He built it from the ground up, recruiting each and every member, gathering us like lost sheep, helping us to hone our powers, giving us a sense of purpose.

And clucking after us like a big, balding mother hen.

The H.E.R.O. program meets three days a week for two periods—not counting special training sessions on some weekends—which for me means skipping gym and lunch. Missing gym is always a bonus, but skipping lunch is hit-or-miss. Today is Wednesday. It's a quesadilla day. So I'm pretty noncommittal.

I walk beside Jenna Jaden as we make our way to the teachers' lounge on the first floor. Her honey-blond hair is pulled back in its characteristic nerdy ponytail. You can't see the bandage on her side because of the baggy sweatshirt she wears. She has her glasses on, of course, with thick black rims and lenses that might help you discover planets. It is all part of her look. Jenna's look. Without the glasses, you wouldn't know who you were talking to. Or who was smashing you in the face.

I always wished I could do that. Just whip off a pair of glasses and instantly be in character. Instead I have to keep my mask in my backpack and run around looking like Zorro's pathetic second cousin with blue spandex on my head and a belt full of homemade gadgets wrapped around my waist. All to compensate for the fact that my powers are not "combat compliant," which is a fancy way of saying I'm next to worthless when it comes to fighting bad guys. Though Mr. Masters says there is more to being a hero than punching people.

"So did your parents say anything about yesterday?" Jenna whispers.

"No. Masters called before I got home."

"Yeah. Me too. Though he just left a message."

Jenna's parents take almost no interest in her life. I suppose it helps her keep her cover, but the way she talks about them, I sometimes wonder if she'd rather it be the other way. I look around to make sure none of the other kids in the hallway is taking an interest in our conversation either. Not that they would. We aren't exactly at the top of the popularity pyramid, though I sometimes wonder about the value of that, too.

"Are you okay?" I motion to her side where the harpoon got her.

Jenna shrugs. "It hurts a little. You?"

I know exactly what she's referring to. She told she me she was sorry yesterday as we made our escape. She really thought he'd show this time. "I'm fine," I say. I know she knows I'm lying, but I know she knows I don't want to talk about it right now.

We meet Eric and Gavin right outside the teachers' lounge. Mike won't be here today. He is still in the hospital, recovering from his "skateboarding" accident. With Mike out, that means we are only missing Nikki. She'll probably show up late, like always.

I wave to Eric, who makes the sign for *bee*, and then spells out the word *awesome*. I roll my finger around in a circle, the universal sign for *whoop dee freakin' do*. Eric Ito has been deaf since birth, but it doesn't stop him from totally kicking butt as a sidekick. There are some days when I think his sense of sight is better than mine, and he's an expert in, like, six hundred forms of martial arts, including one he calls the Dance of the Striking Viper, where his hands move so fast even I can't see them until he pinches my nose. Once at lunch he caught a fly between his fingers, Mr. Miagi style. I found one in my cheese dip last week, but it was already dead.

I try to make up a sign showing a person dangling from a rope and then plummeting to his death, using my first two fingers as little legs kicking. Then I strangle myself. Eric laughs and flashes a sign that I think means something like *moron* or *doofus*. Or maybe that's just how I feel about having to be rescued by someone else's Super.

"Hey," Gavin says, giving Jenna a smile that is irritating in ways I can't really describe. "I heard you got stung yesterday?"

"We really shouldn't talk about it here," Jenna says, though she returns Gavin's smile easily enough. He looks at me with that one cocked eyebrow of his, and I just glare back at him.

It's this little game we play where we pretend not to like each other to hide the fact that we *really* don't like each other.

Gavin McAllister is my antithesis. I think that's the best way to describe our relationship, at least if I'm keeping it PG. He came here from Chicago at the start of the school year, at Mr. Masters's request. I guess he thought we could use a little more muscle in our group. Or less brains.

Gavin's taller than me—by quite a few inches—and better looking, I guess, if you believe in that whole blond hair, creamy complexion, straight white teeth thing. He looks like the kind of person who plays six sports and kicks puppies, though I think he really only plays two and I'm making the puppy thing up. He does lick his lips a lot, which I guess means something—maybe they taste better than other people's lips or something, I don't know. It's still annoying.

Oh, then there's the fact that he can secrete a substance from his pores that causes his skin to turn to granite, making him nearly invulnerable. At first I thought it was a pretty stupid power, but the truth of the matter is that it is way better than mine and I am just insanely jealous.

"They got a great shot of the Fox on the news last night. It was wicked cool how she managed to break your . . . I mean, break *those* chains, blast that missile, and cut off that dude's wings, all in, like, one move."

"Yeah. She's pretty good," I say, trying to remember the last time I had heard anyone say "wicked cool" and *not* get beat up for it. But Gavin is on the football team, which means he has bully immunity, even without the turning-his-skin-to-stone thing.

"She certainly saved your butt," Gavin says. "By the time Hotshot got there, there was nothing left to do."

Hotshot is Gavin's mentor and one of Justicia's regulars. He's a flamer—one of those guys who shoot fire from whatever body part is most convenient. A common sight on the vigilante scene, he was considered by many to be Justicia's most powerful Super until the Fox came to town. He still looks cool shooting through the sky, though, and thinking about him and Gavin working out on the weekends just makes me even more irritable.

I start to say something not nice about *Gavin's* butt and how it probably bears an uncanny resemblance to his face when I catch a look from Eric telling us to shut up as Mr. Masters appears behind us, watch already in hand.

"Talking about the latest vampire movie, I hope?" The stripes on today's vest zigzag and hurt your eyes if you stare at them too long. We all look down at our feet. We aren't supposed to talk H.E.R.O. business in the halls.

"It's time," he says, his eyebrows arched in disapproval. He puts a hand on Jenna's shoulder, and the rest of us stand close enough together so that at least a part of us is touching the next person. Like a lot of things in the hero business, it only works if you are connected—otherwise we will be frozen just like all the others. I put my shoulder next to Jenna's. Eric's foot is touching mine. I take a deep breath. Gavin reaches out and takes Jenna's hand.

Now they're holding hands.

I can see the little beads of sweat in between his knuckles.

I can smell coffee on his breath.

I can hear her heart speed up ever so slightly when he touches her.

What kind of thirteen-year-old drinks coffee?

He licks his lips again.

I decide I hate coffee.

Mr. Masters clicks the button on his watch once, and everything is suddenly silent and still for everyone but us. I shake my head a little and regain my focus. This is, like, the hundredth time I've had time stopped around me, but it still leaves me a little disoriented.

"One minute," he says.

I glance down the hallway to see the horde of students completely frozen in place. Some girl I don't know is about to get pummeled by a pile of books that are tumbling out of the top of her locker. My instinct tells me I should go stack them back up and save her the embarrassment, but I know what Mr. Masters would say. That it's not a life-or-death situation. That the books were meant to fall and she was meant to pick them up, and him stopping time for a moment doesn't change that. Masters opens the door to the teachers' lounge, and I feel Eric pull me inside.

The lounge is deserted, as it always is at this time of day, all a matter of careful scheduling. Mr. Masters takes one last look at his watch and then tucks it back into his pocket. Even if he wanted to stop time again, he couldn't. It takes the watch three full minutes to reset. It's the law of the universe, he says. Every power comes at a price.

Outside the door, I hear the commotion of Highview Middle School kick back in. The girl with the tumbling books curses as one lands on her foot. Three or four people nearby snicker.

"Does anyone know where Nikki is?"

Mr. Masters looks at me specifically. I concentrate a little bit to see if I can hear her characteristic shuffle run in the hall outside, but there is too much other noise. I shake my head.

"She'll show," he says, and fishes in his other pocket for a couple of quarters while the rest of us stare silently at the school's only snack machine.

We all watch the pork rinds. Salt-and-vinegar flavor. Even the name is revolting. Nobody else ever eats the pork rinds. In fact, most of the teachers have apparently complained to the administration, suggesting that the vending machine space would be better served by some peanut M&Ms, but Mr. Masters insists that he loves them, and he has a way of convincing people to forget what they were complaining about anyway.

So when Mr. Masters drops his sixty cents into the snack machine and presses B-1, it is with every confidence that he is the only person who ever does. The pork rinds drop to the bin, and Mr. Masters pulls them free.

Suddenly the vending machine slides back along the wall, revealing a hole and a steep staircase spiraling downward into a gray hall lined with fluorescent lights. Mr. Masters opens the bag of Pete's Vinegar Spice Pork Rinds and pops one into his mouth. I hold my breath. Even without my super senses, those things would make my stomach turn.

"Let's go," he says. "We have a lot to talk about today."

THE SUPERHERO SIDEKICK
CODE OF CONDUCT

I walk down the familiar stairs into the basement of my school—a place that very few non-Supers even know about. The head of the CIA, probably. The president of the United States. The bigwigs at Homeland Security's S.A.D. It's important to keep our training under wraps, to help protect our identities and the identities of the Supers we serve. Our principal, Mr. Buchanan, is oblivious. As are the rest of Highview's teachers and students. It's all very hush-hush. Even the mayor of Justicia doesn't know there's a training program for sidekicks being run out of the basement of a neighborhood middle school. "Your identity is your most important possession," Mr. Masters is constantly reminding us. Of course we don't own magic watches, so maybe he's right.

Though it has the same cement walls as the rest of the school, the Highview basement looks more like something out of a science-fiction film. Filled with the kind of technology that would make FBI agents drool, with monitors and tracking devices and lasers and satellite imaging equipment, all state of the art, and all for a group of kids barely in their teens. A basement I have been coming to for about a year now. Ever since I promised to uphold the Code.

1. A SIDEKICK MUST ALWAYS USE HIS POWERS IN THE SERVICE OF JUSTICE AND HONOR, TO DEFEND THE GREATER GOOD AND TO HELP THOSE IN NEED.

2. A SIDEKICK MUST NEVER SAY OR DO ANYTHING TO COMPROMISE HIS SUPER'S SECRETS OR HIS OWN.

3. A SIDEKICK MUST NOT ENDANGER THE LIVES OF INNOCENTS AND SHOULD NEVER TAKE A LIFE SO LONG AS THERE IS ANY OTHER RECOURSE.

4. A SIDEKICK IS SWORN TO ACCOMPANY HIS SUPER IN ALL ACTS OF HEROISM, TO PROTECT HIS SUPER WHEN THE OCCASION ARISES, TO WALK THE PATH THAT HIS SUPER SETS FORTH, AND TO TRUST IN HIS SUPER ABOVE ALL ELSE.

The Superhero Sidekick Code of Conduct. That's it hanging on the back wall, engraved in stone and illuminated by a single fluorescent light. The four simple rules we all promised to play by when we joined. Our shalts and shalt nots. Like the Girl Scout motto or the Pledge of Allegiance or the four or five commandments from the Bible that people still pay attention to. The thing has been around for ages. I read the last one again to myself as I enter the room. *Above all else.* Even above a swimming pool full of acid, apparently.

Compared to the Code, the H.E.R.O. program is pretty new. In the past, Supers who were interested in taking on an apprentice usually went out and found one themselves. A traveling circus, an orphanage that mysteriously burns down, a bus full of tweens that takes a wrong turn and plows into a toxic waste dump—all prime opportunities for recruiting a sidekick. But over time, Supers started complaining that sidekicks took too much time to train and ended up being more trouble than they were worth. Like the Sparrow, who accidentally hit "accelerate" rather than "override" on the conveyor his Super was chained to at the meat processing plant, sending Nighthawk to a too-early retirement. Or Velocigirl, who ran away from her first fight so fast that the resulting sonic boom caused Mr. Molecular to lose his balance and fall right into the clutches of Professor Von Callous. In fact, there was a whole string of incidents involving rookie sidekicks who couldn't cut it. Hence the need, Mr. Masters said, for apprenticeship programs to help us learn to control our powers and acquire a few of the more rudimentary skills—basic tumbling, self-defense, mind control resistance—so that when we eventually did pair up with our Supers, we wouldn't *always* lead them into traps.

I'm not quite there yet. Jenna is. Maybe Eric. Gavin, I guess, except he's only been working with his Super for a month or so. The truth is, we aren't ready for the front lines. Unlike our mentors, we aren't supposed to be chasing down the bad guys. Our job is to learn: to master our powers, to follow orders, to work as a team.

And to keep a secret.

Someday, Mr. Masters says, the time will come when each of us will stand back-to-back with his or her Super, twin beacons of light in the darkness, providing the great fuzzy comforter of justice that the ordinary citizens of the world snuggle up with at night. We will fight side by side against the forces of evil, until, one day, we decide to strike out on our own and become Supers ourselves.

This is me not holding my breath.

"Come on, people," Mr. Masters chides. "The world isn't going to save itself."

I find a seat in front of the giant screen on the far wall, and Jenna settles next to me. H.E.R.O headquarters takes up the entire school basement. In addition to the central hall, where we go to get lectures, there is a large room that runs team combat training simulations and a laboratory for the kinds of science experiments that would give Mrs. Williams, the seventh-grade science teacher, a heart attack. We also each have our own specially engineered rooms that are designed to test our unique abilities. Most of them are filled with practice explosives, lasers, and weapon-toting robots, all meant to simulate the dangers faced by Supers and their sidekicks in the real world. Eric's room, for instance, looks like a mini dojo, even down to the Japanese scrolls on the wall. Jenna's has a holographic projector that can generate a posse of gun-wielding hoodlums for her to disarm.

My room has perfume. And eye charts. And dog whistles. See some evil, hear some evil, smell some evil: that's my motto. Last week I read the fine print on a credit card application from forty feet away. I identified the sound of a feather landing on a pillow. I smelled one part lemon juice in five hundred parts water. Sharks around the world, eat your hearts out.

Thankfully, H.E.R.O. training isn't all about mastering our powers, or I would be totally bored. Every other Monday we have a half hour of forensics—fingerprinting, bullet caliber identification, CSI stuff—and a half hour of martial arts, led by Eric, whose sidekick name is Shizuka Shi, or Silent Death. A little dramatic for someone who refuses to squash spiders, but it sure sounds cool in Japanese. Wednesdays usually offer at least a half hour of lock picking, bomb defusing, police procedure, or something else fun. Friday is usually pizza day. All in all, it is pretty cool, even if I have to spend ten minutes each session just sitting around smelling stuff.

On days after an "event," however, being a member of H.E.R.O. isn't much fun at all. It doesn't happen often—hardly at all, really—that a supervillain puts one of us in genuine danger. But when it does, Mr. Masters's face is fixed frown-ways as he ushers us down the stairs.

"All right, people," he says sternly. "Let's get started."

Mr. Masters crunches his final pork rind and then fires up the screen. Before he can get going, a light-brown hand appears out of the wall, followed by an arm, a pair of sandals, and a T-shirt that says FAB-U-LUS in glittery white sequins. All of this is connected eventually to the head of Nikki Walters, aka the Wisp, who wears the same nervous expression as always, like a deer about to bolt. Her short black hair is braided into a hundred strands that dance like wind chimes as she shuffles through the wall.

"Sorry, sorry, so sorry." She apologizes to each of us individually, saving a "Really sorry, Mr. Masters" for last.

"It's all right, Nikki. Though in the future, it's probably safer to just use the stairs."

Nikki nods and sits down in the seat in front of me, and I hold my breath, still expecting her to just fall through it, even though I've seen her sit down a hundred times before. I shouldn't worry. She has terrific control of her powers already—mostly because she uses them every Friday to sneak out of the house. If her parents ever caught her with half of her body hanging out of their brick siding, it would probably be the end of her career as a superhero sidekick. But she has a boyfriend—or at least she is in a perpetual state of being somebody's girlfriend—so her priorities are a little out of whack.

My priorities, on the other hand, are chiseled in stone in the back of the room.

"As you all are aware," Mr. Masters says, "and as two of you are *intensely* aware, yesterday saw the capture of yet another

45

villain by the forces of goodness and light." Mr. Masters says *goodness and light* the same way my mom says *cream and sugar* when ordering coffee. Automatically. Like it's a foregone conclusion. He presses a button on the remote in his hand, and an image pops up on the screen behind him. The first slide shows a photo of the Killer Bee, wings clipped, being turned over to the police.

"His name is James Cooper. Though we don't know a great deal about him as yet, we have picked up a few details. Adult male, age thirty-three. Lives in the basement of his mother's house. Can anyone guess what he did for a living . . . that is, before he became a missile-toting, sidekick-capturing maniac?"

"Honey factory?" I venture, a little sarcastically.

Eric spells out *postal worker.* I think he's trying to be funny, too.

"Chemist," Gavin says, looking at me because he knows I'm good at chemistry.

"Entomologist," Jenna guesses.

Mr. Masters smiles and points. "Right. More specifically, an apiologist. Those drones of his were under the influence of some substance manufactured from the chemicals used in bee communications and were not actually acting of their own accord. They are being treated and will be thoroughly interrogated, but as of now, it seems they were innocent, following orders against their will.

"The rest of the facts of the case are these," Mr. Masters

continues. "Sometime around four twenty-five yesterday afternoon, the Killer Bee's drones intercepted Jenna and Andrew on their way home from school, luring them into a trap by fabricating an armed robbery."

I look over at Jenna. This was technically her fault. She was the one who spotted the three drones in the alleyway, armed with harpoon guns, huddled over a fourth figure who was struggling against them. By the time I fumbled my mask out of my pack, she was already in costume, ready for anything. We didn't know it was a ruse—that the struggling figure was just another drone, or that two more of them were hiding behind the Dumpster—though I probably should have heard them breathing. I guess that one's on me. I have a bad habit of listening to Jenna's heartbeat whenever we walk home together, and it kind of washes everything else out. I still think maybe we could have beaten them, but six against one and a half isn't good odds.

Besides, Jenna wasn't worried. She had faith.

Mr. Masters clicks his remote and a second slide pops up, showing Jenna and me helplessly hanging over the pool. Seeing it on the news, it was kind of cool. Now, sitting in front of Mr. Masters, it's just embarrassing.

"The Silver Lynx and the Sensationalist were taken by force and transported to the Justicia community pool, where the perpetrator had assembled an elaborate execution involving a crane and a thousand gallons of hydrochloric acid."

"Told you so," I whisper. Jenna smiles.

"Whether he really intended to kill you," Masters says, looking at Jenna and me specifically, "or was simply *using* you is moot."

I want to object. *Moot* is not a word I would use to describe my death. *Tragic*, perhaps. *Premature*, definitely. Definitely not *moot*. But the look on Mr. Masters's face suggests I should keep my mouth shut. A third slide clicks into place, showing the Fox in all of her blazing, electric, sword-wielding glory, holding her latest prize aloft. "At precisely five thirty-two, the Fox arrived at the scene and quickly dispatched the drones and apprehended the villain. The Sensationalist and the Silver Lynx managed to escape with minor injuries and without being identified, and all the drones were eventually rounded up."

Mr. Masters sighs again. "All in all, it was a successful act of heroism," he says, motioning again to Jenna and me. "Our two members of H.E.R.O. acted with courage and poise, maintaining their secret identities and following the Code at all times." I glance back at the wall behind me. Courage, maybe. I don't remember exhibiting any poise. "That you two were apprehended is understandable, given that you were ambushed and outnumbered."

"Thanks, Mr. Masters," Jenna says a little sarcastically.

He ignores her. "Yet the question remains as to *why* you were targeted in the first place. Could be coincidence. Or it could be that the Killer Bee was already *aware* of your identities and your whereabouts and captured you with the express purpose of setting a trap for the Fox. . . ."

"Or the Titan," Gavin says, falsely earnest. The newest member of our group turns and smiles at me, and I really feel like punching him, except it doesn't seem like a good idea to hit someone who can instantly turn his face into a slab of rock.

Mr. Masters runs his hand over his crown. His frown deepens. "Clearly, Mr. McAllister, one Super was more than capable of dealing with the likes of the Killer Bee. What concerns me more is how he knew where to find you to begin with." Mr. Masters's voice seems to drop an octave. "I would hate to think that any of our identities have been compromised, that maniacs like him have access to that kind of sensitive information. The H.E.R.O. program—in fact, the entire superhero community—depends upon us all working together, trusting one another, no matter the circumstance."

Mr. Masters looks at me when he says this. I mean, he stares right at me. I don't know why. Not sure what I did wrong. I managed to get my mask on. Nobody IDed me. My parents still think I'm their bright and shining star. The other kids at school still think I'm a total dweeb. What has changed? I stare right back, concentrating so hard I can see the capillaries in his eyeballs. I wait for him to blink first before I look away. It's a small victory.

Still, he has a point. If the drones were waiting for us specifically, if it really was a trap, then that can only mean they knew who we were, maybe even knew about H.E.R.O. itself. The list of people with that kind of information is a short one, with Mr. Masters pretty near the top of it.

"I will keep you informed as I learn more," he says. "But the incident only reinforces the need for all of us to be at our best, which is why we will spend the rest of the day working through our individualized training programs."

I groan. I was really looking forward to disarming a bomb or two.

We all stand. Nikki and Gavin start whispering to each other. Jenna takes off her glasses and slides them into her pocket, then pulls the scrunchie out of her hair. I really don't feel like spending the day stuck in my room, smelling test tubes. Somehow it feels like I'm being punished for something I didn't do.

"Come on, people," Mr. Masters bellows, clapping his hands. "One day your Supers will call on you to do some *real* crime fighting, and I don't want them calling *me* to tell me how you nearly got them killed."

He doesn't look at me when he says this part at least.

I head to my own training room, the last one on the left, thinking about *real* crime fighting, thinking that nine hundred gallons of acid seemed pretty real, and the barb of the harpoon Jenna got jabbed with looked pretty real, and the bruises around my wrists felt pretty real. I open the door when Mr. Masters stops me.

"Andrew, can I have a minute?"

I nod. The man can stop time. If I don't give it to him, he'll just take it anyway.

"I understand this can be difficult," he starts, but I put my hand up. I know exactly what he is going to say.

"I know, sir. And I'm sorry about yesterday," I interrupt. "I left my belt in my locker. And I guess I had other things on my mind. I didn't think . . . I mean, you don't expect a bunch of nut jobs in bumblebee suits to hijack you on the way home from school."

Mr. Masters puts a hand on my shoulder. You don't realize how tall some people are until they put their hand on your shoulder and you realize you can probably fit snugly under their armpit. I can smell the vinegar on his breath.

"That's not it," he says, "though I do think leaving a bandolier full of chemical weapons in your locker violates the school's zero tolerance policy. But believe it or not, this isn't even really about you."

The OCs. Somehow I put them in danger. Here comes the speech about the public good. "I know. I should be more careful. People could get hurt," I say, shrugging my shoulders, hoping his hand might slip off, but he just grips it tighter.

"No, really, I mean it. *It isn't about you*," he says carefully, his Lurch-like eyes boring into mine, wrinkles lining up along his sloped and shiny forehead.

Mr. Masters is talking about *him*. About my hero.

He seems to scramble for the right words. "He's going through . . . how best to put this . . . a kind of *identity* thing. But I want you to know that I've asked the other Supers to keep an eye on you."

Like the Fox.

"I don't need a babysitter," I say, with less conviction than I would have liked. That earns me the raised eyebrow again.

"We all need saving every once in a while," he says.

I nod. Hard to argue given yesterday's whole pool/acid/dangling/bumblebee thing

"He'll come around eventually," Mr. Masters adds.

"I know," I say, though I'm sure Mr. Masters can see right through me. If he does, he doesn't call me on it. Believe it or not, there's nothing in either the sidekick or the superhero code about lying. There can't be. Superheroes lie all the time. It's the cost of doing business in our line of work.

Still, there is nothing Mr. Masters can say that will convince me that the man who is supposedly my Super will ever save me from anything. Not anymore.

"Just be patient," Masters says, trying hard to smile and failing miserably. "And work on your listening skills." Then he turns and heads for his office and I duck into my room, thinking that "Be patient" should definitely be part of the Code. Rule number five, I guess. Alongside "Don't panic," "Don't leave your utility belt in your locker," and "Stay away from people dressed up like insects."

But what do I know?

I spend the last hour of H.E.R.O. training in a fog, allegedly practicing my surveillance techniques, listening to snippets of conversations taking place on the floors of the school above me. Normally this is a favorite exercise of mine, as Mr. Masters pretty much gives me permission to eavesdrop on anyone, even the other teachers. "Especially the teachers," he sometimes says. It's how I found out that Debbie Mansfield has a crush on Steven Eldred, which is unfortunate since Steve has a crush on Mark Fizer. It's how I found out that Eli Cummings, our former resident computer nerd, was hacking through the school's internet security system and then charging guys five dollars apiece to sneak into the computer lab during lunch to play Call of Duty.

It's also how I found out that Margaret Sabo thought I was "kinda cute." I couldn't return the compliment, of course—I wasn't supposed to know—but it was nice to hear, even if it was followed by Caitlin Brown's comment of "Seriously? Beanhead? *Seriously?*"

But today I'm not interested in spy work. I just sit there, thinking about yesterday, and Jenna and me dangling on that line, and how there was absolutely nothing I could have done to save myself or her. I wonder what it would take to get him to show. Wonder if he even knew I was in trouble. Or if he cared.

The alarm in my soundproof room rings. In ten minutes, classes will be released for sixth period, and we all have to make it up and out of the teachers' lounge before the classrooms vomit students into the halls.

As I walk out, I see Gavin hand Jenna a towel to wipe her face with. They were both battling laser-blasting androids.

I can smell the heat from the scorch marks on the walls of their training rooms. He wraps the towel around his neck and flexes just so his biceps will bulge through his shirt. I didn't know seventh graders had biceps. I thought we didn't get them until high school, when they were passed out with shaving cream and pamphlets telling us to say no to drugs. I can't help but wonder if I haven't been fooling myself the past year or so. Maybe biceps are a requirement for being a sidekick. If so, I still have a lot of work to do.

Eric stands next to me and follows my gaze.

Box of rocks, he signs. As in, *dumb as a*. As in, don't worry about Gavin McAllister. He's not worth your time.

"Easy for you to say," I say, turning so he can read my lips better. "You know kung fu."

Eric shrugs, conceding the point, then punches me playfully on the shoulder, which actually hurts, though I resist the impulse to rub it because Gavin's looking in my direction. We all head up the stairs.

As I leave, I glance back at Mr. Masters, who is looking after us, hands clasped in front of him as if in prayer. I think about what he said, about bad guys targeting sidekicks to get at their Supers. What if he was right? What if there was someone out there who wanted a shot at the Titan and somehow knew who I was and that he and I were connected?

As soon as I think it, I snort. If anyone out there is thinking about using me to get at *my* Super, they are going to be sorely disappointed.

IT'S NOT A DISEASE

I suppose you'll want to hear about where I come from, and where I got my powers, and what radioactive bug I was bitten by, and all of that junk. You'll want to know that my father was a researcher for a top-secret government program studying the properties of dark matter or that my mother was really an Amazon princess blessed with godlike powers. But the truth is, my father is an accountant—not a fake accountant masquerading as a costumed vigilante, but a real honest-to-god, dull-as-a-dictionary accountant with a closet full of white shirts and a carefully managed pension. My mother is an aide at Brookview Elementary—an aide because she got pregnant with me while in college and never finished her teaching degree. Neither of them has any super-powers, unless you count my father's ability to calculate tips instantly or my mother's uncanny ability to forget I'm not four anymore, sometimes still wiping the corner of my mouth with a napkin damp with her own spit the way she did when I was a toddler.

The truth is, I was born the way I am, without gamma rays, without cosmic intervention, without a flashback episode explaining my secret origins. I was born with a condition—doctors were careful to call it a condition and not a disease—called *hypersensatia,* which basically just allows me to see and smell and hear things better than most people. And when I say most people, I mean better than six *billion* other people. In fact, there are apparently fewer than five hundred people who have this condition, and none of them to the same extent as me. That makes me special, I suppose, though I prefer to think of myself as one of a kind.

My parents know about my condition, of course. There's no way they couldn't. I spent most of the first twelve months of my life screaming my head off and breaking out in rashes. The doctors thought I was allergic to just about everything. Perfume, pollen, lotion, bubble bath, strawberries, sugar, nuts, milk, wheat, laundry detergent, polyester, plastic, dogs barking, you name it. They thought I was photophobic—afraid of bright lights—and ligyrophobic—afraid of loud sounds. As the appointments continued, I was wrongly diagnosed with all kinds of phobias: cheimatophobia (cold), chiraptophobia (touch), chromatophobia (color)—just to name the Cs. Pediatricians turned to specialists, who turned to even more highly specialized specialists, and I spent most of my first three years undergoing one test after another while my parents turned their house into a quarantined safe zone, complete with special air filters, noise-reducing insulation, and allergen-free everything. For the next two years they ate like prisoners of war, eschewing foods with sharp odors, cleaning with unscented dish soaps, muting the television and watching it with closed captioning while I slept.

I made their lives incredibly difficult, until they were referred to a neurologist named Dr. Avian, who finally made the correct diagnosis. He ran a few tests and kept saying the word *extraordinary* a lot. When he was finished, he said that I was an absolutely remarkable human being and that my parents should be very proud.

He was the first doctor to tell them that. He then gave me some specially designed earplugs and a pair of sunglasses that I could wear to dampen the effects of sound and light until I learned to control my senses. He told my parents that my acute senses were actually a blessing, provided I could learn to manage them. That they might even come in handy someday.

And from the age of five, I worked with Dr. Avian to do just that. He taught how to dampen my senses—to shut everything out—and how to concentrate and heighten one sense at the expense of another, so that I could close my eyes and hear the sound of a mosquito's wings or smell an apple orchard from five miles away. When I was ten, Dr. Avian told me that if I concentrated hard enough, if I focused my senses to pinpoint accuracy, I would be able to hear and see things that no one else had ever experienced. But as he said this, I could smell the bit of tuna sandwich that was caught in his teeth from lunch, and I didn't exactly jump at the idea.

I did learn to control the intensity of my senses, though. Touch was not a problem, as my sense of touch is only a little above normal, making me more ticklish than most people and causing me to avoid wool like the plague, but not as intense as the others. Sight, sound, and smell (and by virtue of the latter, taste) were trickier. I learned to block out most of the input, managing to override the overload. At night I would stay awake and count the crickets or listen to the chatter of the chipmunks in the tree trunk of the neighbors' yard. I would wake up to the smell of coffee—which my parents refused to give up drinking—and would try to identify what kind of cereal my dad was eating based on the crunch it made.

And I grew up feeling helpless. Because for all I could see and hear and smell, I could do almost nothing about it. I couldn't hit a baseball to save my life, though I could count the stitches in it as it missed my bat. I never learned how to play the piano, though I could hear my friend Angie Mathers practicing her scales a block away. And the night I woke up to the acrid smell of gas, I was still too late to prevent our neighbors' house on the next street over from burning down. My only consolation was that the Tomlinsons were away for the weekend, so no one was hurt.

Lots of things have happened that I could do nothing about. When I talked to Dr. Avian about this, he told me that every gift has a price. I asked him if I could get my money back. That I wanted it to be *good* for something besides making me feel helpless all the time. He replied that he knew of a way, but that it wouldn't be easy. It would require an intense commitment and the ability to keep a secret, even from my parents.

He asked me if I ever dreamed of being a hero. Not one of those once-in-a-lifetime, baby-drowning-in-a-river, bystander-turned-savior types, but a real hero.

He asked me if I believed in the forces of light, sworn to forever battle the forces of darkness.

He asked me if I was ashamed to wear tights.

I told him yes, yes, and maybe a little, but that I would if I had to.

And that's when he introduced me to Mr. Masters. Mr. Masters, whose shiny skull gleamed like a buffed bowling ball. Mr. Masters, who told me about the vast network of superheroes stretched across the globe, fighting evil wherever it raised its ugly head. Who told me of the need for some of those Supers to have sidekicks, and for those sidekicks to learn as much as possible from their mentors, so that they could one day become Supers themselves.

And Mr. Masters, who ran a program, specially designed to train those sidekicks, that just happened to be in the basement of a local middle school.

I'm not sure how they knew each other—though, later, learning that the good doctor spent his evenings turning himself into a bird and soaring over the city offered some explanation—but Dr. Avian told me I could trust Mr. Masters. That the program would do me good. It would not only help me to control my powers even more but would provide me with a sense of purpose.

I told him to floss more often.

Once I was in the program, Mr. Masters took over my training, though he was a little skeptical at first. After all, most of the kids he had worked with before could shoot heat beams from their eyes or had titanium-reinforced skeletons or human growth hormone XKY that let them triple their size. Mr. Masters had already helped train half a dozen sidekicks and sent them out to serve the forces of "goodness and light." When he met me, Mr. Masters wasn't sure what I was good for. Or who I would be good with.

I spent several months in training before I was even assigned to a mentor. He needed to find just the right Super, he said. Someone who could best complement my own special set of skills.

In other words, a Super who could do most of his own butt kicking and didn't really *need* a sidekick.

What Mr. Masters didn't know—or didn't admit to, at least—was that my mentor, my Super, my *hero*, not only didn't need a sidekick. . . .

He didn't want one, either.

THE LAST HURRAH

No one ever thinks anything strange about a superhero without a sidekick. In fact, most Supers choose to go completely solo or join teams of equals, just like most sidekicks eventually turn out to be Supers. The annals are full of Supers banding together to form legions and leagues, like OCs with their poker nights and book clubs. The Legion of Justice is probably the most famous, of course. And the Eradicators, back in the day. And Los Luchadores. Some heroes timeshare, like Helios and Nocturne, who conveniently split day and evening shifts on account of one is solar powered and the other is half vampire. Others just get married, like Mr. and Mrs. Magnificent—though my good friend and fellow H.E.R.O. member Mike says that well over half of all Superhero marriages end in divorce, so that's probably not the best example.

Still, the vast majority of Supers don't have sidekicks. I guess for them, a sidekick is just a liability. Just someone else to be saved. That's why it's sometimes difficult for Mr. Masters to find mentors. Why Gavin McAllister had to move halfway across the country. Because for every Fox willing to nurse a Lynx to herodom, there's a Super who just can't take it. Who, for some reason or another, can't handle the responsibility.

So it's not unusual to find a Super without a sidekick. A sidekick without a Super, though.

Those are one of a kind, too.

The Titan is "off the grid." That's Mr. Masters speak for "doesn't want to be found." The other Supers don't know where he is. Mr. Masters doesn't know where he is. The forces of darkness and eviltude don't know where he is.

But I do. At least I did. I just hope he's still there. After all, some deranged man in a bee costume went through all the trouble of capturing me and dangling me out to dissolve, maybe with the hope of luring him out of his hole. There's a chance somebody is gunning for him. It seems like something he should know.

Besides, I have a bone to pick. I don't care if Mr. Masters is right and the Titan is going through a little identity thing, there's still a Code. He has one. I have one. It's one thing not to show up to special H.E.R.O. training sessions. To never take me out on weekends the way the Fox does with Jenna. It's another to ignore my signal and leave me hanging. That's just unprofessional. And a little bit rude. Not to mention life threatening. Which is why I took off this afternoon with the hopes of hunting him down again.

The Last Hurrah is open, even though it is only four thirty, and I push my way in, having told my parents that I was staying after school to go bowling. I know what you are thinking, but the Last Hurrah isn't one of those hot spots for the differently powered. It's not a front for a top-secret headquarters that is accessed by an elevator that appears when you pull on the center beer tap. There are no poles you can slide down to get to your secret cave. It's just a beat-up hole-in-the-wall bar tucked away in a grimy strip mall, next to a nail salon and a Laundromat. For all I know, the Titan lives here.

The last time I was here, he made me promise not to tell anyone else where he was, and then he told me never to come back. He knew the Superhero Sidekick Code of Conduct forbade me to share his whereabouts—rule number two—but there was nothing in the Code about *me* coming to see him.

The bartender takes one look at me and frowns. I point to the corner, and he frowns again.

He sits in the exact same place as he did last time, nearly two months ago—when I spent every afternoon for two weeks walking into every bar, tavern, and pub the city had to offer before I found him. I was only operating on a hunch, based on the first day we met. Based on the smell of his breath and the look in his eyes. I knew I would recognize him if I saw him. I'm pretty good at picking up on the little details, and he hadn't failed to make an impression. Still, Justicia's not a small city, and I must have peeked into thirty dives just like this one before I found him.

That day I hadn't said much. Only reminded him that I was his sidekick and he was my Super and that, in general, that meant we were supposed to hang out, trade witty remarks, strike cool poses, and battle evil and stuff. I told him that he had missed our last three special training sessions. Suggested that Mr. Masters had expressed concern about his continued absence. I had tried to be cool about the whole thing. No pressure. Not wanting to push him away even further. Just letting him know I was still around. I remember him burping, and the sheer force of it shaking the glasses that hung behind the bar, clinking them together.

He had been in bad shape then. I could only imagine things had gotten worse.

I walk in and take everything in briefly, instantly, letting my senses open up, but just as quickly battening it all back down. There's nothing to see except peanut shells and a few construction workers calling it an early afternoon. There's nothing to hear except the dull thud of glass on wood after every swallow and the hum of an announcer calling a baseball game on a television. There are lots of things to smell, but none of them merit a second whiff.

He sits at the far end of the bar, his giant frame taking up the equivalent of two spaces. It's a wonder the stool holds him. It's a wonder he can still sit upright. I can't see the look in his eyes because of the sunglasses he wears, but the slight twitch at the corner of his mouth tells me that he saw me come in the door. He takes a long drink, emptying his mug, and motions for the bartender to give him another.

"Hey," I say, walking up beside him. Playing it cool.

He just grunts. This is exactly how our last conversation started.

He looks worse. The wheel around his middle has inflated more. He hasn't shaved, a thick beard adding a whole other dimension to his already expansive face. He hasn't bothered to change clothes in a while either, judging by the spread of the armpit stains on his dingy gray T-shirt and the smell that assaults me even though I'm mostly breathing through my mouth. If I took off his sunglasses, I'm sure I would be knocked over by the bags under his bloodshot eyes. This doesn't look like a man who once destroyed a giant mechanical spider by leaping onto it from a plummeting helicopter and driving his fist through the beast's armor plating. Still, his nearly seven-foot frame dwarfs mine, and his log-sized arms still bulge through his shirt.

I look at his hand to see if he is wearing the ring—my sidekick locator device. It's how Supers keep tabs on their charges. A ring or a chain or some other kind of trinket that acts as a tracker and communicator. The day after I took my oath to become a part of H.E.R.O., I had a nifty little computer chip implanted under my thumbnail that I can activate whenever I'm in trouble, sending my signal directly to his ring and allowing him to hunt me down. He can do the same if he ever wants to send me a message. Of course it doesn't do any good if your Super is so passed-out drunk that he doesn't notice. The Titan's knuckles are tufted in hair and thick with scars, but there's no ring.

"Mind if I join you?" I ask, acutely aware of how loaded this question is.

"You really shouldn't be in here," he says, staring straight ahead as I take the stool next to him.

He said that last time.

"You really shouldn't be here either."

I said that last time, too.

I try to somehow peer past the tinted lenses, to get just one glimpse of what is going on back there, but it's no use. His breath makes my eyes water.

"I've been busy," I say.

"Yeah, me too," he murmurs, raising his hand in appreciation as the bartender sets down a full glass.

"You're not wearing your ring."

"I didn't know we were married," he replies, taking a swallow.

I start to lose my cool, spinning around to face him. "Did you even see what happened yesterday?" I venture, bringing my voice to a whisper and speaking through gritted teeth. "At the swimming pool? All those bees and stuff?" I realize my hands are shaking, and I drop them to my sides.

"I heard about it," he says.

"I could have been killed."

"It turned out okay," he says matter-of-factly.

"No thanks to you," I snap.

I shut my mouth. The man sitting next to me could bench press sixty tons, though it seems to be an effort for him just to lift his glass today.

The Titan shrugs.

I feel the warmth working its way up my cheeks. "I played by all the rules," I say. "And instead I end up getting saved by the Fox while you probably just sat here and watched the whole thing on television."

"There was a game on." He nods to the TV in the corner, then takes a drink and sets the glass down gently. "Besides, you didn't need me," he adds.

And suddenly I want to hit him, too. But if hitting Gavin McAllister would be a bad idea, then throwing a punch at the man who once tucked a live hand grenade under his own armpit to protect a group of OCs should be at the bottom of my list. He shifts his weight on the stool, and I can feel a slight tremor through the floorboards, reminding me of exactly who I'm dealing with. When he speaks again, it's more of a growl.

"Listen, kid, I've told you before and I'll tell you again. I'm not your daddy. I'm not your savior. And I'm not your friend. Besides, even if I wanted to, there wasn't much I could do to help you anyway. You got rescued. That's what matters."

"That's no excuse," I say.

"I didn't know I needed an excuse," he snaps back.

67

"I was counting on you."

"There are plenty out there better able to do the job."

I look at him, slouched there in his stool, foam in the stubble on his chin, the scars on his face, hands, and arms like bookmarks keeping tabs on every chapter of his life. In his prime, he was the Super to beat. Nearly indestructible. Fists of iron. Nerves of steel. Heart of gold. At least that's what the T-shirts said. The leader of the Legion of Justice. More than a hundred captured criminals to his credit. Kids around the world worshipped him.

Or at least one did.

But that was the Titan. Not this huge, soft shell of a man, sitting on this stool in his dark corner of the world. I realize he's right. There are plenty of heroes ready to take his place. Which is just fine for practically everyone else.

"Mr. Titan," I whisper, looking around to make sure nobody else in the bar is paying attention.

"George."

"Okay. Whatever, *George*. I didn't ask to be paired up with you, okay? It wasn't my idea." Though I do remember practically peeing my pants the day I found out. "But I'd like to know that the next time some whack job captures me and plans to feed me to sharks or toss me off a cliff or drop me in a vat of bubbling toxic goo, you are going to come get me. Because if not, I need to find somebody who will. Someone who will stick to the Code." I take a deep breath. My heart is pounding. I can feel the blood pulsing all the way down into my feet.

The Titan looks at the bartender, who is either ignoring us or is very good at pretending to. Then he turns to me, cocking his head to the side. It's the first time he's bothered to look at me squarely, and suddenly I'm thinking I should have listened to him the first time and not come back. He points a finger, a finger that, even now, would probably be all he needed to snap my neck.

"Forget the Code, kid. It's just a bunch of made-up nonsense designed to make things simple and easy. But nothing is simple and easy. Nobody's perfect, and I can't be there to pick you up every time you slip and skin your knee. So do us both a favor, and go save yourself for a change."

He keeps his eyes on me a moment longer, then takes another long drink from the glass, leaving only the foam on the sides. He taps the bar.

And I can tell that's it. The conversation is over.

I should tell him what Mr. Masters said. About the possibility that I was captured in order to make him a target. That someone out there still considers him a threat. But then I look at him. And I realize that no villain with half a brain and an ounce of self-respect would bother to battle the man slumped across the stool next to me.

I stand up and sling my backpack across my shoulder. I make it halfway to the door before turning around. This time I don't bother to whisper.

"One day you're going to regret all the things you could have done differently."

He doesn't look up. "Already there, kid," he says. "Don't let the door hit you on the way out." He smiles weakly, then buries himself back in his mug.

I do let the door hit me on the way out—only because he asked me not to—then hop on my bike and head for home. I don't know why I even bothered. What a waste of time. I pedal faster, the wind bringing tears to my eyes, listening to the police sirens in the distance.

REMEMBER THE TITAN

Deep down, all superheroes have problems. Mr. Masters says that's why they fight crime—because it's easier than dealing with their personal drama. The Scarlet Maiden spent two years hunting down the Posse of Doom just to avoid confronting her failed relationship with Captain Crimson. Angus "The Arrow" McClean admitted in his memoir that every criminal he puts away reminds him of his neglectful father. And Dr. Phil once told Titanium Man that his suit of armor is a metaphor for the barrier he puts around his emotions—causing T.M. to weep uncontrollably behind his metal mask on national television.

At some point, Mr. Masters says, most Supers come to a crossroads where they have to choose between saving the world or saving themselves.

Exhibit A: George Raymond Washington Weiss.

He was born George Raymond Washington to parents Thomas and Jenny on May 5, 1962, though admittedly Jenny did most of the work. Upon delivery, baby George weighed twelve pounds, four ounces. When he came out, he gripped the nurse's finger so hard it bruised, and the first time someone tried to draw blood, the needle broke against his skin.

It was clear from the start that George was not an ordinary child and would require special attention. So Thomas and Jenny Washington did what most OCs do when saddled with a superhuman baby—they gave him up for adoption. Better than putting him in a basket and shipping him downriver, at least.

So George grew up under the care of Jim and Janet Weiss, a middle-class Midwestern couple who knew nothing of superpowers, sidekicks, or capes, but who had open hearts and minds. Jim worked as a foreman for a construction company, and Janet tried to convince herself that selling cosmetics was more than just a hobby. They had been trying to have children for years, so to them baby George was a blessing, even though he once split their dining room table in half during a fit over having to eat cooked carrots.

Jim and Janet quickly adjusted, and baby George somehow managed to grow up without destroying everything around him. By the age of eight, he was accompanying his father on construction sites, and often, when nobody was looking, Jim let the boy carry cinder blocks or bust up cement with his bare hands. George could drive nails into lumber with his thumbs and pull trees out by the roots. They knew the boy was special, but they also knew that it was something they should keep to themselves. At least until he was older. Before they knew it, though, little George was a strapping teen, capable of lifting their truck with one hand.

Unfortunately, George was at school when the scaffolding surrounding a new office building gave way, sending three construction workers tumbling through six stories of steel. Had he been there, he might have been able to do something. Had he been there, he might have braced the beams somehow, or steadied the platform. Instead, Jim Weiss's neck snapped when he hit the ground. He didn't feel a thing.

George snapped too, apparently. Not long after his father's funeral, he said good-bye to his adopted mother and left the only house he'd ever known, on foot, heading nowhere in particular. Janet Weiss passed away a few years later from a heart condition.

That's almost all that is known of his childhood, and most of that comes from medical records or interviews with Jim's sister, Betsy. Little is known about George's young adulthood—only what reporters have been able to glean from very short and very rare interviews with the secretive Super himself. The next time he showed up, he was no longer George. Wearing his soon-to-be-trademark jacket and sunglasses, he had become the Titan. Saving Captain Marvelous from the hands of the Nullifier, he kick-started a career that would rocket through the next ten years.

The Titan wasn't your typical Super, though. He was a recluse. He didn't stick around after a battle for a photo op, and he often phoned in anonymously to the police, who would drive to some intersection to find a couple of thugs with a lamppost wrapped around them. He never took on a sponsor or shilled for soft drinks or milk. He declined all the awards people tried to give him. Mayors mailed him keys to the city, which supposedly sat in their peanut-filled boxes in a storage closet. It is said that anyone who ever got close to him had the snot knocked out of them. Still, he was good at his job, and with the retirement of Captain Marvelous, the Titan found himself leading the new Legion of Justice, perhaps the greatest group of crime fighters the world over. Venus. Kid Caliber. Mantis. Corefire. You could find a poster of them lining the wall of every eight-year-old boy's room from here to Seattle. But even in a crowd like that, the Titan stood out. For a while he and his team cleaned up crime, not just in Justicia, but all over the world, putting away the likes of Dr. Terminus, the Gemini Squad, the Nullifier (again), and a host of other scoundrels still banging on the walls of prisons across the globe.

And then came the Dealer—a particularly nasty villain who dogged the Legion for over a year. The Titan made it his personal mission to stop this man and his gang—a group of equally vicious thugs known only as the Suits. In the end, the forces of goodness and light were triumphant. The Dealer was gone. His henchmen dead or captured. His crime spree ended. It was the pinnacle of the Titan's career. His crowning achievement.

And the beginning of the end.

Something happened after the Titan's battle with the Dealer. He lost his edge. The bad guys started slipping through his fingers. The Titan stopped showing up for work. The OCs started to lose faith. Not long after, he stepped down as leader of the Legion of Justice, promising that he would still be an integral part of the superhero community. That he would continue to make the world a safer place.

And then he all but disappeared. Nobody knew where the Titan was. Nobody saw him around. He was a legend, but he wasn't super anymore.

What none of them will tell you, none of the papers or talk shows or cereal-box biographies, is that about a year ago, George Raymond Washington Weiss waited in the shadows outside Bob's Bowlarama for a then-twelve-year-old boy to appear.

That boy was me, less than a year into my training as a sidekick. Time spent honing my powers and biding my time, reciting the Code that would govern how I would behave. The Code that told me that my Super was more than just my role model—he was my partner in the quest for truth and justice, freedom and happiness, goodness and light, and all the things at the end of the rainbow.

George Weiss showed up with a bottle of whiskey in his hand and another on his breath.

"Andrew Bean?"

He stood in the shadows. I couldn't see his face, but I knew who he was just by his size. I knew who he was because I had been thinking about him all week. I knew him before, of course—I had the poster, the button, the commemorative stamp—but I had spent the time since finding out I was going to be his sidekick intensely studying him. Staring at his picture. Watching old news footage of him online. I had been preparing for this moment, the moment when I would meet him and shake the mighty hand that brought down the Dealer.

"I'm Drew," I said.

He stepped out into the faint glow of the setting sun so I could see his pale skin and stubbly cheeks. He didn't look much like the pictures. He had shaved his head but not his jaw. His stomach spread out over the top of his pants. He was massive, though everything was a little out of proportion from how I pictured it. He still wore his sunglasses, though.

The Titan held out a hand that could crush my head like an olive, though it only held a crumpled piece of paper.

"I got this," he said.

He handed the paper to me, and I tried to smooth it out. It was printed on official H.E.R.O. stationery. It was addressed to the Titan and signed by Nathan R. Masters.

I already knew what it said.

It said that my life was about to change. That I would no longer spend my weekends playing video games. Instead I would be patrolling the streets, sniffing out danger with my hyperkeen senses, fighting crime alongside one of my childhood heroes, a man who could chew glass and punch through the hull of a submarine with his bare fist.

It said that I, Andrew Macon Bean, aka the Sensationalist, had been officially assigned as apprentice to the Titan, to serve him in the name of all things good and just, and to uphold the sacred codes of Super and sidekick alike.

I knew what it said because I had a nearly identical letter folded in my back pocket. It had been there for days. I had it memorized. The afternoon after Mr. Masters handed it to me, I ran straight home and pulled out my copy of *Portraits of Justice* and memorized every detail of the Titan's career. Right up until the moment he disappeared.

I couldn't begin to imagine what had happened since then.

But even in the state he was in, leaning against the wall of the bowling alley, reeking, his clothes stained, I didn't care. He was my mentor.

The Titan shook his head.

"Listen, kid. I can't . . ." He didn't bother to finish the sentence.

I just stared at him. Holding his crumpled copy of the letter in one hand, my other arm limp by my side. I could hear the

77

purr of cars on the interstate two miles away. I could smell the four-day-old scrim of sweat under the Titan's shirt.

"You don't want to be my sidekick," he said finally.

I felt in my back pocket for my own letter, wondering now if they *were* the same, wondering if I had missed something. Some fine print.

"No. That's not true," I said. "I do. I mean, I don't really know what I can do, yet, but I'll try . . ."

The Titan held up a finger, and I shut up. "I understand what you all are trying to do, and I appreciate the thought, but you should tell Nathan Masters that he needs to find somebody else. I'm sorry. I just can't right now. If something . . ."

He stumbled again, chewing over the words, eyes glazed, as if he were trying hard to remember something. Or maybe the opposite. He didn't finish the thought.

"Wait. Hang on a minute. Is it me? I know Mr. Masters says that I really don't have enough combat training, but I thought that with my powers and your powers, you know . . ."

The Titan took hold of my hand and pulled his coat free. His hand felt huge and cold wrapped around mine, and I was suddenly scared that he was going to break my arm.

Instead he just gave it a squeeze. Just hard enough that I winced.

"You'll thank me someday," he said.

I looked down at my hand, still wrapped in his, and held my breath. And then he let go and disappeared around the corner.

I shook my fingers out, then clenched them into a hard

little fist. I had been imagining this moment for days. In some ways, I had probably been imagining it for years.

I slumped against the wall, letting myself drop, hands over my ears, closing off.

It wasn't him, I told myself. Not really. That was somebody else. The Titan would come around. There was the letter. And the code. He would come around. He had to. He was my hero.

Behind me I heard a car pull up to the bowling alley entrance. I recognized the rattle of the engine. My mother honked the horn, and I put my real mask back on.

TESTED

It's Thursday.

I wake up in a haze. My normally acute vision is blurry, and somehow I've managed to sleep through my mother's coffee grinder. Today I actually wake to the sound of her voice telling me it's after seven and I'm going to be late for school and am I feeling okay?

I'm not, actually, though I don't tell her that. I'm running on less than four hours of sleep. I was up all night reading *Julius Caesar* and finishing my presentation on Hannibal for history class. Those two megalomaniacs carried me well past midnight.

The hours from one to two had been spent staring up at my ceiling and counting the crags and crevices in its stucco, thinking about all the things I should have said back at the bar, if there was anything I *could* have said that would have pulled him off that stool. I didn't come up with anything. Though I did think of several things that probably would have gotten my face smashed in.

The hours from two to three had been spent listening to infomercials from Mrs. Polanski's too-loud television next door, learning about the wonderful, specially formulated stain-fighting power of Vamoose. Finally, around three fifteen, I fell asleep and dreamed about the Titan being slowly lowered into a pit of poisonous piranhas somehow swimming in a pool of molten lava, with no one around to rescue him.

And somewhere in there—before midnight, I guess— Jenna called. She was busy finishing her report on the sack of Troy. She wanted to know if I thought Hannibal could defeat Achilles in a one-on-one death match. I said it probably depended on what kind of shoes Achilles was wearing.

"I saw the Titan today," I told her.

It was a lot more than I should have said, I know. It was more than he would have wanted me to say, but I needed to tell someone. And wasn't he the one who told me the Code was just a bunch of hokum?

There was a long pause. When she spoke again, she sounded hesitant, skeptical. "Wow. I didn't think anyone even knew where he was."

"Yeah. He kind of wants to keep it that way," I said. There was silence on the other end. I took it as my cue to continue. "He looked terrible. All pale and pasty. And he smelled . . . I don't know, just *stale*."

"Disgusting," she said. "Where did you find him?"

"I probably shouldn't say," I told her, finally drawing the line. "Besides. It doesn't matter anyways." She said she understood, but I could tell she was disappointed. There were very few secrets between us, but I didn't want her doing anything crazy, like trying to go talk to him herself. I didn't trust him. Didn't know how he would react.

"Does he know what happened yesterday, at least?"

"Yeah," I said. "He told me I should go save myself for a change."

"What a loser." Jenna groaned, then quickly backtracked. "Sorry, Drew. I know how much it meant to you . . . working with him."

I thought about the tire around the Titan's waist. The glazed look in his eyes. I'm not sure he could have saved me if he'd wanted to. "Mr. Masters told me to give him time."

"Yeah, Gavin said he saw you two talking at H.E.R.O. and that Mr. Masters looked concerned."

I paused. "When did you talk to Gavin?" About me, I wanted to add.

"Today after track practice. He walked me home."

"Oh," I said.

"What?"

"Nothing."

"You told me you had something to do after school, and I didn't want to walk home alone after what happened yesterday, so I asked him to come."

"*You* asked *him*?" For some reason, I assumed it was the other way around.

"Yeah."

"No. That's good," I said, coughing to try and cover my lie. "I'm glad. I mean, the guy can sweat limestone."

"Granite."

"Right. Whatever."

"He's nice, Drew. Just because he's new and he's on the football team doesn't mean you have to give him a hard time."

I snort.

"What?" she said.

"A *hard* time?"

I couldn't miss the exasperation in her voice. "I'm serious, Drew. Give him a break."

I'd have to use a sledgehammer, I thought to myself, but I didn't say it. "Sure. Okay. Well, listen, it's late, and I've got that stupid presentation to finish."

"Yeah, me too."

"I'll see you tomorrow."

"'Kay."

I started to hang up.

"Drew?"

"Yeah."

She paused. "You don't need him," she said.

"That's easy for you to say. You're sidekick to, like, the best Super in the world." There was another pause.

"Yeah. I guess so." She sounded somehow resigned to the

fact. "Okay. See you tomorrow."

"See you," I said, hung up, and tried in vain to fall asleep.

Seven hours later, I am frantically getting dressed for school. My head is throbbing. It happens when I'm distracted. I can't focus. The result makes my head throb. I can sense everything around me.

The smell of the laundry in my hamper.

The weather report downstairs.

My father's dandruff shampoo.

The Hungs' yappy dog.

The incessant ticking of the grandfather clock in the living room.

The mildew in the shower.

The trash truck two blocks away.

The humming buzz of the electrical sockets.

I try to concentrate on what I'm doing, which is putting my socks on. The fuzz of the socks tickles the soles of my feet. I careen down the stairs and inhale a bowl of plain Rice Krispies, grab my bag, and head for the door. My mother lassoes me back with her grappling hook of a hand in order to give me a kiss on the cheek. I can tell by the vitamin-y smell on her lips that she is back on Slim-Fast again. She is already skinny, but apparently she wants to look like a supermodel. We all have expectations to live up to, I guess.

I set out at a quick jog and just manage to make my bus, nearly tripping and dropping my history presentation—poster, elephant, and all. The Lego man that's supposed to be Hannibal loses his spear, and it rolls under the seat. I hope that Mr. Broadside doesn't mind that Hannibal is bald and dressed like an astronaut.

The bus smells like exhaust, gym socks, and old leather. The bus driver smells like gym socks and smoke. I close my eyes and hope the day will be over soon.

No such luck.

The trunk breaks off my model war elephant ten minutes before my presentation on Hannibal's invasion of the Roman Empire and has to be reattached with Eric's chewing gum. Then I somehow manage to trip over the only line I have as Servant while reading Act II of *Julius Caesar* in English class. Everyone laughs, including the teacher. I laugh too, hoping that makes it more of a "with me" than an "at me" thing, but I don't think it works if you're faking it.

Oh. And it's Thursday, which means taco salad day at the cafeteria. It also means I actually have to eat lunch in the cafeteria—it's a no-H.E.R.O. day today.

Still, it could be worse. I don't have any harpoons or missiles to worry about. Today I'm just a normal kid with normal problems going to his normal math class waiting for his normal day to end.

Mr. McClain walks through the door, two or three students trying to squeeze in past him. "Put your books away," he says.

I look at my backpack. My book *is* put away. I look at everyone else's books. Open on their desks. I look at everyone else's face. The pale, hollow look of resignation on some. The flush, flustered, frantic look of mad concentration on others. I hear Reggie Townsend whisper a prayer behind me.

I look up at the stack of papers in Mr. McClain's hand.

It's Thursday. Taco salad day.

Math test day.

"Make sure you have a pen or pencil and keep your arms and hands where I can see them. Robert, take that hat off. Ms. Greenway, please place your notebook *all* the way into your bag. This will take most of you the whole period."

I managed to keep up with it all. The papers and the presentations and the loser superhero and the secret identity and the not dying. But somehow I forgot about the math test.

I look around me. I can see sweat bubbling on foreheads. I can hear heartbeats accelerate as the tests are passed back. Angela Locksford comes in late and hurries to her seat. I can smell the wintergreen Tic Tac in her mouth. Behind me, somebody moves his chair, and the sound of the metal feet scraping the hard floor causes my spine to quiver.

I think about Mr. Masters's watch. One minute is more than enough time to make it to the fire alarm and stop this thing.

One row across and two seats ahead, Natalie Cross, last year's mathlete champion, has her two mechanical pencils lined up beside her folded hands.

The girl in front of me whose name I can never remember hands back the test. It smells like printer ink and Mr. McClain's cologne. It's six pages long.

"You may begin," he says.

From four rows away, Catherine Chow says, "I am *so* going to tank this thing," under her breath, where only she and I can hear.

Someone in the back of the class emits an S.B.D.

I try to focus.

I look at the first problem. Something about xs and ys. There's a cube in there, too. I can only assume I'm supposed to solve something, reduce something, or balance something.

I should know this. I'm actually pretty good at math. Math is important to chemistry, and chemistry is important to sidekicks who have to wear utility belts full of gadgets and grenades to compensate for their crappy powers. But for some reason my brain is fried and the numbers look like a foreign language.

I glance around. Everyone has their heads huddled over their papers, pencils working furiously. I pick up my pencil, unsure of what to do with it.

And then my eyes stop on Natalie. Or at least the back of her head. And the brown hair that she just got cut a week ago, making it much easier to see over her shoulder. The way she is sitting, the angle that I'm at, I catch a glimpse of her answer form, but it's pretty far away. There's no way any normal person could see what she has written from here.

I look back down at my paper and try to concentrate.

I can't concentrate.

I close my eyes.

When I open them again, I look a little harder.

Natalie looks up for a moment and then writes something. The answer to number five, according to our class's top student, is twenty-four.

As it turns out, I don't have anything written for that one yet. I chew on the end of my pencil.

The Superhero Sidekick Code of Conduct is fairly clear about when a sidekick should or shouldn't use his powers. It's all pretty much spelled out in the very first rule.

He should use them to defend the greater good.

He should use them in the service of justice and honor.

He should use them to help those in need.

But when you think about it, that's all a little loosey-goosey, really. I mean, who defines *greater good*? Or *those in need*, for that matter? Right now I need an answer for number five.

I look at number five and try to work through the formula in my head. Twenty-four seems like a decent answer.

If I fail this test, then my grades might slip. If I don't get good grades, my parents won't let me stay in the Highview Environmental Reclamation Organization any longer. And then how am I supposed to learn to defend OCs from the forces of darkness? The pattern is clear. If I don't answer number five correctly, there is a very good chance that someone will die.

Natalie answers another one.

Besides, that girl is *really* good at math. Almost superhuman, you might say. She's using the natural gifts God gave her. I'm sure Captain Marvelous didn't let his super strength interfere with his ability to climb the rope in gym class. Do you think Invisilad ever got hit by a spitball? I doubt it. And how do you think H.E.R.O.'s own Jenna Jaden came to be captain of the gymnastics team? Sure, she holds back considerably, but she's still the only one who can do a double backflip.

Natalie Price is already on number eight. That means she is about to the turn the page.

I hear the Titan's voice in my head.

Save yourself for a change.

I focus on Natalie's paper.

Then I quickly answer the first seven problems. I wait a bit for the last one, the answer to which, apparently, is eleven point five.

Natalie turns the page.

I turn the page.

I finish my math test about the same time as she does, though I go back to change one answer in the middle, just in case things look suspicious.

I hold my test out to Mr. McClain with two minutes left.

He reaches out for it.

Our eyes meet.

He gives me a funny look. Head cocked to the side. I can see the gray hairs starting to infiltrate the legions of black ones in his mustache, can trace the growing path of the crows' feet by his eyes. He squints a little, a look of confusion or concern.

"Are you finished, Andrew?"

He looks down at my test, and I realize what the problem is. I won't let go.

"Oh, sorry," I croak. And the paper slides through my fingers.

Mr. McClain smiles. I smile. The bell rings.

Take that, forces of evil.

That afternoon Jenna walks home with Gavin again. She says there's a book he wants to borrow. I ask her why she doesn't just bring it to school tomorrow. She says she guesses she could, but she already told him to just come by and pick it up today. I ask her if, you know, everything's cool. She says, "Yeah, why not?" She asks me how the math test went. That's pretty much the end of that conversation. She smiles, and I can see by the look in her eyes that something's bothering her.

As she walks away, I can't help but wonder if I've said or done something wrong, something that would push her away. If so, I need to figure it out and make up for it. The Titan I can deal with. At least for a little while. So long as I stay out of trouble.

But I don't know what I'd do without Jenna.

UPPING THE ANTE

By the end of the week, everything seems to be mostly back to normal. The hole in Jenna's side has healed. The Justicia community pool has been encased in concrete; the drones have been released from custody and gone back to their OC lives; the Supers are back to thwarting car thieves and purse snatchers, changing the spark plugs on their jet packs, or editing their memoirs; and the news has gone back to coverage of the growing number of politicians' scandals and exposés on the fat content of school lunches.

Don't get me wrong. I'm still miffed about the whole my-Superhero-mentor-is-a-beer-swilling, sidekick-abandoning-lout thing, but there isn't a lot I can do about it right now. Jenna says I may be better off without him. Mr. Masters says he will come around. I don't really know what to think anymore.

I *did* manage to ace my Spanish quiz, even studying only the fifteen minutes I had in homeroom. And despite my elephant's lopsided schnoz and my bald, spearless, spaceman general, Mr. Broadside said my history presentation on Hannibal was excellent, though he pointed out that the opposing Roman general who defeated Hannibal was named Scippio, not Scorpio, which is the problem with spell check, I guess.

I don't know how I did on the math test yet, but I asked Natalie how she thinks she did and she's pretty sure she aced it, so I'm pretty sure I aced it.

The bell rings for fourth period, and I gather my stuff and head up toward the teachers' lounge. Time to H.E.R.O. up. Today we are supposed to practice hacking into computer mainframes. Finally something that Gavin's big biceps won't give him an advantage in.

Plus it's Friday. Pizza day. Mr. Masters is probably paying for the pies now and handing them off to Nikki, who will use her powers to sink into the ground and sneak them into the basement so that the other teachers don't see. I still can't figure out how she does it—something about autonomic molecular reconfiguration—a fancy way of saying she "just walks through stuff." I figure of all of us, she's the most likely to change her mind about the whole sidekick thing, drop out of school, and become a bank robber.

I run into Jenna waiting outside the door of the lounge. She looks the same as always. Glasses perched. Hair pulled back. Tiny mole on her chin. Every time I see her, I kind of feel like I'm just waking up.

My eyes start to water.

Something's not right.

I look around to see if it might be someone else, but I can pinpoint exactly where it's coming from. There's no mistake.

Jenna's wearing perfume.

Jenna *never* wears perfume. In fact, it was Jenna who once told me that only old ladies and middle-aged soccer moms wear perfume.

I start to say something when I suddenly hear familiar foot-falls behind me. I turn to see Mr. Masters with Eric, Gavin, and Nikki in tow. No one is carrying pizza, and Mr. Masters does *not* look happy. The sleeves are rolled up on his canary-yellow shirt. His sweater vest is all angry zigzags again.

"Come on," he says, removing his watch and looking at Jenna and me. "Something has happened."

I know, I want to say. Jenna Jaden is wearing *perfume*. But I'm pretty sure Mr. Masters is thinking of something else.

Sixty cents later, we are descending the stairs. For once I can't smell the pork rinds. All I can smell is Jenna. As we take our seats, Eric spells out the word *lunch*, but the head of H.E.R.O. isn't paying any attention. He takes his spot front and center, and I take my usual spot next to Jenna.

"Did you hug your grandmother or something today?"

"What are you talking about?"

I make an exaggerated sniffing sound.

"Oh. It's just body spray. Sorry. Is it too much?"

She really looks concerned, raising her eyebrows at me.

From the moment she found out about me, Jenna has always been sensitive to my abilities. When we listen to music, she doesn't crank it up, even when it's a song she likes. When we go out to eat together, she doesn't overdo it on the pepper. She doesn't *have* to do these things, of course, but I let her, because I like that she thinks about me.

"No, it's fine. Don't worry."

"Do you want me to move over?"

"No, seriously, don't worry about it," I say.

She smiles, but still she scoots in her chair, closer to Gavin, who sits on the other side.

I'm about to lie to her and tell her how much I like it, in fact, when Mr. Masters clears his throat.

"What I am about to tell you is top secret, though I'm certain it won't be for long. Two hours ago, there was a breach at the maximum security prison in Colton, two hundred miles north of here." The lights go off and the screen flashes to life, showing a photo of a veritable fortress, complete with guard towers and barbed wire and an outer wall of solid steel at least twenty feet high. Mr. Masters clicks to another picture of the same building from a different angle, this one a satellite shot. Part of the outer wall is obscured by white smoke. "At approximately ten thirty-five a.m., an explosion tore through the outer perimeter. A figure wearing a gray mask, a dark gray hat, and a business suit subdued a handful of guards and bypassed several other security measures with ease, infiltrating the prison's supranormal security wing."

I'm only half listening to him. Something about a break-in. I'm sure there are Supers out there cleaning it up. Probably the Fox already has this all under control. I lean closer to Jenna.

"It's flowery," I whisper.

"It's called Purple Passion," she whispers back, sounding just a little annoyed.

Nikki turns to give us a dirty look. Apparently whatever Mr. Masters is talking about is kind of important, but I'm still curious why Jenna's decided that the smell of her honey vanilla body wash and melon berry conditioner that I've grown accustomed to over the past year isn't good enough anymore.

Mr. Masters continues. "When the smoke cleared, twelve guards had been knocked unconscious and three prisoners freed."

"It's nice," I say, realizing that *nice* isn't the word you would use to describe something with the word *passion* in it.

"Gavin gave it to me," she whispers.

Sudden loss of cabin pressure. Stomach dropping. Eyes blinking. I have no idea what to say to that.

I look at Gavin, who turns and smiles.

Yes, I do.

In that case, I think it smells like crappity crap crap crap.

"All three prisoners shared the same name," Mr. Masters says.

I stop glaring at Gavin momentarily and turn to see the photo on the screen, showing four figures escaping through the outer wall and into the forest beyond. The one in the gray suit leads the way. The other three are all dressed in orange prison uniforms. From here they just look like three faceless thugs, though one of them is much larger than the rest—looks more like a boulder with legs, in fact.

"The escaped prisoners are all named Jack," Mr. Masters says.

Suddenly I forget all about Gavin's purple passion.

Three Jacks.

The three Jacks.

I know these guys.

I mean, not personally know them. Anyone who knew them personally is dead or in prison. But I know them the way some people know generals from the Civil War or famous serial killers. I know them because it is my job as a sidekick to know them. I know them because I wasn't hiding under a rock my entire life.

These are the guys the Titan took down almost six years ago. The Dealer's henchmen. His Suits.

"Those of you who have bothered to study your criminal history probably have a guess as to who *this* is, then," Mr. Masters says, pointing to the figure in the gray hat and suit. Now I recognize the outfit from the front pages of so many newspapers. I take a closer look, and a chill works its way through me.

"But I thought he was . . ."

"Dead?" Mr. Masters says, finishing Nikki's thought. "So

96

did the rest of us. But obviously we were mistaken. Apparently the Dealer is back in the game."

I can't tell if Mr. Masters is trying to be funny or not, but the look on his face suggests not. Eric takes a long breath. I look over at Jenna, who huddles a little closer to Gavin. The room is graveyard quiet all of a sudden. No one says anything as Mr. Masters brings up brief dossiers of the escaped convicts. They are all pictures I had seen a dozen times on reruns of *America's Most Notorious Criminals*.

The first is a photo of a man who looks like something out of a 1920s silent film where damsels are tied to train tracks and rescued by Canadian Mounties. The figure in the photo has coal-black eyes and thick white scars on both cheeks, bisected by a long, black handlebar mustache that twists upward at the ends. The mustache looks plastered on, too big to be real. But the hollow, deathly look in his eyes seems all too real.

"Jack Candor," Mr. Masters says, "aka the Jack of Clubs. Weapons and demolitions expert. An unforgettable face and a notorious reputation. He was an accomplished hit man for three years before signing on with the Suits. Carries around a baton that he tosses like a boomerang so it can hit you twice, just to be sure. Most of the time you're unconscious before you even know he's there."

Mr. Masters brings up the next photo—a behemoth of a man with no neck and a body like a bulldozer. He's the boulder from the surveillance photo. His picture fills up the screen.

"Jack Voshel, aka the Jack of Spades. The bruiser. Easily

identified because he is seven and a half feet tall and weighs four hundred twenty pounds. Carries a shovel as his only weapon. Seldom needs to use it. Not the sharpest knife in the block, but not to be underestimated, especially when barreling toward you."

Mr. Masters clicks. The third photo shows a perfectly normal looking man by comparison to the other two. His close-cut blond hair is carefully styled, his thin, angular face drawn into a wry smile. Unlike the other two, he carries no weapons. His only odd feature is quite noticeable, though: a chunk of glass where his left eye used to be.

"Jack Coal, aka the Jack of Diamonds. Once an international jewel thief and playboy. He lost his eye when he was twenty-six and had it replaced with what he believed to be a rare, one-of-a-kind diamond. Turns out it was actually a small chunk of meteorite that quickly bonded to his molecular structure, making him nearly impervious to pain and just as hard to take down . . . not to mention he can use it to shoot energy beams."

Suddenly I'm wishing I had joined the chess club.

"And finally . . ."

The last picture shows the man in the mask, the one who freed the others—eyes like sapphires peering through the mask's only two holes, his dark-gray fedora, like the color of a storm cloud, cocked to one side. Cold and confident, with more than a hint of malevolence. For well over a year this guy was the poster child for a successful life of crime, wreaking havoc everywhere he went. Until the Titan finally brought him down.

"The Dealer," Mr. Masters says. "Real name, date of birth, place of origin, all unknown. No one even knows what the guy's face looks like. He's the one who brought the Suits together the first time. A mastermind and scientific genius, he purportedly engaged in illegal experiments designed to enhance the kinds of extraordinary abilities found in people like you. No known superpowers himself, though, save for his astronomically high IQ and his uncanny ability to stay one step ahead of everyone who ever tried to catch him. Up until today, he was believed to be dead, killed in the battle with the Legion of Justice so many years ago."

Mr. Masters touches a button and the lights come back on.

"We don't know where he's been hiding all these years, but the fact that he has most of his original gang in tow makes him a top priority for all Supers in the area."

Most of the gang, I think to myself. He's only missing one Suit. The Jack of Hearts, who died in the confrontation with the Legion of Justice. Though "dead" doesn't mean as much as I thought it did. If the Dealer is back, there's no guarantee he doesn't have another surprise up his sleeve.

Mr. Masters steps out from behind the podium and walks over to stand right in front of us. "That makes the Dealer our top concern as well. For that reason, I'm putting Jenna, Gavin, and Eric on ready reserve status."

In front of me I see Erik sink in his seat. Gavin actually says the word *oh*. Only Jenna seems unfazed. Ready reserve means that your Super can actually call on you to accompany him on patrol whenever he deems it necessary. Not just weekend training exercises—the real deal.

"The rest of us," he says, referring to Nikki and me, "need to keep our eyes and ears open. We don't know where the Dealer has been all this time or what he's been up to, but it can't be good."

I look at the photo of the Dealer. It's blurry and far away and the mask covers everything but the icy blue eyes. Cool and calculating.

I glance over at Jenna. She is looking at Mr. Masters, who stands in front of the image of the man in the gray mask. Her eyes look pretty much the same. Like she already has a plan to take the Dealer down.

EAVESDROPPING

"What's the big deal?"

We are huddled in a circle eating crackers with circles of what might once have been peanut butter between them, a gift from Mr. Masters, who apologized for not buying pizza and apologized yet again for having to interrupt our training to go make some calls, leaving us to fend for ourselves and to cope with the fact that, only two hundred miles away, one of the most notorious criminal gangs in history had just kicked off a reunion tour. I am just about to open my crackers when Gavin shoots off his stupid mouth.

"What do you mean, what's the big deal?" Nikki replies through chomps of strawberry bubble gum, beating me to it. "Are you nuts? These guys are totally hardcore. The Dealer was a criminal mastermind."

"*Is* a criminal mastermind," I correct. I figure you use the present tense when talking about someone *back* from the dead.

"Right," she says. "The Suits went on a crime spree that lasted three years. It took the entire Legion of Justice to bring them down. And you're asking what the big deal is?"

Gavin straightens up stiffly. "I just don't see what Mr. Masters is getting so worked up over. So a couple of bad-dies break out of prison? Happens every day. The Supers will round 'em up and stick 'em back in—and if we're lucky, *some* of us might get to help." He looks at me and smiles. All confidence and straight white teeth.

I glare back. It is bad enough getting it from Mr. Masters. I don't need to take it from Purple Passion McAllister.

Eric starts signing rapidly.

Gavin shakes his head. "What did he say?"

"He says you're crazy," I translate. "And ignorant," I add, though Eric didn't sign that, "and that these guys are *way* out of our league."

Jenna sits cross-legged next to me. She has taken off her glasses and let her hair down—halfway through her transformation to the Silver Lynx. "Eric's right," she says. "These guys were the most dangerous supervillains in the world. Even without the Jack of Hearts," she adds in a whisper.

"Right. What happened to him again?" Gavin asks. I can't tell if he doesn't know or just doesn't remember. Or maybe he's just playing dumb. Or maybe he's not playing.

I look at Jenna, who is fidgeting with the laces on her tennis shoes. I watch her tug on the loops, waiting for the whole thing to unravel. "Nobody really knows," she says. "Like the Dealer, the Jack of Hearts wore a mask, so no one knew his true identity."

"Though they say he was the most powerful of all the Suits," Nikki adds.

"All we know for sure is that the Legion of Justice tracked the Suits back to their secret hideout and there was this huge fight."

"They were all there," Nikki says, "Corefire and Mantis . . ."

Venus, Eric signs.

"Venus, Kid Caliber . . ."

"The Titan."

Nikki pops a bubble.

I realize everyone is looking at me, and then just as suddenly making an effort not to.

"Can't forget him," I say. There is another long pause, and then finally Nikki speaks.

"So they had this big battle. And everybody kind of gets split up. And the Titan and Kid Caliber chase the Dealer and the Jack of Hearts into this lab. And the next thing you know, the whole place goes up in flames." Eric's hands fly wide in accompaniment, the universal sign for *kerplowy.* "The Titan emerges from the smoke with an unconscious Kid Caliber in his arms and says it's all over."

"Supposedly the Jack of Hearts and the Dealer were both

caught in the blast," I add. "The other three Jacks were captured and imprisoned."

"End of story," Nikki says.

Gavin shrugs his shoulders. "Right. See. My point exactly. Good guys win. We did it the first time, we will do it again."

I stare at Gavin. If it's true that we all have a little voice inside our head, I'm pretty sure his is a bubble-headed cheerleader. "Sure," I say. "Except the Legion of Justice doesn't exist anymore. They've all retired or gone solo."

"Or disappeared," Jenna says, looking at me sideways.

I don't bother to say anything back. I think about the Titan straddling his stool at the bar. What would he say if he knew the Dealer was still alive? If he knew the Suits were on the loose again? Would it make any difference? And what about the others? The ones who may still be around somewhere? Kid Caliber? Venus? Corefire? Would they even care?

"So maybe they'll come back," Gavin says, somehow reading my thought. "Like old times."

Nikki rolls her eyes. "*Tcha*. Last I heard, Corefire was in Australia and Venus was retired out on the West Coast, using what's left of her fame to convince kids to say no to drugs," Nikki says. "And Mantis, didn't he die . . . ?" She can't bring herself to say it. She looks at Eric.

He solemnly holds up two fingers. I remember reading about it in the paper. Turned out his chitinous exoskeleton was actually a form of skin cancer that slowly spread to his lungs and then to his brain, taking him, finally, in his sleep.

He died two years ago.

"All the more reason for the Dealer to make his comeback now," Nikki says. "Now that nobody who stopped him the first time is around to try again."

Or almost nobody, I think to myself.

Gavin shrugs. "Whatever. Forget those guys. *Our* Supers are just as good as them. Screw that, they're even better. Hotshot would toast those guys in seconds flat, and especially with the Fox—"

Of course. Justicia's knight in tight white armor. Jenna says nothing. Gavin's about to launch into another spiel, probably about how he could take the Dealer down himself with one hand tied behind his back, when Eric stomps his foot and points emphatically to the window of the office on the other side of the room. Mr. Masters is pacing back and forth, gesturing frantically, talking on the phone. He looks like he's about to pop. We all just sit and watch him for a moment.

"Wish I was a fly on *that* wall," Nikki says.

"Maybe it has something to do with us," Gavin adds.

Jenna leans next to me. She looks concerned. "You could . . . you know." She tilts her head behind her, toward the room.

"What? Seriously? On Mr. Masters?"

Eric sits up a little straighter, having read our lips. Nikki pauses in midbubble. Gavin looks at me, then at Jenna, then back at me.

We all huddle a little closer together. "Aren't you the least bit curious?" Jenna asks. "I mean, with everything that's just happened, Gavin's right. It *could* be about us."

"Could be about *you*, you mean," I say, reminding her of her new upgrade in status.

"He looks really worried," Nikki says. Eric nods.

Jenna is staring at me.

"Yeah . . . I don't think when Mr. Masters told us to keep our eyes and ears open, he meant we should spy on *him*."

But I already know I will.

In part because Jenna asked me to.

In part because, for once, my powers would come in handy.

In part because of the look that Gavin is giving me.

But mostly because I want to hear what he is saying as much as anyone. I look over my shoulder at Mr. Masters's office. "All these rooms are soundproof," I say. "Believe me. I've tried to listen in on what you guys are doing, and I can't."

"That's from inside *your* room," Jenna says. "This is different."

She offers up one of her pouty smiles.

"Forget it, Jenna. He already said he can't do it. Leave him alone," Gavin says.

That clinches it.

"Okay, fine, everybody shut up."

Nikki locks her mouth shut with an invisible key and swallows it. Eric sits on his hands.

I close my eyes to block everything out.

I hear Gavin snort, and I give him one open eyeful. I guess it looks evil enough, because he doesn't make another sound. I take one last glance at Mr. Masters.

Eyes shut again, I let in all the sounds around me.

A hundred voices talking all at once.

The loud ones are teachers, but there are many more softer voices trying to drown the loud ones out, or at least ignore them, whispered voices creating an acoustic fog, a kind of white noise. I hear shouting from the gymnasium and the sound of balls being dribbled. I hear a volcano erupting and an announcer discussing the properties of lava. *"The molten rock reaches temperatures up to twenty-two hundred degrees Fahrenheit and can travel great distances before cooling."* I hear the squeak of shoes and the hum of the air conditioner, and the sound of chalk scraped across a board, and the click of keys from the computer lab.

And I start to slowly filter it all out. Everything. The lawn mower outside on the school grounds. Ms. Kyle finally snapping and telling everyone to sit down and zip it. At least a half dozen *"oh . . . my . . . god"* squealed almost simultaneously.

I push it all out.

And I open my eyes and stare at Mr. Masters through the soundproof glass. Still pacing. Still shouting. I concentrate on the door, on the window, on the slightest crack or hole I can find. And I feel like my eyeballs are going to pop.

But I can hear his voice. Muffled at first, then louder.

I hear the word *"Dealer"* and the word *"impossible."*

I hear *". . . told me he was dead."*

I catch something that sounds like *"only one who knows for sure"* and something else that sounds like *"can't find him"* and *"we really don't know who it is."*

He says, *". . . possible that all of our identities have been compromised."*

And then he says something that makes my heart stop.

"I think they're watching me."

Then he quickly hangs up the phone, turns to the window, and looks at us.

At me.

I quickly look over at Jenna, away from Mr. Masters, my heart racing. There is a look of concern on her face. She is pointing at me.

"Your nose is bleeding," she says.

I touch my hand to my nose and smear a streak of red across it, then chance one last look at Mr. Masters.

He's still standing in the window. Watching *me*.

Jenna hands me a tissue from her bag, then turns and stares right back at Mr. Masters, who eventually looks away.

PART TWO

IN WHICH I ALMOST DIE . . . AGAIN

PROMISES

I met Jenna Jaden a little over a year ago.

We just ran into each other. Or she ran into me, is more like it.

At the time, I wasn't a part of the Highview Environmental Reclamation Organization. I had just started middle school, of all things, and my biggest concern was suddenly having no recess for the rest of my life. Not that I loved recess. Just that it usually smelled better outside school than inside it. Imagine being able to hear *and* smell it every time a kid loses his lunch in the trash can, and you'll know what I mean.

And of course there was all the other junk that came with the move to middle school: having to learn how to operate a locker; having more than one teacher to suck up to each year; organized sports teams, which gave guys who like to pick on guys like me even more occasions to bond and slap each other on the butt; having to get up early to catch the bus; having to stay up late finishing homework; girls whispering and pointing even more than usual; guys who like to pick on guys like me picking on me even more than usual to impress girls who whisper and point . . . that sort of thing.

I ventured into middle school with very few friends in tow. Being able to hear everything that anybody says about you tends to make you selective in who you hang out with, and I was cagey about my power even before I became a member of H.E.R.O.

Most of my friends from Crestwater Elementary split during the summer. My friend Max headed to private school, and my neighbor Josh had to move to North Carolina when his father was reassigned to a new army base. The other kids in my neighborhood—the few who were even my age—were more casual acquaintances than friends, which left me basically alone going into a new school.

Then along came Jenna.

When we first met, I didn't know she had a fifteen-foot vertical leap. That she had lightning-quick reflexes. Or that she could bench press twenty of me stacked one on top of the other. Maybe that's because Jenna couldn't. The Silver Lynx could, and I didn't meet *her* until later.

When I met Jenna, we made an instant connection. It was sixth-grade gym class—unfortunately, not yet being a member of H.E.R.O., I still had to go to *all* of my classes—and we were playing kickball. They let me play catcher, because in kickball almost nobody misses, and nobody really throws the ball to a base, preferring instead to chuck it at the runner, so there really isn't a lot to do if you are the catcher except stand behind home plate and hope that Davy "Biohazard" Hutchinson doesn't let one rip in front of you when he comes up to kick.

Then Jenna stepped up. Her hair was pulled back in a ponytail that bobbed with each step. Her green eyes peered through her thick glasses, homed in on the ball like a sniper's sights; her freckled arms flexed. She was new to town, and nobody knew very much about her. I think she preferred it that way. Crouching behind her, I stared up at the long curve of her neck and shoulders, trying not to look at her butt, which fit nicely in the tight red-and-blue gym shorts, unlike a lot of girls there. I didn't even realize the ball was coming toward us.

And then she took a shot all the way to the back of the gym, actually hitting the ceiling, nearly busting one of the lights. The ball bounced twice before the outfielder could grab it and toss it in. By then Jenna had already rounded second base.

Of course somebody tried to throw it at her and missed. Instead the ball bounced right to me.

And I actually managed to grab it, just as she was rounding third, me standing directly in her path. And I could hear all the other sixth graders shouting for her to stay on third and for me to throw the ball at her already. And I could hear the slap of her tennis shoes on the hardwood floor. And I could smell *everybody*, because it was near the end of the class and our secretions had mixed together into a miasmatic fog of B.O. that made my stomach do the mambo.

And I could see the look in her ocean eyes. And I could see the wicked and determined smile on her face.

And I knew she wasn't going to stop.

I should have gotten out of her way, but I held the ball out in front of me and closed my eyes and prepared for impact. In three . . . two . . . one.

I felt the red rubber of the ball in my face, in my mouth, up my nose. In fact, that ball was all I saw and smelled, as if it had been a bloodred moon eclipsing the sun of Jenna's face.

I heard the air rushing past as I fell.

I was vaguely aware of everyone in the room, even the sixth-grade gym coach, saying "*Oooh.*" I hit the floor hard, and for a moment, I didn't hear, see, or feel anything.

Then it all came rushing back, and I saw her on top of me. Her glasses slightly askew. Still smiling.

"I guess I'm out," she said.

I tried to breathe.

She stood and offered me her hand. I let her pull me up, which she did without the slightest strain. There was a hornets' nest buzzing in my ears and I was still having trouble focusing, but I could see a look of worry on her face as she pointed.

"You're bleeding a little," she said.

I wiped my nose on my sleeve. "No biggie," I said, sniffing.

"Sorry about that. You should have thrown it."

"You would still have been out," I said.

She shook her head. "You would have missed." I believed her. Jenna bit her lip and scrunched her nose and smiled, and I forgot the blood, and the sweat, and the hornets.

It was like she knew me already.

A month later I found out that, had she wanted to, Jenna Jaden could have kicked the ball so hard that it exploded. She could have rounded the bases and been sitting back on the bleachers before it even came down. She could have hit me hard enough to send me to the emergency room with a blood clot in my brain.

But that's not Jenna. That's the Silver Lynx.

The Silver Lynx is the only one of us who has seen any real action, unless you count last Tuesday, which I'm trying hard not to think about. Of course the others have trained with their Supers. Cryos and Eric spend every third Saturday in his secret cavern working through combat scenarios. Supposedly Hotshot took Gavin out one Friday night to help foil a suspected robbery of dangerous chemicals at the university science lab, though it turned out to be a gang of student activists looking to free the lab mice. And Mike and the Rocket were almost spotted flying over the Justicia football stadium during halftime last year. But for the most part, Jenna's the only one of us who really knows what it's like to be out there, on the streets, in the shadows. She's the only one whose Super trusts her enough to let her help, who's close to being able to do the whole superhero thing on her own.

The Silver Lynx is a hunter. Fierce. Determined. Nearly unstoppable.

But Jenna's different.

The day she bloodied my nose, Jenna asked if we could be friends.

And she promised she would never hurt me again.

UNLIKELY HEROES

It's Saturday. Saturday night, actually. Somewhere out there, a gang of immaculately dressed criminals sharing the same name, and their back-from-the-dead leader, are probably planning to take over the world. Nobody really knows. There have been no grand announcements. No interrupted broadcasts. Though the Dealer's face gets plenty of airtime regardless. The Jacks' escape from prison is the leading news story for the twenty-four hours, and every station dredges up footage of their past crimes. It's all rehashed, especially the climactic final battle between the Suits and the Legion of Justice, showing the smoking remains of the Dealer's headquarters and the Legion in front of it—one of the last pictures taken of all five of them together.

It seems like every time I pass the television I see him—not the sad sack jockeying a bar stool on Thirty-fourth Street, but the *real* Titan, leading the Legion into battle, duking it out with the Dealer, and generally looking all heroic and stuff. When I see him like that, I can't help myself. I just stand and stare, breathless and confused, wondering if he's watching himself too. If he sees what I see.

He has to know. But that doesn't mean he has to care. He made that clear enough last time. So I just stand and stare until my mother notices me, catches something in the look on my face, and asks me if I'm all right. Then I have to turn it off and pretend I don't care.

So it's Saturday. And if my Super was half the man he once was, he would be pounding the streets looking for the Dealer and his three remaining Suits, and I might very well be beside him on ready reserve status, mask and belt on, nose to the ground. But he's not. So I'm not.

Instead I'm going to the mall with Mike to spy on girls. It's a favorite pastime of his, and he deserves it, his first day back in the world, considering what he's been through.

I met Mike my first day at H.E.R.O., when he shook my hand and made my hair stand up. Aside from Jenna, Mike is my best friend. He's the only other member of H.E.R.O. that I hang with outside of school. Nikki has her revolving boyfriends and Eric is involved in, like, thirty clubs. And Gavin—I'm not sure who he hangs out with. Maybe kids from football. Or maybe he has groupies who follow him around. Or maybe he spends his weekends flexing in front of the bathroom mirror. I don't really care.

Mike and I have a lot in common. We both are slightly worse than mediocre at sports and both like pineapple on our pizza. We both enjoy watching B-grade horror movies when our parents aren't looking and despise sitcoms. We both think girls are cuter when they don't wear makeup, and we are both afraid to take our shirts off at the pool when the high school kids are around. We both grew up worshipping the same Supers.

And we've both been let down.

Literally. Though my Super never broke my arm.

Mike got out of the hospital on Wednesday, and he's spent the last three days holed up in his room, calling me this morning to say that if he didn't get out of the house, he was going to electrocute himself.

It was possible. With Mike, self-electrocution is never entirely out of the question. He's an energy manipulator, high voltage class, which is a fancy way of saying he can create balls of electricity by summoning the natural charges in his own body. I told him I'd not only hang out with him, I'd sleep over at his house and catch him up on all the latest gossip. After all, my parents are growing fidgety, constantly checking in on me no matter what I'm doing. Even though the break-out happened hundreds of miles from here and nobody has heard a peep from the Suits since, I can sense the apprehension bubbling. My mother's furtive glances. The way my father mumbles to himself. So the mall sounded like a great idea.

I meet Mike outside the bookstore. It's the first time I've seen him since the accident, and he looks mostly back to normal.

His frizzy blond hair still sticks out all over the place (worse when he's walking on carpet), and he looks like maybe he lost a few pounds. The cuts and bruises have healed, but he's got a cast on his right arm that reaches from wrist to shoulder. He already told me it took several metal pins screwed directly into the bone to get his arm straightened out. The doctors told him he shouldn't even think about skateboarding for several months—and he should never skate down the bleachers at the football field again.

That was the story. That Mike Vanderbolt was stupid enough to surf down the handrails of the metal bleachers before slipping and smashing his arm on the stone sidewalk below. I guess it was the best Mr. Masters could come up with when he took Mike to the emergency room after a frantic call from the Rocket. After all, he couldn't really say that Mike was a superhero sidekick and was dropped out of the sky a full forty feet by a grown man with a jet pack strapped to his chest on what was supposed to be a routine training exercise. Mr. Masters was ticked. It wasn't the first off-duty accident in H.E.R.O. history—apparently Cryos once accidentally froze Eric to the ceiling during one of their training sessions, giving him a mild case of frostbite—but it was bad enough that Mr. Masters spent a full thirty minutes lecturing to the rest of us about following proper procedures when engaging in extra-curricular training with our Supers.

Not that I had to worry about it. But I still had to sit and listen to it.

"We weren't using the safety harness," Mike explains as we head toward Mr. Twist's for the first half of our traditional mall dinner of soft pretzels and jelly beans. "It was my idea. I thought we were ready. I didn't think he would drop me."

You never do, I almost say. "Have you heard from him? The Rocket, I mean?"

Mike shakes his head. "Not for a few days. He took it pretty hard."

"I think you took it harder," I say, pointing at the cast.

Mike shrugs. "Mr. Masters told me that he won't even come out of his house. He won't return anyone's calls. Hasn't been on patrol. Even with all the recent craziness. I kind of feel bad for him," Mike adds. "Dropping your partner out of the sky probably doesn't look so good on the superhero resume."

"Yeah, probably violates the no-almost-killing-your-sidekick rule," I say, wondering if there even was such a rule. I don't know the Supers' code, though Mr. Masters says it's pretty similar to ours. You don't learn it until you decide to become one and take the oath. "He's going to come back, though, right? I mean, he's still your Super."

"Not sure. I hope so," Mike says, then holds up his cast. "Not that I'd be much help to him now anyway." We pass by a group of teenagers huddled together. One of them asks me what I'm looking at. I just smile and wave, eager to avoid confrontation.

"How long?" I ask, pointing to the cast.

121

"At least ten weeks." Mike looks at his broken arm like it's not even a part of him, just some strange plaster appendage hanging from his shoulder. "I asked Mr. Masters if we could just chop it off and get me one of those cybernetic jobs, you know, like the kind Eric's Super has?"

I nod appreciatively. Cryos is a cyborg—a product of American military spending, German engineering, Chinese-manufactured parts, and way too many science-fiction movies. He has this killer cybernetic arm, which not only fires these cool freeze rays but also has, like, more apps than an iPhone. I've only met him a few times—at those special H.E.R.O. training sessions that my own Super never bothered to show up to—but each time he let me touch his arm. It was pretty awesome. If Mike got one of those, I'd catapult myself down the stairs until my own arm broke. But I know Mr. Masters would never go for it. "We are given the gifts we're given," he'd say, "and our job is to make the most of them."

"I'm guessing he said no."

Mike shakes his head. "Not even a flamethrower."

"But can you still . . . you know?" I make a motion with my hands, pretending that I'm summoning currents of electricity, thinking it's funny how we all imitate each other. Like how Jenna looks like a zombie when she's imitating Nikki walking through walls. Or how Eric looks like he's constipated when he imitates me looking at something far away. I've seen Mike generate lightning a hundred times, but the motions just look silly when I make them.

"Yeah, I *can*," he says, "but I still don't really have *any* control where it goes."

"Oh," I say. "That's really not good." It really isn't.

Mike doesn't argue. The ability to launch electricity from your fingertips is one of those signature powers—the kind that you can really design a persona and a costume around. Unfortunately Mike, aka Kid Shock, has terrible aim. In the two years we've known each other, his spastic use of his power has led to a few incidents. And while I fondly remember him accidentally blowing the school's generator, resulting in me, thankfully, missing a Spanish quiz, I try not to recall what he did to his neighbor's cat.

"In that case, you should try to keep it to yourself," I say.

We order three packs of cinnamon sugar twists to split and two blueberry slushies, then head toward the fountain at the center of the mall to feast. Sitting on the bench, licking the sugar from my fingers, I fill him in on what he's missed, from the whole bee incident to the jail bust, though he's seen more news than I have and knows most of it already. I leave out the part about Jenna's new body spray—he would only roll his eyes—but I mention what Mr. Masters said on the phone yesterday about identities compromised and being watched.

"You think he meant me?"

"Maybe." Mike shrugs. "Or maybe there's something else going on. You said the Killer Bee might have set you and Jenna up in order to get to the Fox. Maybe someone out there is spilling secrets to the other side."

I think about it. It's possible, I guess. It seems Mr. Masters suspected as much. Though selling secret identities is tantamount to treason. It'd be like tearing the Code into a hundred little pieces, gluing them back together all wrong, setting the whole mess on fire, and then peeing on it to put out the flames.

And yet Mr. Masters has been looking at me a lot lately. Surely he doesn't think . . . he couldn't, *could he*? After all, *I* was the one dangling from the hook last week. Why would I leak my own secret identity to somebody who would try to kill me?

"It's not one of us," I say emphatically.

"Not one of *us*," Mike says, pointing to the two of us. "But I wouldn't rule Gavin out."

That's another thing Mike and I have in common. Though I think Mike doesn't like him only because I don't, which makes me feel guilty for not liking him, but not guilty enough to stop. Especially not after yesterday. If I try hard enough, I can still smell it.

"But it might be best if you didn't eavesdrop on Mr. Masters's telephone calls anymore," Mike says. Then suddenly his eyes light up. "Speaking of which," he says, "six o'clock. Brunette. Green top. Group of three." I finish my last pretzel and then look for this girl in green. I spot her and her two friends standing outside the Abercrombie, laughing. She's cute. And old.

"Dude, she's like, seventeen, at least."

"She looked right at us, and I'm pretty sure she smiled at me."

I look at Mike. His face is covered in cinnamon sugar, his hair is sticking straight up, and with the cast on, he looks like he's just got pummeled by the entire football team. "I don't think so," I say.

"Then maybe she smiled at you. You're good-looking . . . compared to equally nerdy guys in your popularity bracket."

"Thanks."

"Just do it, please."

I groan as a matter of formal objection and wipe my hands on Mike's shirt. Then I take one last look at the girl in green to get my bearings. This is why we come here. Reconnaissance. I find out what girls are saying about Mike, and he uses that information to decide whether or not to go and talk to them. Of course in about twenty trips to the mall, he has never once spoken to a single girl.

Still, I suppose it's good practice for me. Trying to pick out one voice, especially a voice you aren't familiar with, in a crowd of hundreds at a shopping mall takes immense concentration. I sift through the thousands of sounds, the shuffle of feet and the soft Muzak, and narrow in on Greenie and her friends. I look closely to match up what I'm hearing with the movement of her glossy lips.

"I would totally date a werewolf, are you kidding? Drinking blood is not sexy."

I look over at Mike. He's a little shaggy, but he's certainly no werewolf.

"You're right," I say. "She just told her friends that she

125

totally digs guys half covered in plaster."

"Seriously?" Mike looks at me like a puppy begging for scraps.

I give him a what-do-you-think? look. But Mike is undeterred, scanning the crowd, hoping to catch another girl's eye. Suddenly he leans in and whispers, "Quick, straight ahead, white sweater, short skirt, ponytail."

I look. The girl in the white sweater is only twenty feet away. She's at least closer to our age. She's also standing right beside a guy who looks about a foot taller than me.

"Dude, she's with somebody."

"They're just friends," Mike says. "It's purely platonic. He's gay. Or her brother. I swear. Our eyes met. There was a spark."

"You just accidentally shocked yourself again, is all."

"Drew . . ."

"Fine," I say, "but this is the last one, okay? I'm just not in the mood." Thanks to Mike, I've now got a sinking feeling that Mr. Masters suspects me of being a traitor on top of being a basically hopeless sidekick.

"I promise," he says.

I take a sip of slushie and then open up to the static again. It's a little easier to filter this time, but before I can zero in on what she's saying, she stops, leans in, and kisses the guy. Rather purposefully. Tongue included.

"Guess it's not her brother," Mike says, and I'm just about to shove him off the bench when I catch something else, another voice, a comment that just kind of sticks out, like a wrong note at a piano recital.

"Just take 'em," the voice says. *"Nobody's looking."*

Mike starts slapping my arm. "Ooh. Ooh. Party of five. Over by the cell phone store. All giggling. I think one of them just pointed at us. Drew? *Drew?*"

"Hush," I say, trying to concentrate. I think the voice came from the left. I scan the crowd, listening for it again, hushed, deep, determined, but Mike is still chirping in my ear.

"Just tuck 'em under your jacket and leave."

That's it. I trace the sound. It's definitely coming from our left, maybe fifty yards away.

"I think something's about to happen," I whisper, forgetting that I'm the only one with extraordinary senses and that Mike can barely hear *me* in the crowd. He reaches up and pulls my hand free.

"What do you mean, something's about to happen?"

"I don't know exactly. Someone's going to steal something maybe. Get ready," I say, trying to stay focused, listening for that voice again.

"What do you mean, get *ready*?"

Just then, two teenagers in black hoodies appear at the entrance to Sam's Sportswear. Both have their hands tucked into their jackets—really thick, blocky jackets. The one voice says, *"Just be cool. Keep walking."*

Then, from inside the store, I hear somebody say, *"Hey, you gotta pay for those."*

The two guys look back once and then take off running.

Somebody, I can only assume the store manager, judging by the bald head, comes tearing out of the store behind them. They are all headed in our direction.

"Hey," the bald man yells. "Stop those two!"

But instead of stopping them, the crowd parts like the Red Sea—OCs doing what OCs do best: watching, frozen, as the two teenagers bowl through them. They are only three stores away.

I suddenly get an image of the Superhero Sidekick Code of Conduct hanging in the basement at Highview Middle School, chiseled in stone. I look at my sugar-crusted fingers and slushie-stained shirt, then over at Mike in his giant cast wearing that bewildered look on his face.

We are the forces of goodness and light.

"We have to do something."

It all happens so fast. I think I hear Mike ask, "We?"—but I'm already up and running, jumping right into the path of the looters, instinctively reaching for the belt that I'm not wearing, because I'm not on ready reserve status, because I'm not even really a full-fledged sidekick, because I left it at home in my closet. Still, utility belt or not, I'm determined to stop them.

Mr. Masters says that when you are faced with moments of danger, time slows down, but he has a time-stopping watch, so I always take it with a grain of salt. Truth is, time moves at the same pace; you just have to think a little faster, is all. Standing in the middle of the mall in the direct path of two stampeding shoplifters, I get a lot of thinking in.

I try to remember my training, particularly the moves that Eric taught us all in martial arts.

I think about a picture I saw once, of a man getting trampled by a bull.

I think about the Code and how, come to think of it, I haven't actually *stopped* a crime. Ever. Not once.

And I think about Jenna, and what she might say if she could see me now, standing in front of these guys, stretching out my hand, ordering them to halt the way policemen always do in movies. Standing firm. Not moving, heroic maybe, even as they barrel straight for me. Even though they look to be twice my size and getting larger.

Bracing myself as the first one lowers his shoulder and plows right into me, catching my chin with his elbow.

Spinning, the pain in my jaw so sudden and intense.

Falling, flat on my butt, as the wind tears right out of me, choking to get it back.

Watching as the second shoplifter leaps nimbly over me, both of them getting away.

Then, suddenly, there is a sound, like someone stomping in mud, and I turn to see a woman in her forties, maybe older, standing over the first boy, a smashed shopping bag in her hand, a look of fierce determination on her face, her three kids slack-jawed and gawking behind her. The second shop-lifter, seeing his buddy suddenly laid out on the floor, hesitates for just a moment, when he's suddenly tackled from out of nowhere by a mall security guard. I lie there and listen to the click of handcuffs . . . the store manager cursing the two would-be thieves . . . recovering his two boxes of shoes.

I suddenly realize there is a hand reaching down for me and see that it's the girl in the white sweater.

"You okay?" she asks.

I stand up and look around. Just about everyone has their cell phone out, capturing the moment on video. Tonight I could be on YouTube, getting bowled over by a sixteen-year-old trying to steal a pair of high-tops, though odds are no one would notice me. I watch as one of the mall cops shakes hands with the mother of three, the hero who leveled the villain with one blow. Then, suddenly, the crowd begins to applaud. Even Mike, who comes to stand next to me, is slapping his good hand on his cast.

"Did you *see* that? She swung that shopping bag like a lumberjack. That was awesome. We've got to get that woman a cape."

"Yeah," I say, brushing myself off. "Pretty awesome."

"You were awesome too," Mike says as an afterthought. "You slowed that first guy down."

All around, everyone is buzzing. I look at the girl in the green shirt. She points to me and then turns to her friends.

"Did you see that kid get tackled? What was he thinking?"

I feel the blood rising to my cheeks. I rub my jaw and just stare at the girl until she looks away nervously.

"Come on, let's go," I say.

As we head to the candy store, I watch the mother of three pull all her kids close to her, hugging them fiercely. I can hear her sobbing.

It's tough being a hero, I guess.

Later that night, Mike and I turn on the news expecting to see something about the attempted theft at the Justicia Shopping Mall. "Mall Hero Mom Comes Out Swinging," or something like that, but it turns out there's much bigger news than a couple of shoplifting teens.

A bank robbery in a small town about a hundred miles north of here. The thief managed to bypass all the alarms and disable the security cameras with ease. A high-powered laser of some sort was used to blast through the locks on the vault itself. No one was hurt, and the robber managed to get away easily.

In place of the missing cash, estimated in the millions, the thief left a playing card.

The Jack of Diamonds.

SOMETHING DOESN'T
SMELL RIGHT

I t's Monday. Grilled cheese day, which is kind of a shame, because I might have actually eaten one of those, provided it hadn't been sitting in its waxy cocoon under the heat lamps too long. At the very least, I would have eaten the soggy fries that came with it, because the salt sticks to the grease like wet snow and I've grown fond of salt. It's the only spice my delicate senses can tolerate, and I put it on everything. Even my applesauce.

But it's Monday, which means lunch will be a granola bar and a banana quickly scarfed down on the way to the teachers' lounge. Normally I move quickly, but for some reason I take my time walking to H.E.R.O. today. The incident at the mall ruined a perfectly good Sunday set aside for lying around. Mike told me not to worry about it. That it happens to the best of us, and that I certainly looked brave jumping in front of those guys. Still, I don't see how I am supposed to go toe-to-toe with an eye-blasting supervillain like the Jack of Diamonds when I can't even tackle a teenage shoplifter. Coupled with the news of the bank robbery and the fact that Jenna was apparently too busy to return my phone calls . . . I'm starting to get the impression that I'm being left behind somehow. That I'm on the outside looking in, like all the OCs huddled in front of their televisions, wondering who's going to save them next.

And Mr. Masters doesn't help, spending the first twenty minutes rehashing everything we already know about the bank robbery, then telling Jenna, Gavin, and Eric that they are to spend the entire day in the combat simulator, fighting robots, while Nikki and I resume our regularly scheduled training, though we can at least sit together. He makes it pretty clear that until I learn to shoot lasers out of my eyes or flames out of my butt, I won't get to play with the other kids. That is, unless all of a sudden the Titan should find his feet below his gut and get back on the streets. Or until Mr. Masters can find a Super in need of a sidekick who can hear a cricket's chirp twenty miles away.

I look through the window of the simulator, watching as Eric and Gavin bash their way through a wave of armored automatons while Jenna leaps over another with lynxlike grace. Just watching her move puts me in a trance. If she had been at the mall on Saturday, she would have mopped the floor with those guys. Even next to Eric and Gavin, she looks like she's in a league of her own, and before long she has a pile of scrap metal at her feet.

There is a loud *thunk* next to me, causing me to leap out of my chair. Nikki has her hand caught inside a chunk of marble and struggles to shake it free. "Sorry," she says, massaging her fingers.

"It's okay," I say. "I get my hand caught inside rocks all the time."

I look at Nikki and smile. At least we're in the same boat. Her mentor, a telepath named Miss Mindminer, has been on loan to the Chinese government for the past month or so, on some top-secret mission, way too dangerous for a novice sidekick like the Wisp to tag along, leaving Nikki Superless until her return. There is talk, Mr. Masters says, of bringing Miss Mindminer back to help round up the Suits, but she is so deep undercover that only another telepath could reach her. There is another *thunk* as the marble hits the floor this time.

"What are you doing, anyway?"

"Composition one oh one," she says, indicating the twenty or so blocks of stone, glass, and metal on the table. "I'm just trying to get a feel for it. Makes it easier when I try to pass through." She picks up the piece of marble again, letting her fingers sink into it little by little. "Some are harder than others. Glass is pretty easy. So are most woods. I can pass through drywall without even breaking a sweat. But platinum—don't *even* try to walk through that."

"I'll cross it off my list," I say, opening the box that contains my activity for the next half hour—a series of forty glass vials, each containing the slightest trace of some substance that I'm supposed to identify by smell alone. I don't know why Mr. Masters makes me do this. I don't know what good it will do me. Will telling a villain that he had burritos for lunch make him let me go? I have my doubts.

Mr. Masters says I may someday be able to sniff out danger from miles away, which is all well and good if I knew what danger smelled like. Gunpowder I've got. I can identify nitrous oxide, acetylene, and chloroform. I can even tell you if Bobby Ellis was stupid enough to bring fireworks to school again. But until bad guys start wearing their own unique brand of cologne, I don't think my nostrils are going to save the day.

"Bubble gum," I say.

"Huh?"

"Sorry. The smell. Bubble gum," I say again, holding the vial out to Nikki, who takes a sniff and shakes her head.

"Can't smell a thing," she says.

"And I can't walk through walls," I say.

I screw the cap off the second vial and take a whiff. "Fresh pear," I say, passing the tube back and forth under my nose as if it were wine . . . and I knew anything about wine.

"You look like a dork," Nikki says to me, and then promptly shoves her head through a piece of wood so that she looks like a hunting trophy displayed on the wall of a cheap hotel.

"Ditto," I say, guessing ginger ale and then checking my answer to make sure I'm right. "Have you talked to your

Super?" I ask, opening the next vial and taking a big whiff. Corn chips, no question. "Or, you know, has she . . ." I put my hands to my head and make a funny humming noise. Because I don't have the slightest clue what using telepathy looks like. If I could read minds, I would know why the Titan won't get off his stool. Why Mr. Masters keeps looking at me funny. And why Jenna has been avoiding me lately. I'd know what my parents were really thinking every time I came home late and what the OCs were really thinking whenever a Super dropped out of the sky.

"Not really," Nikki says, shaking off a cement block. "I don't think she likes me much. I've read somewhere that telepaths prefer to work alone. I don't know why she even signed up to take on a sidekick."

"I know *exactly* what you mean," I say.

Nikki looks over at me and frowns. "It kinda sucks, doesn't it? Being tacked on."

"Yeah. Kinda," I say. "Though at least you have a boyfriend."

Nikki holds up two fingers and smiles slyly. I shake my head, then look back through the glass of the simulator just in time to see Jenna drive her fist into one of the robot's sensors before flipping it over and smashing it with her heel. I can see the intensity in her eyes. The concentration. It's a little frightening. I take a sniff of my next tube and guess fish, then read the label.

ICELANDIC COD. Now, apparently, I'm supposed to identify

where the smells *come* from, too.

"I don't know," Nikki says, looking down at the metal table, dipping her fingers into it, and stirring them in a way that is mesmerizing. "I think it's different with you. I mean, with everything that's happening, and what happened before, with the Dealer back, you would think . . ." She doesn't finish the thought. She doesn't have to.

You would think he'd come back.

"You can't make someone be a hero," I say.

"Whatever," Nikki counters. "But if it was me, if it was *my* nemesis come back from the dead, breaking those guys out of prison and robbing banks and stuff, you can best be sure I'd be out on the streets kicking some *serious* tail." She thrusts her fists clear through the table for emphasis.

She's right. I think she's right. But it doesn't matter what I think.

I reach for the last vial in that row, twist off the cork, and bring it just under my nose. "Oh, *gyyyahh, gross.*" I choke and hold the tube away from me, grimacing.

"What? What is it?" Nikki asks, alarmed.

I hand the tube over to her and she takes a sniff. Even she can smell it—that's how bad it is.

"Oh. Oh, god. What is *that*?" She hands it back.

I look at the label on the back. The words MACINTOSH APPLE are crossed out. In its place is written *Eric's Fart.*

I look back through the simulator window at the rest of H.E.R.O. standing triumphantly over their imaginary foes.

Shizuka Shi turns and waves to me.

"I am *so* going to get him back for that."

I make it through all forty vials, only missing two. I couldn't identify cauliflower or arsenic. The first doesn't bother me—I can't imagine any villain who would try to kill a superhero with a head of cauliflower, unless the superhero was a toddler and the villain was his mother. Arsenic, on the other hand, seems like something I should be able to identify. I think about how in demand I could have been, like, four hundred years ago, when everyone went around poisoning everyone else. I could have been the royal sniffer, sitting beside the king, shoving my snout into his pot roast and pomegranates. But most bad guys don't bother poisoning anyone anymore, now that it's so much easier to shoot them. Though the worst kind just find someone else to do their work for them.

At the end of H.E.R.O., Eric, Gavin, and Jenna emerge from the training chamber, laughing and clapping each other on the back. I see Gavin throw his arm around Jenna and whisper in her ear, and even though it's probably none of my business, I listen anyway.

"You rocked today," he says.

That's actually what he says. I resist the urge to vomit in my mouth. I wonder if that will be his catchphrase, the one they print on fan T-shirts when he becomes a famous Super ten years from now. "Hi. I'm Stonewall, your friendly neighborhood Super, and I totally rock!"

I wonder what mine would be.

"I'm the Sensationalist, and I smell better than you!" Maybe I have a future as a deodorant pitchman.

Mr. Masters calls out a few reminders as everyone heads back to the stairs. This Wednesday is small blade disarmament training and we only have three days left to decide if we need our costumes altered—turns out some of us are already outgrowing our spandex. Then he reminds us all to be especially careful, that the Suits are still at large, that evil never sleeps, and to always follow the Code. He adds a "good work today," but I don't think he's talking to me. I head to the stairs, hoping to catch up with Jenna, to offer to walk her to her next class, when Mr. Masters intercepts me.

"Number forty?" he pries.

"What?" I try to crane my neck to look over his shoulder and see if Jenna is waiting for me, but the man is just too blasted tall.

"Number forty. What was it?"

Mr. Masters always saves the hardest scent for last. It's the only one he ever asks me about, and he never puts the answer on the back. "Sodium chloride," I venture. "My guess is one crystal dissolved in about two ounces of water."

"The Sensationalist does it again," he says, smiling.

Yeah. Goody, I think to myself. Somewhere out there a teenage shoplifter is having nightmares about a mother of three with a heavy shopping bag and a wicked left hook, and I'm in here smelling salt.

"And you," I say, "had doughnuts for breakfast. Jelly filled." There's a spot of jelly on his collar. It doesn't always take a superhero.

Mr. Masters drops his smile. "Listen, Drew," he says. "We need to talk."

I step to the side and watch Jenna disappear, listening to her footsteps on the stairs. I know her walk. I could pick out the sound of her step in a crowd of hundreds. I could find her anywhere.

"I'm concerned," Mr. Masters says, stooping a bit to make eye contact.

This snaps me back. When adults tell you they are concerned about you, what they usually mean is that they think you are up to no good and are about to have you tested, or increase your medication, or transfer you to military school. The lines on Mr. Masters's face all crease downward.

"About me?" I ask.

"About the Titan," he says.

"Oh," I say. I unconsciously glance sideways at the giant stone tablet hanging on the wall.

"I know in the past I've told you to be patient. To see if he won't come around. But things are more serious now. The Dealer. The Suits."

"That was a long time ago," I say. A lot can change in six years. Mr. Masters should appreciate that. He can change a lot in sixty seconds.

"But some things aren't easily forgotten," Mr. Masters

presses. He takes a moment to just stare at me. I take the time to count the hairs that just barely poke out of his nostrils. I'm not sure what he wants from me. Why he keeps holding me back.

Mr. Masters's hand lights on my shoulder again, holding me. "I'm afraid the Titan might be in danger," he says. "If you have *any* idea where he is, or if he has tried to contact you at all recently . . ."

I look into Mr. Masters's burrowing brown eyes, see the little bubbles of sweat forming above his brows. Why is he even asking me this? He knows the Code as well as I do.

And yet part of me feels like I should just tell him. About the shape the Titan is in. I should tell him because Mr. Masters was the one who assigned the Titan to me to begin with—and maybe he is the only one who could convince him to put the outfit back on.

But I can't. I made a promise. I can't tell anyone where he is if he doesn't want me to. If the Titan had wanted Mr. Masters to keep tabs on him, he wouldn't have gone off the grid.

"I don't think I can help you," I say.

Mr. Masters stands up straight and hovers over me. I can hear him grinding his teeth. He doesn't believe me. He doesn't say anything, but I can see it in his eyes. And I'm pretty sure that he knows something I don't. Maybe a lot of somethings.

And I start to wonder a bit.

Mr. Masters, who runs the H.E.R.O. program. Who is tapped directly into the network. Who knows all our secret identities. Who has access to tons of classified information. Mr. Masters, who once worked for the Department of Homeland Security's Supernormal Activities Department. Mr. Masters's hand grips my shoulder, a little harder than last time, and I look for his other hand, the one that is tucked into his pocket. The one with the watch.

"Are *you* okay?" I ask.

His expression softens; his hand releases me. He musters a smile, though I can tell it is a challenge for him. "Just worried, is all. If you *should* see him, tell him that I'm looking for him. That I he needs to come find me."

The bell rings again.

"You're late for class. Better hurry," he says, turning to head back into his office.

I nod again and take off for the stairs, but when I'm at the top, I pause, thinking maybe I've heard my name.

It's not a mistake. I hear Mr. Masters whisper, *"I know you're listening, Drew."*

And then I hear him whisper, *"Be careful who you trust."*

And I feel a chill sweep over me as I slide out from behind the snack machine and into the hall, deciding that from this point on, I will take Mr. Masters's advice.

Maybe starting with Mr. Masters.

THE CALL

Being a Super isn't easy. Just think about the stress. To be available at a moment's notice. To drop everything you are doing and squeeze into your tights when nobody's looking, cramming yourself into the backseat of an unlocked car because there aren't any phone booths anymore, trying to pull your jeans off over your spandex and getting them caught around your ankles, pulling your mask clumsily over your head and somehow getting it twisted around one ear. Seeing your signal blaze in the night sky while you are in the middle of your ravioli al forno, taking one last sip of wine as you grab your jet pack and leap out your window, accidentally frying a pigeon on the way. Missing the end of a movie or your favorite show, coming back to find that your coffee is cold or your boyfriend got tired of waiting for you and left, slamming the door so hard on his way out that it knocked pictures off your walls. Canceling Thanksgiving dinner because some whack job in a mole costume decides to sabotage the city's generators to send the world into total darkness so that only *he* can see. It's always something. Your time is not your own, unless you have a magic watch, and even then your life is measured out in minutes.

Add to that the fact you've got lives in your hands. Trains with failed brake systems and jumbo jets full of panicked passengers plummeting into the ocean. Reporters falling off buildings and little kids somersaulting over the Hoover Dam. And that always-nagging thought that maybe *this* time, you aren't going to be able to save them. Maybe *this* time, your laser vision will fail or your vulcan hand cannon will jam or the lace on your boot will come loose and you will trip at the last moment while the reporter does her best pancake impression on the sidewalk before you can catch her. Not to mention the bad guys always giving you the "choice" between chasing after them or rescuing hundreds of OCs who are about to have a building fall on them or the cables on a suspension bridge snap, knowing full well that you will follow the Code, that you aren't going to just sit back and let civilians *die* (though imagine the look on the bad guy's face if you did. "Sure," you'd say, "six hundred innocent people drowned today, but at least I caught you, you jerk").

Oh. And then there's the money. Being a Super is expensive. Over half of all Supers are funded through grants from the National Endowment for Superheroes and Crime Fighters.

But still, even your average-sized 7,500-square-foot top-secret underground headquarters, modestly outfitted and reasonably priced, runs at least two mill in the burbs, and twice that if you want to be downtown for easy access to crime and shopping. Then there're uniforms, gadgets, weapons, upgrades, computers, jet planes, personalized body armor, nuclear reactors, guided missile systems, global tracking satellites, grappling hooks, utility belts, utility hooks, grappling belts, butlers, blasters, bunkers, cryogenic containment labs, and all that other junk. It just adds up. Time. Stress. Money.

Yet every Super who has ever been asked about the hardest part of the job will tell you it's not the deadly combat or the sleepless nights or the pressure of thwarting giant alien death rays aimed at the planet. It's keeping the secret. They have manuals on how to deal with all that other stuff. How do you deal with the loneliness? The fact that, on some basic level, you do *everything* for *everybody* and no one even bothers to say thanks, because they don't even know who you *are*?

So you let something slip. Maybe while having a drink after work, you say something about the time you punched a hole through the roof of a car or accidentally set your living-room couch on fire with your heat vision. Sometimes you forget a little detail. The scorch marks on your boots or the radioactive goop that is still somehow tangled in your hair from your run-in with extraterrestrial terrorists.

Sometimes you do it on purpose—a casual comment to someone you care about, hoping that maybe, just maybe, she will figure it out and guess your secret. Because then you no longer have to bear the burden alone. Because *somebody* knows. Somebody else has to carry it with you. But by then it is too late. Your secret is out. You've been compromised. The best Supers are the ones who can stay behind the mask. Who never show their hand.

Take the Fox. Nobody knows very much about her. *I* only happen to know her secret identity because Jenna told me, swearing me to absolute secrecy. In fact, it's the only time I know of that Jenna's broken the Code. And if she hadn't told me, I would never have guessed. The Fox has short, flaming red hair, sparkling blue eyes, and stands about five foot seven. Kyla Kaden has long, flowing raven-black hair, light-brown eyes, and stands at least six feet, though if you looked in her closet you'd probably find rows of high-heeled shoes and a few wigs. Kyla wears sharp business suits and lots of makeup. The Fox wears a white-and-red jump suit and a matching white mask that covers half of her face. Stand them next to each other, and you would swear you were looking at two different people.

A disguise is about playing to expectations. Helping people believe what they want to believe. Kyla Kaden is the founder and CEO of Kaden Enterprises. She came to this country at the age of twenty-two to start her own business. The heiress to a huge estate left to her by a father who supposedly died in a fire when she was a teen, Kyla applied her genius-level IQ to the field of weapons engineering, developing satellite-guided missile systems for the army. She was wealthy, accomplished, and beautiful.

She couldn't possibly have time to be a superhero too.

But that's the thing about the Fox. Like the best of them, she's hard to pin down.

That night, as I'm finishing the third act of *Julius Caesar* (*Et tu, Brute?*), I hear my father groan from the living room. My mother asks him what's wrong, and he tells her the crazies are on TV again. They've interrupted *Jeopardy!* for some kind of special announcement. I wonder which group of crazies he's talking about—there are a lot to choose from—but then I hear the Fox's name mentioned and practically trip over myself careening down the stairs. I turn down the hall to find my parents sitting on the couch, staring at her. Her wavy red locks stream out from beneath the white mask she wears. Her blue eyes blaze. Though her sword isn't strapped on, she still looks every bit as dangerous as she did when she was cutting down drones back at the pool. She stands at a podium, her hands gripping the sides as if she's about to tear it out of the ground. She could, of course. With ease.

My mother notices me and pats a spot beside her on the couch. As I sit, she puts a hand on my knee, comforting and uncomfortable all at once.

On TV the Fox stares into the camera. A small crowd stands behind her—all stars from the forces of goodness and light. The mayor and the Justicia police commissioner stand to her left. Cryos stands behind her, his cybernetic eye glowing like a hot coal, his cold-fusion blaster arm hanging by his side. And beside him, Hotshot, Gavin's Super, is dressed in his customary orange and yellow, with swirling red flames trailing down the sleeves of his fireproof suit, a halo of blue flames flickering from his crown. No sign of the Rocket. Apparently Mike's Super still hasn't left the house.

No sign of the Titan either.

Not that they need him. There's enough power behind that podium to take down a deck full of villains. It's actually kind of thrilling to see them standing there together.

But they aren't really together. This isn't the Legion of Justice. The other Supers stand behind the Fox, like backup singers waiting for the chorus. The camera is focused on her.

"Hello, citizens," she says in her growling, gravelly voice that Mike calls sultry. "Please excuse this interruption, but I want to take this opportunity to assure you that, despite recent events, there is no cause for alarm. The superhero community is doing everything it can to assist both government offices and local law enforcement agencies in apprehending the criminals known as the Suits." The Fox takes a moment to acknowledge the mayor and the commissioner, both of whom look down at their polished shoes. Then she continues. "I promise that it is only a matter of time before the Dealer and his men are brought to justice. Until then, I ask all of you to remain calm and go about your ordinary lives. I also ask that *all* Supers and anyone charged with supporting their efforts remain vigilant and answer the call that their Code commands. I give you my personal assurance that those responsible will answer for their crimes. Thank you."

The camera zooms in and freezes for a moment on Justicia's white-masked crime fighter and she does that thing again, with the little wreathes of electricity around her eyes. I try to imagine the Dealer, sitting in his cave or his secret hideout or whatever hole he's found, watching her. It would be enough to make me pack up the Suits and find an island volcano to retire in.

"Oh, well then, I guess we have nothing to worry about, do we?" Dad says. "The electrified vixen in the white suit's going to take care of everything."

It doesn't take extraordinary senses to detect my father's sarcasm.

"I wouldn't call her a vixen, honey. Vixens are mean. She's not mean."

"She certainly *looks* mean," Dad says. "Did you see that thing she did with her eyes? It's a wonder she still has any eyebrows left. And that man with his head on fire. These people are a walking hazard."

"I think the mayor looked worried," Mom adds. "Do you think he looked worried? And who was the robot man in the background? Not sure I've seen him before."

"Cyborg, Mom," I say, though I realize maybe that's not something I should know.

"Cyborg, of course," Dad says. "I always said we needed a

good cyborg in this city. Not enough of *them* around." Dad shakes his head and changes the channel, but the Fox is everywhere. The message is being replayed and analyzed. Finally he just turns it off.

"Who's up for a game of cards?" he says, slapping his knees and standing. He looks down at me and smiles, but I can't help but stare at the television, still picturing the Fox, standing there, commanding everyone to answer the call.

"Sorry, Dad," I say. "I've still got work to do."

CAUGHT IN THE ACT

It's Tuesday, the third Tuesday of the month. And according to the menu magneted to our fridge, that means it's chicken nugget day, which is all well and good providing you don't think about all the parts of a chicken you wouldn't eat if you knew better, which is a lot of it, really. It doesn't matter how much fried batter you put around a thing, it can still be awful at the core.

It's Tuesday, and the Fox's announcement seems to have restored some of the public's faith. The morning headlines are boldface, all caps. FOX VOWS TO BRING DOWN DEALER. CITY'S CHAMPION PROMISES JUSTICE. There's even a quote in one article, supposedly from the Fox herself, saying that she will do "what the Supers who came before me never could." I suppose if anyone can, it's her, yet I can't seem to shake this feeling in my gut. That there's something we're all missing.

Which is why I'm on my bike when I should be at school. Riding to the south end of town, past the graffiti-covered tunnels and the stinking sewer grates, wondering what my parents would say if they knew what I'm doing. If they knew that I am skipping school to go to a bar. To meet up with my superhero mentor. Again.

Twice we have spoken since he dumped me outside Bob's Bowlarama. Twice I have tried to convince him that he has a responsibility—if not to me, then at least to the Code, to the community. To truth, justice, freedom of assembly—I don't care, as long as it's something. Both times he's blown me off, swatting me away like a gnat. The second time, I swore it was the last. I gave up.

But that was before Mr. Masters pulled me aside. Before the three remaining Jacks escaped from prison. Before the last villain the Titan ever faced, the man who had supposedly died at his own hands, came back from the dead.

Mr. Masters was worried, and though I still felt like there was something the head of H.E.R.O. was hiding from me, I couldn't deny the logic. Whatever happened between the Dealer and the Titan so many years ago was enough to send the leader of the Legion of Justice into a downward spiral. Now the Dealer was back. And the group of heroes who stopped him was no more, its members either retired, missing, or dead.

Except for one.

Which is why I'm skipping school.

Convincing my parents to let me stay home was the easy part. I only had to throw up. Twice. All I needed was a trigger—something to get the stomach rolling. Like the smell of rotting garbage in the Randals' driveway, tipped in the night by a raccoon. Eggs overdue and a gallon of putrid milk plus one finger in the throat, and last night's dinner is on the esophageal express to toilet town.

"No fever," my mom said, shaking the thermometer the way she has seen them do in old movies even though it's digital and goes in my ear. "I guess it's just something you ate."

I told her I'd be fine. That she was late for work. She told me she'd call me at lunch to see how I was feeling. I made a note of it, then waited for the sound of her van turning the corner before I bothered to get dressed.

The ride to the Last Hurrah seems to take a lot longer this time. Along the way, I plan what I'm going to say. Something about the Dealer and the three Jacks and Mr. Masters, and how the world needs the Titan to come back and do his job. I won't make it about me. He's made it clear that I'm not one of his priorities. I'll appeal to his sense of justice and honor. And if that doesn't work, I'll tell him he's in mortal danger. And I suppose if *that* doesn't work, I'll call him a chicken and make those squawking noises like we did in first grade to kids who wouldn't jump off the swings. I hated that.

My bicycle is the only thing parked outside the Last Hurrah at nine thirty in the morning. The sign says OPERATING HOURS: NOON TO THREE A.M. I peer through the window.

The lights in the bar are off, but I can make out a faint glow coming from the back hall, enough to see that the place is empty.

I sit on the steps, letting my back slide down the door, my head resting in my hands. I don't know what I expected. To find him still on the stool, maybe, or passed out on the floor. Or maybe sleeping on a bench outside. I look around. A man walking his dog. An older woman carrying her basket of clothes from the Laundromat next door. Two guys in black jackets standing at the corner. One of them looks at me, and I quickly look away.

I think maybe I'll just sit here for the next five hours and hope he shows up.

Or maybe I'll just walk around the seediest part of town I can find until somebody mugs me or kidnaps me, on the off chance that *this* time he will show up.

I'm debating my options when there's a *click* and I nearly fall backward as the door I'm leaning against swings open. I turn to see the Last Hurrah's bartender standing in the frame. He's wearing a bathrobe cinched tight and a hat that says PICK UP THE TAB.

"Little early to be lookin' for a drink," he says. "Little young, too."

"Sorry," I say, standing up and straightening myself out. "I was . . . I mean, I *am* looking for someone. I think he comes here a lot."

The man scratches his chin and then rests his hand on the

natural shelf of his belly. He smells like cigarettes, beer, and maple syrup. "A lot of people come here a lot," he replies.

"Yeah, but this guy you'd remember. Tall. Big arms. Big chest. Big everything. Sits back in the corner . . ." I can tell by the look in the man's glossy eyes that he knows exactly who I'm talking about.

"Sorry, kid, but I haven't seen him in almost a week. Not since *you* came in last." The bartender smiles, and I see he's got one silver tooth, like a pirate. If I look hard enough, I can see my reflection it. "Don't get too many customers your age," he explains. "Besides . . . he told me you might come lookin' for him."

"He did?" That doesn't sound like the Titan.

The bartender nods. "He said to tell you to just stop already. Stop botherin' him. Stop lookin' for him. Stop even thinkin' about him. He says you're better off if you just forget about him entirely."

Never mind. That sounds *exactly* like him. I look down at the steps for a moment, then back up at the silver tooth.

"I don't suppose you know where he went or where I could find him?"

The pirate bartender shakes his head. "You don't hear too well, do you?"

"Actually, hearing is a strength of mine," I say. "It's listening I have trouble with."

He grunts at my joke, then sighs. "Not that it's any of my business," he says. "I don't know that he *lives* anywhere. But

155

I do know he's got a friend picks him up sometimes when it's closin' time. Don't know who this friend is or where he lives—only that his name's Red."

"Red," I whisper. Color of fire trucks and apples and that really great sweater Jenna wears sometimes with the three buttons. And my eyeballs in just about every family photo. Also the name of guys in Westerns, usually cooks, who end up shot about halfway through. I have no idea who Red is.

"Okay. Thanks." I turn to mount my bike, but the bartender stops me, motions for me to come back. He leans against the door and kind of squints at me with one eye.

"Listen, kid. I seen a lot a men. Good men. Strong men. *Proud* men. But they come through this door all beat down and bowled over by one damned thing or another. They come through that door with that somethin' lodged inside 'em, so they can't swallow. And they try to drown it, fast as they can. But it doesn't work. They leave with it still stuck there." The bartender points to his chest. "I don't know your friend very well, and I don't know what's goin' on between you two, but I hope it's that you are lookin' to help *him* and not the other way round."

The man straightens up and leans in the doorframe again, arms crossed. I mean to say thanks, but it feels like there's something caught in my throat too, so instead I just nod and get back on my bike.

"And don't come back here until you at least know how to shave," the bartender shouts behind me.

I start for home with only a color. When I get back I can search online, but with no last name, I'm not hopeful. I could always ask Mr. Masters. He might know something, though I'm still not a hundred percent sure I trust him, either. Or that he trusts me.

It's all just a big jumble in my head. The Titan. The Dealer. Mr. Masters. The Fox. Jenna. The Suits. I feel like a spectator watching it all unfold. And every time I *try* to do something, I run into a dead end. A pool of acid. An empty bar. A new body spray.

It's starting to tick me off.

I pass the entrance to Ellis Park and check my phone. It's only ten o'clock. I've got two more hours before I need to be home to intercept my mother's call. I let my bike drop in the grass, and I drop down beside it.

On the weekends, the park is swarming with kids, but on this Tuesday morning it's mostly empty. I find a spot in the shade to cool off. The breeze feels nice, and I open up a little. I can smell the moisture in the air, laced with the perfume of the clover in the field below. I lie back in the grass and let it tickle my ears. I try to block out the sound of traffic and construction crews filling potholes and concentrate on what's right around me. Squirrels fussing. Bees humming. I can hear the trees talking, their branches creaking, stretching their limbs, the whisper of the leaves holding out for October, less than a week away.

Then I close my eyes and let it all drift. One by one, the sounds disappear. I take deep breaths and let them out as slowly as possible. Until there is nothing. Only the coolness of the ground on my back and the suggestion of light beyond my eyes. I try to let go of everything. The Titan. Mr. Masters. The Suits. *Julius Caesar.* The math test. The homework I didn't get done. The shoplifter I didn't tackle. Even Jenna. Just let it all go.

And drift away.

The buzzing wakes me up. It's coming from my pocket. I fish out my phone. Two missed calls. And a text.

Where are you?

The text isn't from Jenna, or Eric, or anyone at school.

It's from my mom. Only parents bother to use proper capitalization and punctuation in their texts. I check the time. It's twelve seventeen. And I'm supposed to be at home sick.

I hop on my bike and pedal as fast as I can, sweating through my shirt, making my legs burn, but it's not fast enough. Her car is already in the driveway. I let the bike fall and try to compose myself, smearing my hair down and catching my breath.

When I walk in the door, she is standing in the foyer, waiting for me. She actually has her hands tucked into little fists on her hips. I didn't know mothers actually stood like that. As soon as she starts talking, though, they launch from their perches and flit around like crazed hummingbirds.

"Where have you been?" she squawks. "I tried calling twice! Both here and your cell, and you didn't answer! I called your father and he didn't know either!" I can actually hear the exclamation points at the ends of her sentences. The hummingbirds come to rest by her sides again. I take advantage of her need to take a breath.

"Sorry, Mom. I just went over to the park for a while, hoping the fresh air would make me feel better." I always like it better when I can tell part of the truth. But she's not convinced. Her eyebrows are still arched, one foot tapping an impatient rhythm.

"You can't just up and leave like that, you know?" she scolds. "Not without telling somebody. You should have called or sent me a message. You know the rules."

Yes, I think to myself. I am well aware of the rules.

"I'm sorry," I say, "I should have called." Hoping the quick apology cuts off her attack. I offer a little smile as icing, but she doesn't bite.

"You don't understand," she says. "I was worried sick." And I can hear it in her voice. The slight tremble. This isn't about me not making a phone call. "Did you even hear what happened this morning?"

I look at her dumbly. Waiting.

"Those lunatics robbed another bank. Right outside the city this time."

I feel myself tense up. Another hit. And closer. The Suits are grabbing cash and working their way to Justicia.

"Were they stopped?" I ask, maybe a little too quickly. "I mean, you know, did the cops show up . . . or anyone?" I think about Jenna and Eric and Gavin, all on ready reserve status. Would their Supers have called on them? Dragged them out of school? Piled them in the backseat of Cryos's car and told them to change on the way? Probably not. They were still just rookies—but if it was an emergency, if the Supers needed all the help they could get . . . then what?

My mother shakes her head. "I heard it all on the radio. Then you didn't answer. I was so worried." I'm instantly swallowed in a bear hug, the life squeezed out of me. "It's stupid. I know. It has nothing to do with us. But I can't help it." She steps back and holds on to both of my shoulders, staring into my eyes with her two blue tractor beams. And there is that moment again, where I start to wonder just how much she knows.

"You don't have to worry," I tell her, trying my best to sound convincing.

She gives me another disapproving look. "I don't want you to go out alone while those . . . thugs are around, understand?"

I want to tell her that they aren't thugs. Thugs carry lead pipes and wear ski masks hoping to steal purses from old ladies. These guys are villains. There's a big difference. But I don't. After all, I just told her not to worry.

"I'm serious, Drew. These people are dangerous. I've heard all about them. I know there are others out there to protect

160

us, but you can't always count on them, you know. You have to look out for yourself."

"'Thanks, preacher,' says the choir," I say, then realize I've probably said too much already. "I'll be careful. Promise." We hug it out some more, and she gives me a parting death stare—akin to saying, "I'm watching you, mister." I manage to escape and tiptoe upstairs to my room, shut the door, and pull up the local news feeds on my laptop.

One headline on the *Justicia Daily Trumpet* website reads: SUITS STRIKE AGAIN! Another reads: ESCAPED CONS CONTINUE CRIMES: CRUSADERS CAN'T CATCH UP. It's another bank robbery, except this one is captured on video and is already streaming across YouTube. In a town less than an hour away. The robber, enormous, dressed in a snug black coat and fancy slacks and size sixteen shoes, walked into a First National with a shovel across one shoulder and a giant bag that he demanded be filled with hundreds only. A security guard, overestimating his chances, drew his gun and emptied his clip—all twelve shots ricocheting harmlessly from the flat face of the shovel. With one swing, the shovel caught the guard in the gut, sending him flying. The robber then made some comment about using that same shovel to dig everyone's grave if the tellers didn't hurry. So they hurried. As he left, the robber handed the bank manager his card.

The Jack of Spades.

According to the news, Hotshot was the first to arrive at the scene, nearly burning a hole in the roof as he touched down—but by the time he got there, the Jack had disappeared. The Super made some offhand comment about remaining vigilant and stopping them next time before launching himself back into the sky, Fourth of July style. Cryos pulled up three minutes later in his souped-up bulletproof roadster, squealing to a halt and poking his chrome-plated head out the window just long enough to scan the scene with his cybernetic eye before thundering away. The police filed in after, though there wasn't much detective work to be done. It's the easiest game of Clue ever. Jack of Spades, in the bank, with the shovel. The Suits aren't subtle. That's the difference between thugs and villains. The villains *want* you to know they did it.

Strike two against the forces of goodness and light. At least nobody from H.E.R.O. was involved.

I think about what Mr. Masters said, about the Dealer's knack for staying one step ahead of everyone, and I can't help but feel like this is only the beginning. That it might even just be a ruse. Maybe they don't even need the money. Maybe they're just trying to put everyone in a panic. Is it any coincidence that this happened less than twenty-four hours after the Fox told us all to stay calm? I watch the bank teller in the video scream her head off.

I scroll down when something else catches my eye. A little patch of news in the corner—an editorial or a blog, only three paragraphs long, but the picture and title get my attention.

The photo is of the Titan, in costume, obviously taken from the archives, judging by how young and trim he looks. He holds a would-be mugger in each hand and is slamming their heads together like he's crashing cymbals. He looks nothing like the man at the Last Hurrah.

I whisper the title to myself.

"Where are you now?"

And I realize that I'm not the only one looking for him.

THE BEST TWO AND A HALF SECONDS OF MY LIFE

It's Wednesday, and I'm back in school where I belong. Or where most people think I belong, anyway.

It's Wednesday, and on this Wednesday the poor suckers at Highview are cursed with cube steak and gravy, which tastes vaguely like grilled Play-Doh and looks a lot like canned dog food. For kicks they get green-bean casserole and Jell-O fruit salad surprise. The *surprise* is usually just some of the lunch ladies' hair—though I did find a fingernail once.

It's Wednesday, and things haven't really improved. If anything, they've gotten worse. The second robbery has everyone whispering, despite the Fox's assurances. I catch snippets. I hear questions. *"Do you think the Jacks will come here?" "Do you think the Dealer is planning on attacking the city?" "Do you think the Fox can stop them?" "Did you know the Jack of Diamonds can melt metal with that crazy eyeball of his?" "Do you think Jeremy*

Whitfield will ask me to homecoming?"

Thankfully, nobody asks, "Do you think the top-secret group of sidekicks-in-training operating out of the hidden basement in our school have anything to do with this?" Not that I can hear, anyways. As far as I can tell, our identities are intact. Then I think about the Killer Bee and Mr. Masters and start to wonder all over again.

It's Wednesday, and I've got my own identity issues: I still have no idea who Red is. I spent two hours searching online, and the one person I found with that nickname living in the city is a ninety-five-year-old man in a nursing home. Of course it's possible that Red is just a pseudonym. Obviously it's somebody the Titan trusts, which means it's probably somebody just as secretive as he is. Which means there is almost no chance of me finding the Titan or talking to him again.

Jenna doesn't have that problem. She texted me last night to tell me she spent most of the weekend on patrol with the Fox, following up on leads, trying to uncover the Dealer's plan. My only consolation is that she didn't spend the weekend with Gavin. The last message I got just said

Sorry.

I wasn't sure for what. For not returning my calls? For having an infinitely cooler hero than me? For smelling different all of a sudden? I guess I probably should have texted back that it was okay, but I didn't. Instead I just said I'd see her tomorrow.

So it's Wednesday. H.E.R.O. day. Mike and I finish history and walk to the teachers' lounge together. He is officially back in school, and Mr. Masters said he could continue to attend meetings even though his physical training is suspended till the cast comes off—the same cast that is covered in signatures already. He insists none of them are forged, but I have my doubts. Mike is empirically more popular than I am, but there is no way Susan Smalls would give him more than a snotty look, let alone grace his arm with her loopy signature. As we walk, I notice some of the halogen bulbs flickering as we pass under them and wonder if he doesn't have some serious pent-up energy. Maybe the Suits have everyone on edge.

The rest of H.E.R.O. is already by the door when we arrive. Mike asks Nikki to scratch an itch on his arm just above his elbow, which she does, easily sinking her fingers beneath the plaster. Jenna smiles and waves. She still smells like Gavin's gift.

"Where's Mr. Masters?"

Eric points to a note on the door.

HIGHVIEW ENVIRONMENTAL RECLAMATION ORGANIZATION CANCELED TODAY. PLEASE ATTEND YOUR ALTERNATIVELY SCHEDULED CLASSES.

MR. M

"What the heck is *this*?" I say.

I reach for the door.

166

"Don't bother," Gavin says. "It's locked."

I listen for Mr. Masters's voice down the hall anywhere but can't catch it. Maybe it's a test of some kind. I turn to Nikki. "You want to take a quick look, just to be sure?" I whisper.

We all gather around her. She bends over to tie her shoe and then quickly slips through the floor like water soaking into the earth.

"It is unusual," Jenna says as Nikki disappears. "Has anyone even seen him today?" I shake my head. The look on her face makes me think Jenna has seen something odd in Mr. Masters's behavior lately too.

"You look worried," Gavin says to me. "Afraid you're going to miss out on some crucial test-tube smelling today?"

"No. I just think it's weird that Mr. Masters would cancel our meeting given everything that's going on."

"So you're just scared, then," Gavin fires back. "Which one of them scares you the most? No, wait, let me guess. The big guy with the shovel . . . nope, hang on . . . I've got it. It's the handsome one with the glass eye."

"It's an extraterrestrial diamond, dork," Mike says. "And he's not scared of any of them, are you, Drew?"

Mike looks at me. I pretend I didn't hear him, which doesn't work so well with me.

"Ah, the Jack of Clubs, then." Gavin smirks, then gives me a wink.

Two minutes later, the teachers' lounge door opens and Nikki slinks through, closing it quietly behind her.

"He's not down there. Everything's shut off. And there's no one in the lounge," she whispers.

What now? Eric says with a shrug.

"I guess we go eat," Gavin suggests. "It is lunchtime, after all."

Sometimes I forget that Gavin's only been at this school for a month. He probably hasn't had the chance to discover buried treasure in the Jell-O yet. I'm about to say something, but Nikki is the first to put her hands up. "Green-bean casserole? You must be outa your mind."

"Yeah, sorry, guys," Mike says, scratching now at the crevice where his cast opens under his armpit. "I'd rather starve."

"Me too," I say. Eric nods.

"We could just hang out by the fields," Nikki suggests.

I look at Jenna. Gavin looks at Jenna. "Seriously. I've got to get something to eat," he says.

I can almost hear the rustle of the tumbleweed. The locker doors closing around us, the soundtrack in the background. I forget all about the Titan and the Jacks and the Dealer and even Mr. Masters. This is between the two of us. Or at least Jenna is between the two of us. Except I have the advantage. The green-bean casserole has mushrooms in it. Or some kind of fungus, anyway.

Jenna puts both hands on Gavin's shoulders.

"Sorry," she says. "But I've tasted Ms. Merkel's celebrated cube steak and gravy once in my life . . . and that is one time too many."

We follow Jenna down the halls to the school's back entrance, having dropped a sour-faced Gavin off at the cafeteria to eat with some of his football buddies. Jenna invited him to come with us one more time, but he refused, probably out of pride. This just means I don't have to be around Gavin *or* cube steak for the next hour, so my day is suddenly looking up.

There are no teachers or kids by the back door, and it's only locked on the inside, so getting out isn't a problem. And we have Nikki, so getting back in won't be either. I listen for the heavy thud of Officer Jenson's heels on the sidewalk. Our lone security guard has a slow, bowlegged gait and wears heavy boots—easy to identify. I can hear him clear around the front of the school. "All clear," I say. Somewhere out there, probably not too far from here, some criminal in a suit is holding a playing card and saying the exact same thing. But there's a big difference between knocking over banks and skipping out on lunch. At least, I'd like to think so.

We head to the baseball diamond behind the tennis courts. Along the way we talk about the thing on all of our minds. Mike thinks the Jacks are just gathering enough cash to fly the coop—maybe head to Europe or South America, even go their separate ways. He figures the Dealer owed it to them to bust them out, but that they aren't really a gang anymore. Nikki thinks Mike is an idiot, even if he is kinda cute in a lost-puppy-with-one-broken-leg kind of way, and that the robberies are just meant to spook the public. Eric says the Suits are planning a big crime spree, though he may have said that they are baking a big cream pie. It's hard to follow along with his signs when we aren't standing still, facing each other.

Then I pitch my theory. That the Suits are out for revenge. After all, the bad guys don't like getting beat any more than the good guys do. The Jacks spent six years in prison thanks to Justicia's Supers, and the Dealer—well, who even knows what he's been up to. Not to mention they lost one of their own— the Jack of Hearts hasn't risen from the dead yet—giving them something else to avenge. I look over at Jenna, but she just looks down at her feet. When she finally notices everyone looking at her, she shrugs.

"The Fox will take care of it," she says with certainty.

Rule number four.

"That's easy for you to say," Mike scoffs, echoing my thoughts exactly.

The baseball diamond is deserted. The ground smells musty from last night's rain, though the sun has at least dried the bleachers. Because Mike won't get the cast off for a couple of months still, Eric decides to teach him the art of one-handed kung fu.

"This should be good," Jenna says, climbing the steps.

"Yeah. Do you think Mike will break his other arm or just electrocute himself first?" I ask, sitting next to Jenna on the top bench of the bleachers, watching Eric show Mike the proper fighting stance down at home plate.

"My money's on accidental electrocution," she says. It's a

figure of speech, of course. Jenna never has any money.

Nikki takes one look at Jenna and me sitting on the bleachers and watches Mike strike a crane pose, though with his plastered arm and unsteady leg he looks more like a gimpy goose.

"I can't watch," she says. "I'm taking a walk. Please make sure Eric doesn't kill him."

"Oh, Mike will do himself in, don't worry," I say, watching the Wisp shake her head, walk straight through the fence, and then disappear into the woods beyond the field. Beside me, Jenna is sitting cross-legged, fidgeting with the pull strings of her sweatshirt, wrapping them around her fingers one way and then the other, cutting off circulation. I watch Eric practice a couple of whirlwind kicks, one right after another. He's so graceful it's almost hypnotizing. Then I watch Mike fall on his butt just trying to get one leg to follow orders. I realize this is the first time Jenna and I have been alone—or at least almost alone—in about a week. Since we hung out together at the pool.

Suddenly she turns to me. Her hands are in her lap, one leg tucked underneath the other. Her eyes are scrunched behind her glasses and she's chewing on her upper lip, which is, I notice, a little chapped. I could count the cracks if I wanted to.

I've seen this look before. She has something on her mind. I hold my breath and wait for it.

"Do you think I'm good?" she asks. "A good person, I mean?"

I literally look behind her, wondering where, exactly, she pulled this one out of.

"You're no Mahatma Gandhi," I say, figuring stupid questions deserve equally stupid answers, but the look on her face tells me I need to try again.

"You're serious?"

She nods.

"You? Jenna Jaden. Straight-A student. Award-winning athlete. Soup kitchen volunteer. Superhero sidekick extraordinaire. You seriously don't know if you are a good person?"

She leans back, challenging me with a smile and one raised eyebrow. "Well, are *you* a good person?"

"Well, yeah," I say. "I mean, I think so, don't you?"

She doesn't answer that one. That's when I know I'm in trouble. She leans forward again. "When's the last time you lied to your mother?" she asks.

Technically I don't think I said anything to Mom that wasn't true in the twenty minutes we spent together this morning over breakfast. So that would make it . . .

"Yesterday," I say.

"When's the last time you did something you knew you probably weren't supposed to?"

I immediately think of the math test. Then skipping school and biking to the bar. Then I realize that I'm probably not supposed to be out here sitting on these bleachers talking to her during fourth period.

"Okay. What's your point?"

"I'm just saying that you do things that some people would consider *not* good."

She's got me fixed with those green eyes of hers. There's no way out of this one.

"Well. Yeah. Sure. I'm not perfect. I screw up every now and then. But when it comes to the really important stuff, I think I do okay."

"You do *okay*." The way she says it, I feel like I'm suddenly six inches tall.

"I don't know. I think I'm basically good, I mean, more or less."

"Well, which is it, more or less?" she prods.

"You know what I mean," I tell her. "You do the right thing most of the time, and you make some mistakes, but you learn from them, and you try to help other people or at least stay out of their way, and you don't kill anybody and you're, you know, basically good."

"And basically good is, what, good *enough*?"

"Yeah, something like that," I say.

"But it's not *good*. Not *good* good. Not the way we mean it when we say things like good and evil, right?"

"I don't know, Jenna. I don't think anyone is good all the time. Being totally good every second is just not . . . well, it's just not *reasonable*."

"So that's a reason not to do it?"

I throw my hands into the air. The universal gesture of *What the heck do you want from me?*

"I'm just asking," she says defensively.

"Well. No. I guess not." I smile, hoping to segue into a different line of questioning or even something resembling a stupid, meaningless, middle school conversation, but Jenna is all earnestness, leaning in, eyes narrow, lips pursed. She's not letting go. "Seriously. What is all this about? Did Mike tell you about my math test?" I knew I shouldn't have told him about that. Of course he said he cheated on his Spanish quiz the week before, so I didn't feel bad. But I'm guessing Jenna never cheated on anything in her life. She's all about hard work and sacrifice.

"This isn't really about you, Drew."

Jenna looks down at her feet. She's wearing sandals today, even though the air is a little crisp, and her nails are painted pale pink. Her feet smell like the wet grass she just walked through. I can see the tiny, soft blond hairs on her legs just above her ankles. She looks back at me. "It's just that some- times I kind of wonder . . . what's the point, you know? I mean, every day most people don't do a single thing for any- one but themselves. And some people, they do terrible things and get away with it. And then there are people who devote their entire lives to being good and doing what they believe in, and they end up forgotten."

"Geez, Jenna. You're only thirteen. I think it's a little early to worry about this stuff."

"I'm not talking about me, either, Drew. I mean, not really." On the field, Mike is desperately trying to land just one punch, but Eric continues to dodge them with ease. I suddenly realize I'm Mike in this conversation. I scoot an inch closer to Jenna.

"Sometimes I don't think there really is a good and bad," she says. "At least, not the way we are always taught. Sometimes I think there are just choices and consequences."

"Okay," I say. "I can see that." I scoot another inch, leaning back on my elbows, all casual like. I can actually smell the leaves turning, drying out, can hear them breaking free, and I'm reminded of that hippie song about seasons and times and purposes and all that. My mom loves that song, which means I am naturally inclined not to, but I kind of believe it anyway.

"But then there must be good and bad choices, right? Or at least good and bad consequences?" she asks.

"Well, sure."

"I mean, if I blow up a building and kill the people inside, that's bad, right?"

I can't help but give her a look. "Um. Yeeaaahh, Jenna. I think blowing up a building full of innocent people qualifies as a *bad* choice."

"And even if I *make* the bomb and *sell* it to the guy who blows up the building, that's bad, too, right?"

"Pretty sure. It's a bomb. What did you think it was going to be used for? It's not like you sold him a pack of gum."

"Okay. Right," she says, suddenly moving close enough to me that our knees bump. It makes me sit up straight. Our faces are probably only a foot apart. I can actually count the pores in her nose. I can't believe *none* of them are clogged. I'm suddenly very self-conscious about my breath. I had oatmeal for breakfast. Apple cinnamon. I wonder how good *her* senses are. Still, I don't dare move.

"So let's say I sell him a pack of gum instead, and as I give him back his change, he says, 'Hey, did you know I was headed over to that building across the street to blow it up?'"

"He just says that?"

"Yes."

"As you're giving back his change?"

"Yes."

"In that girly voice of yours?"

"No, fart head. He sounds like Kermit the Frog." Jenna scowls at me, but she doesn't scoot away.

"Really. Because I can't imagine Kermit the Frog blowing up a building." I realize that I'm trying to be charming, which isn't a strength of mine, but I can't turn back now.

Jenna hits me on the shoulder. It's meant to be playful, I think, but it actually hurts quite a bit. "He says he's going to blow up the building."

"And you say?"

"Nothing. I don't say anything. Or I just say 'oh,' and I go back to restocking the snack cakes."

"You say 'oh'?"

"I say 'oh,' that's it, and then half an hour later the building explodes."

"That's one vicious frog."

"I'm serious," Jenna says through gritted teeth. I'm afraid she might punch me again, less playfully this time.

"Okay. Okay. It blows up. And you never did anything to stop him? Never called the police?"

"I didn't say a thing to anyone."

"Well, then, yeah. That's definitely not good."

"Right. Because I could have stopped it, right?" She shifts a little, and our knees bump again. "Okay. Except let's say there were no people inside, so nobody really got hurt."

"Still bad," I say. "Destruction of property. Maybe not as bad—"

"Except one. There's one person," she says, interrupting. "A terrorist."

"Miss Piggy?" I ask.

"Drew!"

"Okay. Fine. There's a terrorist in the building. Whatever."

"Thank you. And the guy I sold the gum to is blowing up the building to get rid of the terrorist."

"Right."

"So that's bad, right?"

"What's bad?"

"That I didn't call the police when the guy buying the gum told me he was going to blow up the building."

I'm a little confused. "And you knew that there was only one person in the building and that the one person was a bad guy?"

"No."

"No, you didn't know, or no, you knew?"

"I didn't know he was a bad guy."

"Then I'm going to have to say not good."

"Then yes."

"Yes, what?"

"Yes, let's say I knew he was bad."

"Who?" I ask, confused again.

"The guy in the building. The one that got blown up."

"And you didn't call the police?"

"No."

"No, you didn't call, or no, you did?"

"No, I did, actually." She seems to be debating it in her own head.

"You called the police?"

"Yes. And they stopped the man who bought the gum from blowing up the building."

"With the terrorist in it?"

"Right. And he escaped."

"The gum guy or the terrorist guy?"

"The terrorist guy. And *he* blew up another building that was full of innocent people."

"I see," I say, but I'm just saying it. I'm completely lost.

"So then which is it?"

"Which is what?"

"Good or bad—me calling the police to stop the guy who was going to blow up the first building to begin with?"

I don't say anything this time. I'm trying to piece it together, more than anything to just try and figure out why she is asking me all of this. I wonder if this doesn't have something to do with me somehow. Or Gavin. Or both of us. I wonder if I'm the chewing-gum guy. I hope I am. I think at least it's better than being the terrorist.

"Good or bad?" Jenna prods.

"I don't know," I say.

"Good or bad?"

"I don't *know*, Jenna. It's neither. You're just a convenience store clerk, not an undercover FBI agent. You sold some guy a pack of gum. He said he was going to blow something up, so you did what you thought was right. You called the police. That's what I would have done."

"Even though the consequences turned out bad."

"Yeah, I think so. I mean, it was still right at the time."

"Even though I later found out that it wasn't."

"Yeah . . . but that's not your fault. You didn't know."

"So then it works the other way, too."

"What works the other way?"

"If I hadn't called the police. And I didn't stop the guy from blowing up the terrorist."

"I don't know. I mean, in retrospect . . ."

"The consequences were good," she says.

"Yeah. I guess."

"So that makes it right, right?"

"Um . . . right?" I offer skeptically.

"Right. Because all those innocent lives were saved. Even

though what I did, by not calling the police, was wrong. Right?"

She is looking at me. And the way she is looking at me . . . it's as if she can't take a breath until I answer.

"Jenna," I say, shaking my head, "what on earth are you talking about?"

She turns around and looks out over the tennis courts and the track and the school and the city and into the clouds that have just formed a thin veil between us and the sun, and I wonder just what it is she sees that I don't see.

"I don't know," she says.

And that's when I do it. I reach out and put a hand on top of hers. It could just be the bravest thing I've ever done in my life. She doesn't turn around, but she doesn't pull her hand away either.

"Don't, some days, you wish you could be . . . you know . . . normal?"

And I want to say no. Because she's not normal. She's remarkable. And I don't want her to change. And if say yes, then she won't know just how remarkable she is anymore. She turns to look at me again.

"Every day," I tell her.

I look at Jenna, and I can see that she is about ready to say something and then stops herself. And there is something about the look she gives me, her head a little tilted as if we've just met at a reunion and she's trying to place me from a picture in our high school yearbook. She twists her hand to hold mine. Then she takes a deep breath and leans in close to whisper something.

And kisses me instead.

It lasts for two seconds. Slightly longer, if you count the half second of hovering afterward, where our lips aren't touching but I can still feel the kinetic energy between them and still feel the moist air of her breath. It's so sudden that I don't have time to pull my senses together to capture it all. But I can hear her heartbeat—I can feel it through the pulse in her bottom lip, and I can just feel the tips of her bangs softly on my forehead. I can taste the remnants of the strawberry yogurt she ate on the bus that morning. And I see things, beautiful things, from behind the closed curtains of my eyes.

And then it's gone.

I blink twice.

I glance down at Eric and Mike to see if they noticed, but they aren't even looking our way.

"What was that for?" I ask, not sure I want an answer, wishing, perhaps, that it was only an impulse. That there didn't have to be a reason.

"I needed to know," she says.

And then she stands up and starts back toward the school, leaving me even more confused than before.

For the next three hours, I don't know where I am. I am vaguely aware of my body walking down halls, into classrooms, squeezing behind desks. I acknowledge that at some point I will have to take control of said body again. But for now it is on autopilot.

She needed to know, she said.

Know what? How she felt about me? That she was a good person? What I had for breakfast?

When she gets up, I try to follow her, but she just smiles and shakes her head.

"I'll call you after practice," she says—the kind of thing she would have said to the other Drew. Pre-kiss Drew. The Drew who was perfectly content suppressing any nonplatonic feelings he might have possibly had for his best friend and fellow sidekick to avoid the risk of losing her completely. Not this Drew. Not Drew, A.K.

Which means I suddenly don't know who I am, either.

So I sit there until Mike shakes me with his good hand, still alive despite his training, and I follow him back to earth. Nikki is waiting for us by the door.

"You okay?" she asks. Somehow she knows. Girls always know.

"I don't know," I say. "I think so."

Nikki squeezes in and unlocks the door. I don't know how Jenna managed to get back in, though I don't think anything she does will surprise me from here on out.

"Hey, did you know that if I hit you in just the right spot I can collapse your windpipe?" Mike says. "I mean, *I* can't, but Eric could."

"That's great," I tell him. I'm still finding it a little difficult to breathe anyway.

In the halls between periods I look for Jenna, but I can't

find her anywhere. I sit in class and listen for her laugh down the hall. For the sound of her footsteps. For a glimpse of her through the window in the door. For once I can't see or hear anything else.

The final bell rings, and I head to my locker to drop off some books and grab my jacket, looking for her, listening for her. It takes two tries to get the combination right. I'm obviously not thinking clearly. Normally I can hear the clicks of each pin when the number hits. I swing open the door and out of the corner of my eye notice something taped to the inside of it.

It's the Jack of Clubs.

THE WORST FIFTEEN
MINUTES OF MY LIFE
SO FAR

The world stops spinning, only for a moment, and then speeds up again. I pull the card free, not thinking that it might be rigged somehow, not thinking that the act of pulling it off the door could cause the whole school to blow up or something.

But I'm just being stupid. Nothing happens. It's just a playing card. A man with a sword stuck through his head. Smiling at me. Suddenly, all around me, the school erupts in sound. I've lost my concentration and let control of my senses slip. Everything is rush and roar, and I feel like I'm submerged beneath a waterfall.

Okay, Drew. Calm down. Remember your training. What do you do when a psychotic villain leaves his calling card in your locker? Panic? Do you panic? Is that what you do?

Yes, I answer myself. Panic first. No avoiding it. Might as

well get it out of the way. I stand there, my hands shaking, the Jack of Clubs bouncing up and down.

Now. Take a deep breath. Try to slow it down. Concentrate. You need to tell somebody. He could be here right now. The whole school could be in danger. Get help.

I look around for anyone. Jenna, Eric, even Gavin, that's how desperate I am.

Nobody. Everybody. Bodies everywhere. I don't recognize any of them. Why is everyone so loud all of a sudden?

Calm down. Get control.

I head to the corner. Jenna's locker is down the hall on the left, but she's not there.

Where is she?

I can usually find her anywhere, but there's no trace of her. The crowd is shoving, pulling, yelling. I need help.

Mr. Masters.

I quickly head up to his room, remembering that he teaches earth science last period, but he's not there. I'm still holding the stupid card in my hand. I'm listening for a familiar voice, but it's the end of the school day and the noise is deafening. I can't concentrate enough to sift through them all. All the conversations bleed together into a chaotic buzz. I'm sweating. My mouth is dry. I feel like I might pass out.

Then I hear a voice I recognize.

It's my former English teacher, Ms. Norris. Three doors down.

"Andrew? Is everything all right?"

I catch my breath. "Ms. Norris, you haven't seen Mr. Masters around, have you? I really need to talk to him about this . . . project I'm doing."

"I'm sorry, but I think Mr. Masters left early this afternoon."

"*What?* What the heck for?" I look around frantically.

Ms. Norris gives me a very strange look. "I'm sure I don't know, though he is an adult . . . with a life . . . so he does leave this school sometimes," she says a little defensively. "Is there something I can help you with?"

I look back at her. She's a nice enough lady and she knows a lot about poetry, but rhyming couplets are no defense against supervillains. I shake my head.

"You can always try and get his home number from the front office," she calls after me, but I am already headed back down the stairs.

All right. Forget Mr. Masters. I need to find Jenna. If I find Jenna, she can contact the Fox. As I run down the stairs, I pull out my phone. Speed dial two.

It goes straight to voice mail.

"Hi, you've reached Jenna Jaden. I'm really sorry I missed you, but I'll buzz you back later."

"Seriously?" I hang up.

Crowds of students bustle past me, shoving me aside with their shoulders and backpacks, oblivious. I scan the crowd, looking for Jenna's pink-and-yellow backpack with the tie-dyed peace sign on it. Nothing.

Everyone's headed out to the buses.

Who can I call?

Neither Mike nor Nikki have phones. Nikki's is in a perpetual state of confiscation and Mike burned through three before his parents realized that he and personal electronics were a bad combination. I never bothered to get Gavin's number, even though Mr. Masters told me I should. So I quickly send a message to Eric, who can text eighty words per minute and keeps his phone on vibrate in his front pocket.

I type SIT and hit send. It stands for Sidekick In Trouble. It's the SOS of the superhero sidekick universe. Dot dot dot, dot dot, dash.

I hope he gets it.

All right, Drew. You're on your own for the moment. What next?

If I was any other sidekick, of course, I would contact my Super. That's the *first* thing I would have done. I would press the nearly microscopic button embedded under my fingernail, and a little alarm would go off on the ring on my Super's finger, showing my exact location. Then my hero would suddenly slip into his suit and rev up the save-my-butt-mobile and be outside the school in five.

But last time I looked, the Titan wasn't wearing his ring—I doubt he even still has it—and I don't have the phone number for every bar in the city. So there's no chance of him showing up for this one, either.

Think.

I could call the police.

I pull out my phone and start to dial 911. It's the last resort of Supers and sidekicks—to have to rely on the lesser authorities. Kind of like asking your little sister for help opening a jar of pickles. But the school could be in danger. At the very least, *I* could be in danger. And I'm willing to take all the help I can get.

Then I stop before I press the last one. Because it dawns on me.

How could a wanted fugitive like the Jack of Clubs—someone who has been on the news and on the front page of every paper since last Friday—walk into a school, of all places, to stick a playing card in my locker . . . without being noticed?

And *why* would he? This is me we are talking about, after all. How would he even know who I am? Or where my locker is? Even if he somehow did sneak past the front office and slink down the halls unnoticed.

But if not him, then who? Only so many people in school know how to break into a locker. There still isn't an app for it. It's the kind of knowledge a criminal would have.

Or a sidekick. Like two weeks ago, when we spent half an hour learning to pick a dozen different kinds of locks, including the spin combination variety. If you were a sidekick, and you wanted to scare someone in order to get back at them for something they did to you, say, around lunchtime.

All of a sudden, standing there, holding my phone in one hand, about to bring the S.W.A.T. team down on Highview, it occurs to me. I hold up the Jack of Clubs and give it a sniff.

Which one scares you the most?

"You're going to miss your bus if you don't hurry, son."

I look around to see a janitor motioning to the halls, which are quickly emptying.

He's right, of course. I should go catch my bus—if it hasn't left already.

But all I can do is stand there and think about how I'm going to get back at Gavin McAllister.

On the ride home, I fume. The fact that Jenna didn't bother to call me back ticks me off, even though she is probably at gymnatsics practice by now and can't get to her phone. And it ticks me off that Mr. Masters wasn't there today, of all days, or that Eric didn't bother to respond to my SIT. Even just a text saying, "Sorry, dude. You're SOL." And I'm still perpetually ticked off that my Super is never anywhere to be found. But mostly I'm mad at Gavin.

And I wonder if maybe he didn't find about what happened on the bleachers at lunch, and if that's what prompted his little prank. I think about telling Mr. Masters. Maybe it will be enough to get Gavin kicked out of the program. Impersonating a known villain? He could have caused mass panic. School lockdown. What a jerk. Not to mention he nearly ruined the best day of my life. I think of Marc Antony getting revenge on Julius Caesar. "The dogs of war shall be set loose," he said, or something like that. The rest of the bus ride home I think about my dogs and how best to loose them. Maybe I'll get

Eric to help me. After all, he still owes me for the apple smell incident.

The bus stops at my block and lets me out. I open the front door using the key under the plastic frog and toss my backpack in the corner. Mom won't be home for another hour, and Dad won't be home for another two. I slip off my shoes, then fall into the couch and grab my phone. I think about calling Jenna again to tell her what Gavin did. I wonder if he wasn't in the halls, watching me, waiting to see the look on my face. Laughing with some of his football buddies as I fled, panicked, down the halls.

No connection.

I look at my phone. Call lost. No bars. Funny. It was working less than an hour ago.

Pressing lots of random buttons over and over again doesn't help. Nor does walking into three different rooms. So I flop back on the couch and stare at it for a while.

Then I pick up the ancient landline phone from the end table beside me.

No signal.

"That's so weird," I say to myself. I'm holding the dead phone to my ear.

No sound at all.

Except breathing. I only hear breathing.

I hold my breath.

And my heart stops.

It's not my breathing.

I turn just in time to see the club flying toward me—like a police officer's nightstick, but rounded on both ends like an oversized, deadly Q-tip. I manage to duck, and it careens into the bookshelf on the opposite wall, sending several volumes to the floor. The club somehow circles back, like a boomerang, and I peer over the edge of the couch cushions to see a hand catch it.

A hand attached to a man in a black suit with a black shirt and solid black tie. With mousy black eyes, a scarred face, and an oily black handlebar mustache twisted on the ends. He is standing by the front door. Smiling. Even his teeth are black. Some of them, anyways.

"The Sensationalist?" the man asks.

For a moment I think he's got the wrong guy. This is the first time anyone I don't know personally has called me that. In fact, pretty much only Mr. Masters uses that name. Someday, he says, it will be famous. Someday it will be in headlines. Staring at the Jack of Clubs standing in my doorway, I decide fame is overrated.

"Who?" I say. I am instantly aware that I don't have my mask on, but it clearly doesn't matter. This guy already knows who I am.

The Jack of Clubs reaches back for another toss. I use the Lord's name, partly in vain, mostly in earnest, and roll off the couch and into the coffee table, catching the corner of it with my head as the club goes whizzing past me again. This time it smashes into the forty-two-inch LED television that was my father's Christmas present last year and gets stuck in the glass and plastic.

Now's my chance. I take off toward the kitchen and the back patio door. Behind me I hear a grunt and footsteps on broken glass. I slide on the kitchen linoleum in my sock feet and slam into the counter, smashing my knees into them. I turn to see him coming down the hall behind me, club in hand.

I look down just to confirm that my utility belt is, in fact, still stashed away in my backpack by the front door and hasn't somehow magically appeared around my scrawny waist. If it *were* there, it would afford any number of solutions to the problem that is stalking me down the hallway. Paralyzing gas, cryogenic bomb, even just a smoke grenade. As it is, I have a used gum wrapper in one pocket and sixty-five cents in the other.

I need a weapon.

I look around frantically.

Knives.

Our block of kitchen knives. Right beside me. I grab the biggest handle—the big butcher knife, the *Psycho* knife—and launch it, but it clatters uselessly off the wall, missing its mark by several feet. The Jack of Clubs stops. I've gotten his attention, at least. I grab two more—a bread knife and the other long, skinny one. The first sails right past. The other he blocks easily with his club. I toss the rest, including the paring knife, five steak knives, and even the scissors (miss, miss, block, dodge, miss, drop, big miss); then I throw the block of wood for good measure. He manages to avoid them all with ease, except the block, which hits him in the shoulder and falls to the floor with a pathetic *thunk*.

Jack looks at his shoulder, then back at me. I think his mustache actually twists around by itself. He flicks his wrist, and the club soars out of his hand again.

I dive to the left, past the center island, headed toward the dining table as, behind me, I can hear the splintering of our wooden cabinets. There is the sound of more glass breaking as I crawl beneath the table, facing the patio door. I can tell from here that it is unlocked. Through the glass I can hear a dog barking, many houses down.

I wish I had a dog. A Rottweiler or a Doberman. With big yellow teeth. And rabies. Dripping, nasty, froth-at-the-mouth rabies. I'd name him Chopper. Or Jack Ripper.

I slide out from under the table and put both hands on the door handle. I pull hard, but it only opens an inch. It's stuck somehow. I push and pull. The sound of metal hitting wood. I look down to see the dowel rod that my parents use as an extra precaution blocking the way, meant to keep the bad guys out.

The sound of air being split as something whisles through it. I duck just in time and squeeze back under the dining table as the club soars past in an arc, nearly taking my head off.

Then I hear something large—probably Jack of Clubs size— landing on the table above me. For a moment I'm paralyzed. I can see the backyard. I can see the Powells' house beyond it. I can even hear the sound of children playing in the street.

There's no way I can make it out the patio door in time, not unless I try to crash through it. He's right on top of me.

I wish I had Nikki's powers. I would melt right through the floor and into the basement. Surely linoleum is no platinum. But I'm no Nikki, either.

I turn and look the other way—back down the hall at the front door.

Which way to go?

I turn to look back at the porch.

I scream.

His face is right there, hanging down over the table. Grinning with all of his black and yellow teeth. For a moment I think his *mustache* is reaching for me.

"Hi there," he says.

I scream louder and scamper backward, kicking out and catching him square in the jaw with one socked foot.

I wish I had been wearing cleats. With three-inch spikes. Coated in poison.

I'm free of the table and see him stand up and spin around, rubbing his jaw with one hand. I manage to pull myself up and head toward the front door, my lungs already burning, my senses kicked into overdrive. I can smell the orange soda seeping into the carpet. Then I hear the slightest grunt of effort and manage to twist sideways and onto the stairs as the club wings past, lodging in the front door. Scrambling up the stairs on my hands and knees, I fall into my room, slamming the door shut with my feet.

The whole world is spinning.

I can hear his footsteps on the stairs.

I stand and lock my door and press my ear against it. He is breathing right outside.

He smells like sweat and licorice.

That, apparently, is what pure evil smells like. Like black licorice.

The Jack of Clubs jiggles the knob. There are very few things more unnerving than watching your doorknob jiggle, knowing there is a crazed killer on the other side.

I scramble into my closet and dig through piles of clothes and old blankets till I find my trunk—an oversized toolbox that I keep most of my sidekick supplies in, including a few gadgets I don't have room for on the belt. Inside the box, at least, is a Taser with enough juice in it to bring down a rhinoceros. It might not be enough to take down the Jack of Spades, but it should at least trump the club.

I open the box.

It's empty.

"What the *what*?"

Suddenly I hear one smashing sound followed by another and watch as my doorknob falls to the floor and the door swings open.

He stands there, looking at me trapped in my closet. His black shoes are dusted with broken glass. There is a spot of blood in the corner of his mouth, presumably from where I kicked him. He grins wickedly.

He opens the bag slung across his shoulder and pulls out some of my stuff, including the Taser and several smoke bombs and even a nifty little device Jenna helped me design for blocking phone signals and radio transmissions. I had kind of forgotten about that. He tosses the gadgets back inside.

"Kids your age shouldn't play with toys like this," he says.

He takes a few steps toward me, his club in his right hand, down by his side. I scoot backward until I am tucked into the corner of the closet, frantically considering my dwindling options.

My closet is filled with dirty laundry, old board games, and neglected sports equipment that my former football-star grandfather buys me every year for Christmas. I grab a hockey stick, figuring it at least makes for a better weapon than a basket full of dirty socks.

"What do you want?" I say, pulling myself into a crouch, trying to make myself as small a target as possible. I wish I had Gavin's powers. I would turn into a mountain. A very small mountain, but solid rock nonetheless. Then I would just let him whack at me until he got bored and left.

The Jack of Clubs stops for a moment, listening. He turns and looks out my bedroom window and then back at me.

"Actually, I was hoping for a little more of a fight. But I guess I'll have to make do."

He takes another step.

I look up expectantly. This is the moment. The one when the Titan comes crashing through the ceiling, all flexed and fisted, tackling the Jack of Clubs and pummeling him through the drywall, beating the snot out of him while I cheer him on. Rule number four, again.

Except he's not here. Nobody's here. Even Jenna's not here. I'm on my own. Though I can still hear the Titan's voice in my head. Like Obi-Wan Kenobi, if Obi-Wan was a drunk, three-hundred-pound loser who smelled like six-day-old sweat.

Save yourself for a change.

So I charge, shouting and swinging my hockey stick like a lunatic. Maybe I'll get lucky. I aim for his crotch.

I miss.

Jack takes three steps backward and then swings once with his club, breaking my hockey stick in half. With his other hand, he gives me a shove, and I'm suddenly reeling back toward my bedroom door, falling into the hall. My head hits hard, and I'm starting to wonder why so many of these encounters end up with me on the ground with my head ringing. Then the Jack of Clubs is hovering over me.

I really wish my grandfather had given me a shotgun for Christmas instead of a hockey stick.

"I'm sorry, kid, really. This isn't about you."

Why does everybody keep *saying* that?

"But it doesn't look like either of us is getting what we want today."

He raises his club to finish me off.

I close my eyes and wait for it. Listening to everything. The children outside. The Hungs' dog barking. The hum of the refrigerator. The creak of a door opening, of feet on stairs. The sound of our heartbeats, his and mine.

Or at least mine.

I crack open one eye to see him standing there, club still raised. Beady black eyes looking down at me.

Not moving. Not an inch. Not even the slightest quiver of a mustache hair.

Then I jump, because I suddenly realize there is someone crouched beside me with his hand on my shoulder.

"It's all right. It's me. Are you okay?"

I nod frantically. Then shake my head.

"All right. Come on. We've only got about forty seconds left."

I somehow stagger to my feet and we careen down the stairs, taking them three at a time. I manage to grab my backpack and shoes as we head out the front door. Down the street I can see kids playing football, except nobody's moving. The ball is frozen in midair. Up above me, two birds are stuck to the sky.

"Let's go. In the car."

The blue Chevy Malibu. I have ridden in this car before. To and from weekend field trips. Saving the environment and stuff. There are empty cans of Mountain Dew on the floor and a box full of papers in the backseat.

Mr. Masters slides into the driver's seat and counts backward from five.

Suddenly the ball comes down into the hands of one of the kids, and I can hear them shouting. Mr. Masters turns the key and throws the car into drive, swinging out into the street.

In the distance I can already make out police sirens. Judging by the sound, they will be here in a minute or less.

"My mom," I croak, twisting around to look behind me.

"Don't worry," Mr. Masters says. "The cops will be there, and he's probably gone already."

"How can you be sure?"

"Because he has no interest in your parents. In fact," Mr. Masters says breathlessly, "I don't think he was really after you."

ALL ALONE TOGETHER

I stare at Mr. Masters the way you stare at anyone who's just said something incredibly stupid.

"What are you talking about? He tried to bludgeon me!" Why didn't anyone ever take my almost dying seriously?

"I'm not saying he wouldn't have *killed* you," Mr. Masters says. "I'm just saying that it wasn't his first priority."

Somehow that doesn't make me feel any better. I don't want my death to be on anybody's to-do list, even at the bottom. I take a moment to catch my breath. Mr. Masters doesn't look at me, just keeps his eyes on the road. He looks more resolute than I've ever seen him.

"He knew who you were," Mr. Masters says. It isn't a question, but I answer anyways.

"He called me the Sensationalist."

"Then he knew what you are. Who your Super is."

I want to remind him that I don't really have a Super, and that if I did, I probably wouldn't have been in that mess in the first place. I turn back around and look in the direction of my house, just to make sure it hasn't exploded or anything. No thick columns of black smoke. No towering infernos. That's good. The TV is bad enough. Dad loved that TV.

"He said he was hoping for more of a fight," I mumble.

Mr. Masters sighs as he pulls up to a red light. He drums his fingers on the steering wheel for a second, then reaches over and grabs my shoulder, pressing the button on the watch sitting in his lap. "Traffic," he mutters, running through the red light, weaving in and out between the now-frozen cars.

"You don't have to worry about your parents, Drew. The Jacks are nasty, but they have purpose. They won't attack unless they have something to gain."

Something to gain?

"You mean the Titan?"

But Mr. Masters doesn't say anything. Just makes a familiar turn. I watch him carefully.

"How did *you* know I was in trouble?" I ask.

He takes a moment to answer. "Jenna," he says. "She said she got your message and was worried. I happened to be nearby and said I would check on you. I rushed over, saw the front door open, heard stuff breaking upstairs, and decided we needed a minute together."

I turn and look out the window, watching the buildings zip past. Finally the streets come back to life, and we fall back into line with the unfrozen cars.

Jenna was worried about me. Outside, the procession of houses, stores, and restaurants grows more and more familiar.

"Where are we going?"

"Back to school. I need to check on the others."

"Others?"

"Yes, Drew. You aren't the only one the Suits hit today."

I have more questions, a lot more, but Mr. Masters says to just wait. We are almost there. He also says I will have to call home. My mother will be worried. I'll have to make some excuse. He will think of something.

I gingerly rub the bump on my forehead from the coffee table.

"Are you hurt?" he asks.

"Could be worse," I say.

He takes a look at the lump swelling under my bangs. "It might be soon," he says, then pulls into the staff parking lot with a screech of tires. He hands me my backpack and puts a finger to his lips. "Come on, and don't say a word to anyone."

Highview is mostly deserted, though there are still a few straggling students. Most of the clubs and practices have been canceled, and I can't help but wonder if the Suits have something to do with it. I try to focus on walking, one foot and then the other, try not to think about the man standing in my very own bedroom about to brain me with the business end of his baton, or my mother opening the front door to find a trail of kitchen knives down the hall. We make our way up the stairs and to the teachers' lounge, Mr. Masters keeping a hand on my elbow so I don't fall over. I lean against the wall, and he tells me to wait.

Even without my powers, I can hear the conversation he has with Mrs. Unser, the art teacher.

"Oh," he says. "If you're in here, then I guess they caught the mouse."

"Mouse? What mouse?"

"They found it in one of the cabinets. Big one. White with red eyes. I told them that it sounds more like a rat and that I'd come look for it—maybe I could use it in science class—but I guess they've already taken care of it."

Ten seconds later I wave to Mrs. Unser, who walks briskly down the hall, eyes wild, whispering something about needing a new job.

"Come on."

Mr. Masters pulls me inside and fishes in his pockets. He counts out what he has and turns to me. "You have a nickel?"

I reach in my pocket and pull out my change. "This one's on me," I say. A bag of pork rinds is the least you can give someone who saves your life. Mr. Masters smiles as I press the button for B-1.

I walk downstairs and realize the magnitude of what has happened.

They are all there, the members of H.E.R.O., or most of

them, anyways. Mr. Masters had broken protocol, leaving them alone in the basement without him for who knows how long—long enough to come rescue me, at least. He would never do that unless it were a matter of life and death.

"It's the only place I was sure they would be safe," Mr. Masters says, reading my thoughts. Safe from what? I think, and then I see what's happened. Nikki is slumped over in a chair, and Mike is bent over with his cast propped on his knee. He looks at me and smiles wanly, but I can't help but look at the other two. Eric has one cheek the size and color of a plum and deep scratches on the other. There is blood on his jeans— his blood, somebody else's, impossible to tell. His right hand is swollen and he has several fingers taped together. He holds an ice pack up to one eye.

Gavin's hair isn't perfect for once, but that's just the first thing I notice. He also has one hand pressed to his side. There is a hole in his shirt ringed in scarlet. Every breath he takes is hitched.

That's it. Just the four of them. My stomach twists. "Where's Jenna?"

"She's safe. She's with the Fox," Mr. Masters says from behind me.

"That doesn't mean she's safe," Nikki snaps.

Gavin snorts, then winces and presses his hand harder against his side. I turn to Mr. Masters. "What's going on?"

He motions for me to sit, which I do, afraid I might fall down otherwise. "It was a coordinated attack," he says, crouching next to Gavin to inspect the bandage beneath the hole in the shirt. "Keep your hand there," he tells Gavin, then turns back to me. "Eric found a Jack of Spades in his gym bag and was ambushed on his way to karate. Gavin found the Jack of Diamonds in his back pocket and was attacked while walking home from school."

"They weren't after us," Gavin mutters. "We were just bait."

"We aren't sure about that," Mr. Masters says, raising an eyebrow, but it falls just as swiftly. "Though it does appear to be the case," he adds with resignation.

I think about what Mr. Masters said in the car. That the Jack of Clubs wasn't even after me. Then my thoughts jump to Gavin's and Eric's Supers. Mr. Masters takes the empty seat next to me. "Cryos and Hotshot are missing," he confirms. "Off the grid, though we shouldn't assume they are dead. The Jacks waited for Stonewall and Shizuka Shi to send out their distress signal; then they attacked. The Jack of Spades was carrying some kind of machine that disrupted Cryos's cybernetic link, making him all but powerless—no doubt one of the Dealer's devices. And it turns out that the Jack of Diamonds is naturally resistant to fire. Hotshot didn't stand a chance."

"And diamond can cut right through rock, as it turns out," Gavin groans. "Or at least a laser can." Nikki scoots her chair closer and puts her arm around him, and I suddenly feel guilty for suspecting him earlier.

"They knew you would notify your Supers once you found the cards, drawing them in," Mr. Masters continues. "What isn't clear is how they knew who you were, where to find you, how they planted their cards on you in the first place." Mr. Masters stares into the distance, talking as if he's thinking out loud. "Or why they wanted to capture the Supers to begin with."

"What about you?" Gavin asks, nodding at me. "Did they get the Titan?"

Usually I'd assume this to be another of Gavin's digs, but the pained look in his eyes convinces me that he's actually concerned this time. I'm about to say something when Mr. Masters answers for me.

"The Sensationalist has no way of contacting the Titan. Nobody does." He gives me a long sideways look that makes me glance down at my shoes. "That doesn't mean that the Titan is in any less danger. Or any of us, for that matter."

"What about Jenna?" Mike asks. "Doesn't that mean they know about her, too? Won't they use her to get to the Fox?"

We are all staring at Mr. Masters. Waiting. He reaches into his pocket and pops open his watch, running his thumb across the glass face, then snaps it closed again.

"Yes," he says finally. "The Jacks are clearing out the opposition. The Fox is now most certainly Justicia's best chance of stopping the Dealer. We will have to keep a close eye on Jenna." He looks at me when he says this. As if protecting Jenna is suddenly my job.

I turn to Gavin and give him a look that for once is not nasty or condescending. It's more of an unspoken agreement.

That if Jenna's ever in trouble and I'm not around—who am I kidding, even if I am around—he's more than welcome to save her. He nods. It's a totally macho, action-movie thing to do, but at least I know he understands.

Mr. Masters puts his Lurch-size hands on his knees and pushes himself to his feet. "I will do everything I can to find out what has happened to your Supers," he says, "but until then, I think it's best if you try not to draw any attention to yourselves. You don't have Supers who you can count on any-more," he adds. "You have to look out for one another."

AN INVITATION

When Mr. Masters drops me off two hours later, there is still a police car in my driveway. I mostly believe him when he says my parents aren't in any real danger for now, but seeing the patrol car here, parked in *my* driveway, makes me sick all over again.

"Remember what we talked about," he says. "Everyone will be fine. Just stick to the script."

I nod.

"Are you all right?"

I nod again. The nod is the easiest lie there is.

Before I even open the door, I can hear my mother on the phone. Probably talking to my aunt Claire. Or maybe to my grandmother.

"Oh, they're here now. They say it's probably just vandalism. No, nothing was stolen. Yes. The TV. There are holes in the kitchen cabinets, too. Knives scattered across the floor. It looks like they broke down Andrew's door. No, of course not. He stayed after school for his environmental club meeting, thank god! Oh, I know, I can't imagine what would have happened if he had been home. No. The cops say whoever it was probably would have turned and run. Rowdy teenagers. Of course they are going to check for prints. No, I don't think there are any DNA samples. You watch way too much TV."

It's Grandma.

"No, we are *not* moving. This is the first thing like this that has happened in our neighborhood. No, I really doubt that. Why would a gang of supervillains break into my house, Mom? You can't believe everything you see on the news. Yes, I know there is a house available just down the street from you. No, Mom. No . . . Mother. *No* . . . Mother. We'll be fine. No, I don't think Andrew wants to come live with you by the lake. Besides, how would he get to school?"

I open the door.

"Hang on, Andrew's home. I'll call you back."

I stand there for a moment.

The place is a wreck. Shattered television bits are stuck in the carpet. Tables knocked over. Holes in the walls. One cop is taking what seems like twenty pictures of everything. I'm paralyzed for a moment by the repeated flash of the camera. Seeing it here, this way, with my parents, makes it different somehow.

My father, who is sitting at the kitchen table with another

cop, comes toward me, but my mother squeezes ahead of him with the interception. I am instantly suffocated in her arms.

"I'm so glad you're safe," she says.

You aren't the only one, I want to say, but I don't. Instead I ask her what happened, trying to sound confused and a little appalled. Mr. Masters said to let everyone else talk as much as they wanted and to say as little as possible. Mom says it was a break-in. Dad says probably just teenagers looking for cash . . . *not* a plotted attempt on the part of an escaped convict and a member of a supervillain gang to ambush a hung-over super-hero by attacking his unsuspecting, nearly powerless sidekick. They hug me some more; then one of the officers needs to ask me some questions. My parents flank me on either side of the kitchen table like bodyguards. If I had to guess, I'd say they will probably both camp outside my room tonight with baseball bats in their hands. Either that or just sleep in my bed with me like they did when I was two and there was a thunderstorm.

"So you were at school all afternoon?" the officer asks.

"Yes, sir."

"An environmental club meeting?"

"We keep trash off the streets," I say, reciting the motto, wondering how many people Mr. Masters will be an alibi for today.

"Andrew, can you think of anyone, maybe somebody at

school, or somebody from your neighborhood, anyone who maybe has something against you?"

You mean the mustachioed psychopath with the boomerang club specifically? Or any of his psychopath friends?

"No, sir."

"No one you've been arguing with or had a disagreement with of some kind?"

You could call it a disagreement. You might also call it attempted murder.

"Not that I can think of."

"Is there anybody at school you don't particularly like or who doesn't like you?"

Sure. His name is Gavin. And he secretes lava rock or something and has real, honest-to-god biceps. Though I feel kind of bad for him right now because *his* Super actually bothered to show up and got kidnapped for it, while he got zapped by some goon's beam-blasting eyeball, so now he has a hole in his chest and his hair's messed up. I wonder which one bothers him more.

"I'd say most people don't care about me one way or the other," I answer.

"Right. Looks like not much has changed since I was in middle school." The officer smiles at my parents, who smile weakly back, then turns to me again. "And you can't possibly think of any reason somebody you know would break in here and do this?"

Now that you mention it . . . there is this one guy, you might have heard of him, the Titan? Six-five, about two-eighty, can bench press a whale. Yeah, well, he ticked off this one guy a while back by supposedly killing him, and now that dead guy and his friends are using me as bait to even the score.

"Nope. Sorry," I say.

"No problem. Well, Mr. and Mrs. Bean. This is normally a quiet neighborhood. One of you is an accountant and the other is a"—he looks down at his clipboard—"teachers' aide for kindergartners. Can you think of any of *them* who would want to break into your house and smash your TV?"

My mother laughs nervously. I'm not sure it's that funny, though. I've met some of her students.

My father shakes his head. "This is the first time anything like this has happened to any of us." He wraps a reassuring arm around me.

I nod.

The officer stands. We all stand. He says something about insurance and paperwork and coming by tomorrow. My parents show him out. After he leaves, my mother gives me another smothering hug.

"Why'd they have to smash the TV?" Dad says, surveying the damage, holding a piece of glass to the light.

"The important thing is that it's over and we are all safe," Mom says.

"Yeah, until next time," Dad says.

My mother scowls at him. "Richard. Stop. You're going to scare your son."

Dad moves in and wraps his skinny little arms around both of us. "Sorry," he says. "You're right. It's fine. We won't ever let anything happen to you." They both squeeze, and I feel like I can hardly breathe.

By the time we get the house mostly back in order and sit down to an unenthusiastic dinner of leftovers, it's ten o'clock. My parents barely touch their food, and they are reluctant to send me upstairs, just as I suspected, insisting that I keep my door open halfway, even though the knob is still busted off and it won't close anyways.

I finally collapse onto my bed and stare up at the ceiling, replaying the day in my head from start to finish. I know I should only be thinking about the Jack of Clubs standing over me, ready to clobber my brains out, about Gavin and Eric nursing their wounds, or about their two missing Supers, but it's the two and half seconds with Jenna that I can't get out of my mind.

What if she really is in trouble?

What if she and the Fox are the next targets?

What if she never kisses me again?

I try calling again. The Jack of Clubs took my bag of gadgets with him, but at least that means my phone works. I get her voice mail and leave another message. This one is short and pathetic.

Finally, at midnight, she calls me back.

"About time," I say. I mean it to sound playful, but instead I sound like a father waiting by the door after curfew.

"Hi," she says. She sounds exhausted. Even more than me.

"Where've you been? I tried to call."

"I know. I got your messages. All ten of them."

I really thought there were only seven or so. I must have lost track.

"I was a little concerned," I say.

"I figured. I was out with the Fox," she says. "We spent half the night looking for those guys."

"Did you . . . ?"

"No, nothing," Jenna says. "I heard what happened, though. Terrible news about Cryos and Hotshot. The Fox is sure they've been kidnapped. She's determined to find them. What about you?" she adds, her voice softening. "You okay?"

I'm not okay. Not exactly. But I'm not sure how to tell her what's wrong with me. "I'm alive," I say finally. "Mr. Masters got to me just in time. He has a knack for that sort of thing."

"Mr. Masters," she says. She sounds disappointed. As if she expected something else.

"He said that maybe you . . . because of the Fox . . ."

"That I was in trouble?" Jenna finishes. "You don't have to

worry about me, Drew. I'm fine. I just wish I could have been there. You have no idea how worried I was," she adds.

"Really?"

"Really."

"Would you say you were worried *sick*?" I ask.

"I almost blew chunks," she says.

"That's really sweet."

There's a pause. I can hear my father snoring two rooms away. And Mrs. Polanski snoring next door. And sirens a few miles away. I've gotten really good at picking out sirens.

"Listen, Jenna, about today—" I start to say, but she cuts me off.

"Actually, I wanted to ask you about this Saturday," she says. "I know it's probably not the best time, but there's this charity benefit on Saturday. You know, one of those fancy dress-up things. Kyla's asked me to be there, you know, to help keep an eye on things. It's a lot to ask."

She waits.

"You want me to come keep an eye on you?" I ask.

"Or the other way round," she says.

And this is how the best and worst day of my life ends. With me being asked out on a date by the girl who kissed me for two and a half seconds.

"So she can babysit me."

So will you come?

She knows the answer before she even asks. Even with

215

everything that's happened today, maybe *because* of everything that's happened.

"What do I wear?" I ask.

"A suit, if you have one," she says. "But leave the belt at home."

PART THREE

IN WHICH SOMEONE ELSE ALMOST DIES FOR A CHANGE

FOR WHAT IT'S WORTH

They have their own trading cards, you know. Supers, I mean. They come in packs of five. Just like baseball players. The first one ever printed was of Captain Marvelous, and they only released a hundred of them. Last I checked, it was going for two thousand bucks on eBay.

There's none of me, of course, though I won't lie and say that I haven't already sketched out what it might look like. I've got a better costume. Midnight blue—that kind that's nearly black—made out of heat-resistant, Kevlar-reinforced mesh, of course, sporting a big red S right there on my chest. I've still got my utility belt, and boots instead of sneakers, and my hair is artistically windswept. I'm posing in a kind of ninja-tiger combat crouch, and my nose is in the air, all feral-like. As if I'm tracking someone. You flip it over and see my stats.

THE SENSATIONALIST
Affiliation: H.E.R.O.
Speed: 2
Agility: 2
Strength: 2
Power: 2
Resistance: 2

This is all out of ten, of course. And that's being generous. But Perception? That one's off the flippin' charts. A 10 easy.

The numbers on these cards are all bogus anyway. Contrived by the marketing department of the company that makes them. It's all subjective. The only way to know which Super is the strongest is to wait and see who's still standing at the end.

I have a copy of the Titan's card from ten years ago, when he was just taking over as the leader of the Legion of Justice. It's one of those cool 3D-effect jobbies where every time you tilt it, the Titan throws a punch at you. The numbers on the back are inflated a little. Mostly nines and tens across the board. But he was in his prime then. The head of one of the most celebrated superhero teams in the world. Citizens' darling and the scourge of villains everywhere. He deserved a little grade inflation.

I think about what the card would be now. A picture of him straddling his stool. And every time you shift the card, he takes another drink.

The Titan. Speed: Zero. Perception: Highly impaired. Resistance to alcohol: Negligible.

I stopped collecting the cards about a year ago. Mike's got one of the Fox. He showed it to me a few weeks ago. Much the same as the Titan's. All nines and tens. The only difference is that next to the word *Affiliation*, the Fox's card reads *None*. There is no Legion of Justice. It seems like there are very few teams left anymore. Everyone's got their own agenda. Everyone's out for their own glory.

I wonder if that will happen to us, to H.E.R.O., once we all graduate from the program. Will we just go our separate ways? Just forget about each other? Will we send each other postcards showing us punching the stuffing out of some villain at the top of an erupting volcano with the caption "Wish you were here"?

Assuming we make it through the program, of course.

Assuming we even make it to next week.

JENNA'S DATE

It's Saturday, and everybody's mowing their lawn. I can hear the symphony of small combustion engines whining and rattling in unison up and down the neighborhood. I can smell the fresh-cut grass, probably the only good thing that comes out of lawn-mowing Saturday. Somewhere, somebody runs over a rubber ball. I can hear the *thwap thwap thwap* as it's shredded to pieces, the first casualty of the day.

It's Saturday, and that means my mother is cleaning. She's still finding pieces of glass in the carpet, even three days later. She still jumps whenever anyone knocks on the door, even though it has two brand-new locks and an eight-hundred-dollar alarm system attached to it. "You can't let fear run your life," she tells my father. And then she checks to make sure the doors are all dead bolted.

It's Saturday, and my suit is hanging on the door, waiting

for me. The tie my father helped me pick out is burgundy. My father owns forty-two ties. He's an accountant, and nobody ever knows what to get him for his birthday. I practice tying the knot that he taught me and notice my hands are shaking.

It's been that kind of week.

Since Wednesday, everyone's been on a tightrope. All of H.E.R.O., of course. Eric and Gavin, who do their best to mask their injuries and check their backpacks for playing cards after every period. The lights flicker whenever someone bangs a locker anywhere near Mike in the hall. Even Jenna—normally so composed, so in control—seems to be constantly looking over her shoulder. And every time I try to talk to her, she finds an excuse to cut our conversation short.

But it's not just us. The students at Highview fill the halls with murmurs instead of shouts. The teachers look out the window constantly, as if they expect one of the Suits to come busting through and take the school hostage. Officer Jenson keeps one hand on his Taser as he walks the school grounds. Even the principal reminds us to be careful walking home from school in the afternoon.

The mayor's been on the news twice in two days, insisting that everyone stay calm, that the authorities have the situation under control, that we should continue to have faith in the city's champions even though most of them are missing or worse. There's still the Fox. And if anyone can find the Dealer and stop him, it's her. Jenna says the same thing. The Fox has a plan, though sometimes I'm not sure even Jenna's convinced.

223

But none of us are as wigged out as Mr. Masters, who came to H.E.R.O. on Friday pizza-less again and still with no news regarding our missing Supers. He looked like a zombie, ambling slowly to the front of the room to give us the empty update. He was making calls. Trying to summon reinforcements, but to no avail. Lady Dynamo. Ultimatum. Black Scorpion. They were scattered all over the globe. They all had their own villains to beat, their own plots to uncover. Nikki's Super, Miss Mindminer, was still off the grid, deep undercover in the Chinese mafia.

Then he told us about the Rocket.

Taken from his underground bunker sometime yesterday. Listed as MIA, just like the others. Mr. Masters had gone to check on him after failing to make contact. There were signs of a brief struggle. Broken glass. Holes in the walls. Deep gouges in the floor. It looked, he said, like the Jack of Spades's work. Just as disturbing—Mr. Masters said he had no idea how the Suits had found the Rocket's secret hideout. Like our identities and who we served, that information was supposed to be classified.

I looked at Mike, who sat in his seat, stone-faced, except there was a burning smell coming from the armrests where his hands were clenched. His Super might have broken his arm in eight places, but that didn't mean Mike had stopped caring.

Mr. Masters rubbed his polished head in frustration. "We will get your heroes back," he assured us, though I wasn't sure what he meant by *we*. The members of H.E.R.O.? The

Fox and Jenna? The fine, upstanding members of the Justicia police department, who, up to now, had been content to provide after-event crowd control?

I'm not sure he knew either.

As we trudged back up the stairs to the teachers' lounge, he told us all to remember the Code, to trust in the forces of goodness and light, to stick with the plan. But if Mr. Masters had a plan, he wasn't sharing it with the rest of us.

And judging by the Supers disappearing left and right, it certainly wasn't working.

So it's Saturday, and I'm getting into costume, the tie pulled so tight I can barely breathe. The dress shoes crimping my toes. My hair is slicked back with too much gel, and I've brushed my teeth three times since this morning. When I walk into the living room, my mother just stares at me for a moment. She looks like she's going to cry.

"I hardly recognized you," she says.

"It's my secret identity," I tell her.

Sometimes it's the thing right in front of our noses that we look over.

Twenty minutes later, she drops me off at the Grand Avenue Hotel and tells me to call her when I'm ready to come home or at eleven, whichever comes first. We apparently don't want the Toyota to turn back into a pumpkin. She adjusts my burgundy tie and kisses me on the cheek, and I wait until she has pulled away to wipe it off. The hotel lobby is full of marble columns and uncomfortable-looking couches. I can smell the chlorine from the hotel pool, but the very thought of a swimming pool makes me queasy. I take the elevator to the top floor.

I step off and am immediately blocked by a man twice my size, holding a handheld metal detector. He waves his magic wand over me twice, like some Secret Service fairy godfather, and then tells me to have a nice evening.

"Leave the belt at home," she said. Now I know why. The gorilla at the gate probably wouldn't have looked too kindly on a kid with containers of nerve gas strapped around his waist. I follow the few other puffins and their dates down the hall and walk through the double doors.

Jenna warned me what to expect. A charity dinner to help stamp out hunger. A bunch of Justicia's well-to-dos spending three hundred dollars on oysters so that some poor family somewhere can get a bag of rice. The dinner is being hosted by Kaden Enterprises, but the guest of honor is the mayor himself.

I've never met the man personally, though I've seen him on TV a lot lately. His slicked-back silver mane of hair and pounding fists have been everywhere since the Jacks escaped. The speech is always the same. "We won't be held victims to acts of villainy." "A thug is still a thug, no matter how he's dressed." "The Dealer and his Suits will be captured and brought to justice." Bold words—especially with a gang of notorious criminals at his doorstep and most of the Supers sworn to defend the city missing in action.

And in the middle of all of it, Kyla Kaden gathers the mayor and a host of Justicia's wealthiest citizens in a closed-off banquet hall on the top floor of a hotel. It's almost like dumping a bucket of chum over the side of the boat in shark-infested waters. Not a great idea.

Unless you're fishing for sharks. I stare into the room full of men in tuxedos and women in dark evening gowns. From here they almost look like pawns on a chessboard. And I wonder if, just maybe . . . But no. It's unthinkable. A Super would never intentionally endanger the lives of so many innocent civilians. Rule number three.

This isn't a trap, I have to remind myself. It's just a date.

Of course, that doesn't make me any less nervous.

It's sensory overload, right from the start. Everyone here seems to be sprayed in something, and I get the same woozy feeling that I get walking through department stores at the mall. The sound I can cope with—a steady rumble of voices competing with the string quartet playing in the center of the room—but the smell is dizzying, like a ten-megaton perfume bomb. Save for the greenery decorating the tables, everything seems to be black and white. Even the ties are black. All but mine.

"Drew?"

Any other time I would have sensed her coming. Her walk. Her smell. But I am so busy blocking out everyone else, she gets the jump on me. I turn to face her.

"Jenna."

But it's not really Jenna. It's not the Silver Lynx, either. This

227

is somebody else entirely. Somebody new. Gone are the cheesy T-shirts and baggy jeans, replaced with a strapless dress, kind of a shimmering black that plays catch with the light. Her hair is tied into a knot, two blond curls snaking down over each ear. Even her glasses are different—slimmer, with gold frames. She is holding a champagne glass, though I can tell by the smell it's just seltzer tinged with lime.

"Wow. You look . . . um . . . great." I wince. Jenna cocks her head to the side.

"Really? Um . . . great? That's the best you can do?"

"Sorry," I say. "I guess I've just never seen this side of you before."

She shrugs, then reaches over and readjusts my tie so that now it looks even more crooked than before.

"Come to think of it, I don't think I've seen you in anything that buttoned up before," she says.

"It's my only suit."

"That's not true," she replies. She reaches out and touches my arm, so I don't really care that I'm being mocked.

I nod to one of the half dozen servers carrying plates of really expensive and disgusting-looking hors d'oeuvres.

"Fighting hunger?"

Jenna sighs, looks out over the schmoozing crowd. "Not everyone's a superhero, Drew. Most people would rather just write a check. Besides, Kyla doesn't really care what she's fighting, as long as she gets to be a hero."

"Where is she, by the way?" I ask, scanning the crowd

looking for the tallest woman I can see. Though I've obviously met the Fox before—have actually been less than three feet away from the business end of her katana—I have never had the chance to meet her alter ego in person.

"Who knows?" Jenna says. "She likes to stay on the edge. There's the mayor over there, though." Jenna points to a tall gentleman with too-white teeth and a really expensive-looking suit. "See the two men standing nearby with earpieces? If you look real close, you can see the bulge in their suits where their holsters are."

She is right. The mayor's two hulking escorts are standing at attention, scanning the crowd, hands folded in front of them, just like in the movies. "I guess they don't know what kind of company they're in," I say.

"It doesn't hurt to be careful," Jenna replies.

I watch her watch the crowd, still not sure who I'm looking at. With the dress and the lipstick and the eye liner she looks like she's home from college or something. And I suddenly sense this gap between us, that maybe is only a crack but feels more like a canyon. I feel like a little boy tugging on her dress, trying to get her attention, afraid if I don't try to step over, I'll never get across.

"So, Jenna, I was thinking. About last Wednesday . . ."

Jenna turns and smiles at me, then looks over my shoulder. She gives a curt wave. My instinct is to turn and look, but I know if I take my eyes off her, I'll lose my nerve and won't say what I want to say.

"Sorry. About Wednesday?" Her eyes literally sparkle.

"Yeah. I don't know about you, but for me, I think some-thing, you know, kind of *shifted* between us."

"Really?" She takes a sip from her glass, looks at me, then behind me again.

The dry-cleaned trousers are itching my legs furiously, and I somehow resist the urge to scratch. "Changed, somehow. I mean, I don't want you to get the wrong idea, but I just felt like maybe you and I . . . we . . . are you all right?"

She keeps looking over my shoulder. Finally she turns back to me and fixes me with her eyes.

"I'm sorry, Drew," she says.

And I can see it in her eyes. Not like "Sorry I'm only half listening to you," but really sorry. Like "Sorry for your loss" sorry. Like "Sorry your dog got run over by a truck last night" sorry. Really, seriously sorry.

That's when I smell him. I smell him before I see him. A blanket of Right Guard and Irish Spring barely hiding a layer of pure testosterone.

"Hey there, Bean."

Gavin McAllister slaps me on the shoulder. His hair is gelled even more than mine, and I can almost taste the alcohol tinge of mouthwash on his breath. He is wearing a grin wider than a mobile home and a black tie.

I turn and glare at Jenna, who pretends there's something interesting in her glass.

"Nice tie," Gavin says.

"You too," I say.

"Jenna, you didn't tell me Andrew would be here."

"Jenna," I say as best I can between clenched teeth, "you didn't tell him I was coming?"

Though he's really only four inches taller, I feel dwarfed standing next to Gavin, the two of us looking at Jenna, who is running a finger along the edge of her glass. I think about what they say about tension so thick you could cut it with a knife. I'm pretty sure you'd need a chain saw for this.

Jenna looks at me, then at Gavin, then back at me.

Then she empties the glass in one swift swallow and hands it to him.

"Would you mind? I could use some more."

Gavin looks at Jenna, then at me, then back at Jenna.

Jenna looks at me again, takes a deep breath, and then glances out over the crowd.

I look at Gavin. *Just* Gavin. I actually *stare* at him. Boring holes through his eyeballs with the laser vision I don't have. Right through his eyeballs and into that big granite head of his, chipping away at the rock of a brain, wondering what it is she can possibly see in the guy.

"Sure," he says. "No problem." He takes the glass and retreats toward the bar. When he's far enough that only I could hear me, I turn on her.

"What's *he* doing here?"

"The same thing *you* are doing here. I invited him. He's my friend."

231

"I know he's your friend, but you can't . . ." The look on Jenna's face stops me cold. Never tell Jenna Jaden what she can and can't do. I've learned that lesson before. "You don't invite two guys to the same rich snooty dinner party charity thingy. Haven't you ever seen a movie in your life? Now one of us has to kill the other one."

Jenna smirks and shakes her head, but I just keep glaring at her. She takes another look at me and stops smiling. "You're serious."

"Yes," I say a little too loud. "I mean, no. I'm just saying he shouldn't be here." Or I shouldn't be here, though I decide not to include that as an option.

Jenna rolls her eyes in disgust. Her hands take off and I'm suddenly outnumbered again, three to one. "You two aren't apes. I'm not a prize." She sticks a finger at my chest. "This is not a date. And you are being way too dramatic."

I don't even know where to get started with all of that.

"What do you mean, not a date?"

She looks around her, palms up, exasperated. "Does this look like a date to you?"

I have to admit I wouldn't expect the mayor to come along on Jenna's and my first date. But then I look at the way she's dressed and her hair all done up, and I think about the fact that the shirt I'm wearing is actually ironed, and I honestly don't know what to think.

"Okay. Maybe I'm overreacting," I say. "But what do you expect? You kissed me. *Me. I'm* the one you kissed, in case you've forgotten."

I stop.

Because she does that thing. That thing girls do where they look sideways and then down and then chew on their bottom lip. I know that look.

"You're kidding me."

"Drew."

"You're not kidding?"

"Keep your voice down."

"I don't believe it. When did you kiss him?"

"Why is it any of your business?"

"Was it the same day? Right before I almost got my brains bashed in? Did you kiss Eric too? Mike?" Please say she didn't kiss Mike. I really would have to kill *him*.

One of the servers walks by and sticks his platter between us, probably in an attempt to shut us up. "Endive?" he asks, pointing to a plate full of white, leafy things wrapped around what seem to be pieces of moldy cheese. I feel like I might throw up. I shake my head.

"No, thank you," Jenna says, much more tactfully, smiling at the server, who shuffles away.

"If I had known you were going to act like this, I wouldn't have invited you."

"If I had known you were inviting him, I wouldn't have come."

She rolls her eyes again. I can feel the heat rising to my cheeks. This could be the moment, right here. If I don't say the right thing right now, then she will transform back into just-a-friend Jenna or, worse, slip away entirely.

"Jenna," I say.

She turns and stares at me. "What?"

"Excuse me. Am I interrupting?"

Gavin is suddenly next to us, holding Jenna's glass in one hand and something on a cracker in the other.

And I smell something. Something besides the champagne and the Gruyère. Something entirely out of place, hidden in the walls or in the ceiling. I recognize it from H.E.R.O. training. From one of my test tubes. It was one that I missed the first few times, and so Mr. Masters drilled it into me. It's cyclotrimethylene trinitramine. Otherwise known as cyclonite.

The most common ingredient in C-4 explosives. I tackle Jenna just as the ceiling comes crashing down.

CRASHED

At least now I know what evil smells like.

We all tumble like dominoes, the whole black-and-white crowd careening off each other. The force of the explosion knocks some of the guests over, causes others to bathe themselves in their drinks, but mostly just results in a lot of smoke and noise.

And a huge hole in the ceiling.

Jenna and I look up at the same time but stay low to the ground. People are screaming and scrambling. One of the waiters is actually trying to pick crab cakes off the floor. It's hard to focus on anything in all this chaos. Then I feel something heavy on my back.

I turn to see that Gavin McAllister is gone. In his place is a creature covered in black-and-gray rock. His pants have ripped; his shoes are in shreds. He has taken off his jacket and torn his shirt, but he's still wearing his tie. I wonder if anyone has seen the transformation, but he had been standing behind us, and all eyes are on the gaping, smoking chasm above us.

Stonewall gives me a nod, and I nod back. I have no idea what we are nodding about, but given the circumstances, I am suddenly not opposed to his being here.

Far to our left, the mayor's two bodyguards already have their pistols drawn and are speaking into their wrists, hopefully calling for backup. The mayor is crouched behind them, pushed back against a wall. Down the hall, you can hear the smoke alarms going off, a pulsing screech that makes my head hurt. I try to peer through the smoke.

Suddenly there is a blast of light from the new hole in the ceiling, and one of the mayor's guards goes down, clutching his shoulder, his gun skidding across the marble floor. The other guard spins around, looking for the source of the attack, when a black boomerang hurtles toward him, knocking his weapon from his hand, then circling back and catching him in the back of the head before returning to its owner.

The three Jacks jump down from the new hole in the ceiling, dressed perfectly for the occasion. When the Jack of Spades lands, the whole floor shakes. The third guard—the fairy godfather from the elevator—bursts through the door, his weapon ready, but another blast from a diamond eye sends him spinning to the floor, unconscious. There is suddenly a lot more screaming. I scoot a little closer to Jenna, who reaches for my hand.

"Everyone. Quiet. Please," the Jack of Diamonds says, patting the air. His voice sounds a little like James Bond, the new one, not the old Scottish guy who everybody likes better. Suave, ponderous, but with a hint of menace. "May I please have your attention?"

The crowd is still frantic, guests scrabbling across the floors, skittering behind overturned tables, like bugs under an upturned rock. With a nod from the Jack of Diamonds, the Jack of Spades suddenly roars and lifts his shovel and brings it down on top of one of the tables, smashing it in two with a splintering crack. Everyone suddenly freezes.

"Thank you," the Jack of Diamonds says. "Sorry to crash the party, ladies and gentlemen. We don't plan to stay long. We've only come for the guest of honor."

The mayor is still pressed against the wall. The guard who had his gun knocked from his hand by the Jack of Clubs is standing in front of him. I can see his pistol about thirty feet away, though I don't imagine it would do him much good even if he could get to it. He'd be zapped, bludgeoned, or pulverized before he even got a shot off.

"We have to do something," Gavin whispers.

"Sure," I hiss. "Remember what happened the last time you faced off against just one of these guys?" I nod to the fissure of chipped white rock along Gavin's side. Even in this form, he still has scars. I turn back to Jenna, who is now crouched beside me. "Where's Kyla?" I ask, though she knows full well who I mean.

"I don't know," she says. "She'll be here."

"But soon, right?"

Jenna doesn't say anything. I can see that look in her eyes, though. She slips off her glasses and slowly sets them on the chair beside her, then kicks off her high-heeled shoes.

"Oh, no," I say.

The Jack of Diamonds takes several steps toward the mayor, his hand extended as if asking for a dance. "The Dealer requests the honor of your presence, Mr. Mayor, so if you would please . . ." The Jack of Diamonds's artificial eye is glowing, a dull orange that pulses in rhythm with his heartbeat. In a blink, it could burn a hole the size of a grapefruit through any one of us.

The mayor doesn't budge. Nobody moves. The servers hide behind their silver platters. Those who are crouched next to doors eye them, calculating their chances. I hear somebody whisper, "Just go," and see a man struggle to his feet and scramble toward one of the exits.

The Jack of Diamonds merely glances that way, and a beam of bright orange light tears through the room, hitting one of the ceiling fans, which comes smashing down at the runner' feet. The man freezes in place, paralyzed. The Jack rubs the temple beside his artificial eye, then turns his attention back to the mayor. "Please, Mr. Mayor, just come quietly. Otherwise one of my colleagues will be forced to make an example."

The Jack of Diamonds raises his hand, and the Jack of Spade reaches under a nearby table and pulls a young woman out by the neck like a baby kitten, lifting her effortlessly into the air, her feet kicking beneath her, her black shoes tumbling free. He really is gigantic—the biggest man I've ever seen. Even bigger than the Titan.

I press down hard on my fingernail. Just in case. Though at this point, I have no expectations. The Jack of Spades lifts the woman even higher. I think he's just going to snap her in half.

"Let her go."

I look up to see Stonewall take two steps toward the three Jacks, his granite hands formed into small boulders by his side.

"You again?" the Jack of Diamonds says. "Haven't we been over this once already?" Beside me, I can see Jenna's muscles tense.

"Get ready," she says.

That's funny, I think to myself. Just last week I found myself saying the exact same thing. Then I got trampled.

Except those were teenagers. These are the Suits. And we aren't even full-fledged sidekicks yet. But I can see the look in Jenna's eyes, and I know it makes no difference to her.

Stonewall takes another step. Jenna pulls herself up onto the balls of her feet, and I see the twinkle form in the Jack of Diamonds's eye.

Then there is that moment again. When I kind of see things just before they happen. Like the twitch of a finger before a gun is drawn or how somebody licks their lips before they are about to say something. I see the mayor about to stand and his guard about to crouch, ready to go for his gun. I see the Jack of Clubs raise his arm for a throw and the Jack of Spades lift the woman higher before tossing her aside.

And then there's a flash of white outside the window, and the moment suddenly shatters with the pane of glass, and everything speeds up again.

The Jack of Diamond fires and Gavin just manages to dive out of the way, collapsing into another table, breaking it in half. Jenna launches herself, full speed, in the direction of the mayor, the Silver Lynx's reflexes kicking in, dodging fallen chairs and crouching bodies.

I turn and see the Fox, the only Super left, swinging in through the broken glass, a blur of red and white delivering a swift kick to the Jack of Diamonds before drawing her sword and turning just in time to parry a blow from the giant's shovel. The Jack of Spades grunts as the Fox ducks and spins, catching him behind the knees, sending all four-hundred-plus pounds of him crashing down. All around us, the guests are back on their feet, running for whatever exit is closest, screaming at the top of their lungs, driving a spike into my skull with the sheer volume of it. Ahead of me, Jenna flips over a table and pulls the mayor out of the way just as another chandelier comes crashing down. I can't believe she can still move like that in that dress.

"Drew!" she yells.

"Coming!" I yell back.

I shake my head, trying to clear it, and then stand up and scramble after her. Everywhere, people are running, tripping, clawing, shouting. The sounds of explosions fill the air as the Jack of Diamonds fires again and again at the Fox, who back-flips and twists her way around the blasts. I manage to make it to Jenna, who has pulled the mayor behind a table. There is an exit maybe fifty feet away.

"You have to get him out of here," she says. She doesn't need to shout for me to hear her, but she does anyway.

"What about you?"

"Don't worry about me. Just take him and go."

The mayor looks at us like we are crazy. His three armed guards have been replaced by two middle school honors students. I guess he doesn't feel like he has a whole lot of options at this point, because he stands up when I tug on his shirt and follows me as we bolt for the exit. Behind us, there is another explosion of glass as two more windows shatter under a shovel's swing. I see a blur of white and hear a splinter of bone as the Fox delivers a swift kick to the Jack of Spades's ribs. The exit beckons to us with its glowing green letters. And for a moment, I think we might actually make it.

Then I hear a familiar sound and skid to a stop, the mayor careening into me as a black baton whistles by and lodges itself in the wall beside us, stuck tight. I look up to see the Jack of Clubs walking determinedly toward us, his wicked mustache curled in on itself, one hand pulling a long, evil-looking knife from his belt. I threw a whole block of them at him just a few days ago, so I'm guessing this is probably some kind of perverse poetic justice. I stand in front of the mayor, frantically considering all my options. The Jack of Clubs raises his blade, and I just manage to step right, nearly tripping over my feet as the slash narrowly misses. A second strike almost scalps me as I duck. It's not too different from self-defense training with Eric, I think. Except Eric's not really trying to kill me.

The Jack lunges, and I somehow manage to not only dodge the knife but also to deliver a kick to the man's shin, though it only elicits a sneer and a growl. The Jack takes a step back, and I frantically run through the list of attacks I've learned, trying to pick the one I have the least chance of screwing up.

The Jack slashes with his knife again.

And I choose to fall on my butt.

Though I at least keep myself from being skewered, I barely manage to get to my knees before he is standing over me again, his twisted mustache curled twice over, his eyes like pools of black ink.

Just as he is about to strike, a rumbling black boulder bowls into him from out of nowhere. Stonewall has both blocky arms around his villain, and the two of them slam through several chairs before collapsing to the floor.

I stand frozen for just one second as Gavin drives one of his rocky fists into the Jack of Clubs's gut. "Go!" he yells to me. I turn and grab the mayor's hand again, pushing him toward the exit, following, quite literally, on his coattails. As we duck through, I chance one look behind me to see Stonewall and the Jack of Clubs back on their feet, trading blows, and Jenna somersaulting away from blasts from the

Jack of Diamonds. And the Fox's sword cutting the Jack of Spades's shovel in half, those little blue electric bolts arcing between her eyes.

We practically collapse into the hallway, falling into the fleeing throng of panicked guests. It has only been a matter of minutes, but already the cops are in the stairways and on the elevators, flooding the twentieth floor behind their riot shields. I can hear shouting and sirens and alarms clamoring along every floor of the hotel. Two officers grab us, one throwing me against the wall, ready to arrest me before the mayor calls him off.

"Who are you?" the mayor asks.

I'm not quite sure how to answer that one.

"Nobody, really," I say, but before he can respond, the mayor is quickly whisked away, taken by no fewer than six armed guards while the rest pour toward the banquet hall. Somebody else in a uniform grabs me and pulls me out of the way, down another hallway toward the stairs, where other OCs are being evacuated.

"It's okay. It's all right. I can go back, I'm a si—"

I stop myself just in time.

I'm not wearing my mask. I'm just Andrew.

"It's okay, son," the man who grabbed me says, the same thing he probably said to everyone. "Everything's going to be all right. No need to panic."

"I'm not panicking," I say, though my eyes are wide and my breathing's heavy and I have a small cut above my right eyebrow and can feel blood trickling down my cheek. I'm probably the poster child for panic.

Still protesting, I suddenly find myself herded down the stairs with about twenty other guests, most of them slack-jawed, or sobbing. By the time we reach the first floor, there is another crowd of policemen and paramedics. The fire department, more SWAT, hostage negotiation, and about a dozen reporters with cameras in tow. Someone in scrubs dabs at the cut on my head once, seems satisfied that it isn't serious, and tells me to hold the gauze there before moving on to the next guest. There is sound everywhere, and I can't make out anything distinctly. I manage to snake through the crowd, down the hall, and out the emergency entrance into an equally flooded parking lot.

The flash of emergency lights hits me first, followed by the sharp sting of the night air. Staring at the top floor, I can see the smoke still drifting from the roof. I think I see someone moving, running perhaps, but even with my eyes, I can't tell who or what it is through the smoke. I make my way along the side of the building to the alleyway, wondering how I'm even going to get back up there, thinking that heroes who can fly have it easy.

I hear a door open and turn to see a half-naked Gavin stumble through the emergency exit, his shoes gone, his jeans torn, but his tie still around his neck. Save for last Wednesday's wound, which is still purple and swollen, he doesn't look like he's hurt.

"Where's Jenna?" I bark.

"It's okay. She's okay," he says. "Come on. We've got to get out of here before someone realizes what we've done."

"What have we done?" I ask him.

Gavin grabs me by the arm and drags me along. I'm surprised by how strong he is, practically lifting me off my feet. "We've saved the mayor's life," he says.

We escape down the alley behind the hotel and then across the streets that are filling with OCs following the sound of sirens like the rats of Hamelin. Gavin points to my suit coat, which is dusted in glass and debris.

"Do you mind?" he says, looking down at his bare chest, no longer covered in granite but now, I see, covered in a few stippling hairs.

I brush the coat off as best I can and hand it to him. His shoulders look as if they are about to burst through the seams. Still, it's better than nothing. At least he stops shivering. I look back at the hotel.

"Shouldn't we go back?"

But Gavin ignores me. He points to a bus stop down on the corner. "You got any money?" he asks.

I nod. "You're sure Jenna's all right?"

"She's fine," Gavin says, still dragging me along. "The Fox has everything under control. Besides, Jenna's the one who told me to find you, make sure you got out safe."

I stop walking and look back at the hotel. There are spotlights dancing across it now. I can hear a helicopter approaching, though it could still be miles away.

Gavin looks ridiculous with his torn pants and bare feet, his too-short borrowed suit coat and no shirt. The starting left guard for the Highview Middle School football team and body spray connoisseur—who, I think, might have saved my life back there.

"Thanks," I say, though I kind of mumble it. I'm not quite sure I said it loud enough for him to hear, but he must have at least read my lips.

"Did you just say what I think you said?" he asks.

"I think so."

"That must have been hard for you," he says.

"You have no idea."

"Yeah. I think I do."

Gavin pulls me over to the bench by the bus stop, and we sit down. I put my head in my hands, and he leans back and winces a little with each breath. Whether it's the old wound or a new one, I can't tell. "You should get yourself checked out," I say.

"It's not serious," he answers. He tries to fasten the coat, but it won't close far enough and he manages to pop a button, then just lets it go.

"And you're sure you're okay?" I ask again, looking over my shoulder.

Gavin nods. "Listen, Drew. I want you to know, I had no idea how tonight was going to turn out."

"You mean the Suits?"

"I mean you," he says. "I had my suspicions about the Suits."

Maybe Gavin's not as dim as I wanted him to be. I think about Jenna inviting both of us. So that she could keep an eye on us. So that we could keep an eye on her. She knew, too.

"You think it was a setup?"

"The mayor makes good bait," Gavin says. "Probably even better than a sidekick. Hard to resist."

"Like zombies at a brain-eating contest."

I think about the looks on the Jacks' faces when the Fox burst through the window. They hadn't been expecting it, at least. Or maybe they had, and they thought they could take her—the three of them together.

And maybe they could have if we hadn't been there.

Maybe, in some messed-up, backward, upside-down way of looking at it, we just saved the mayor *and* the Fox.

"If it was a trap, it was only half sprung," Gavin says. "Two Suits managed to escape back through the roof. The Fox only caught one."

"Clubs?" I ask, hoping she made that that malicious little baton-throwing worm squirm.

"Diamonds," Gavin answers, then points at the headlights of the oncoming bus. "Still. A win's a win. Score one for the forces of goodness and light, right?"

He holds out a fist, and I cringe for a moment before I realize what it's for. I give it a bump. "Win's a win," I repeat.

"You'll want to clean off that cut before you go home," he says. Then gets up and waits for the bus to stop. I look back at the smoking hotel. One Jack down.

All part of the plan. But I'm still not convinced. Can't quite believe that the Fox would purposely endanger so many people, the mayor included, just to get a shot at the Suits.

I think about what Jenna said. Back on the bleachers. That it works the other way, too.

Then I follow Gavin onto the bus, smoothing my bangs down over my forehead to hide the cut. "So is that why she invited both of us?" I wonder out loud as we board, but Gavin shrugs.

"Or maybe she just did it because she's a girl," he says. "And girls are nuts."

By the time I get home, Mr. Masters is already sitting in the living room with my parents. Chatting and drinking tea. I can hear him before I even open the door. He's always in the right place at the right time, not a minute before. He looks better than he did yesterday. At least he has shaved. And the sweater vest is paisley this time.

"Drew. You're home early," my dad says as I open the door.

I try to look normal. I spent the bus ride cleaning myself up as best I could, though I let Gavin keep the coat.

Mr. Masters stands when I walk through the door. I catch the look in his eye.

"So, how was the party?" my mom asks. "And where's your jacket? Isn't it cold outside?"

They don't know.

Mr. Masters puts one hand on my shoulder. The other is tucked in his pocket.

My mother puts her hands on her knees, as if ready to get up, probably to hug me again, but she suddenly stops. The look on her face is chiseled in stone. My father's too, his cup halfway to his lips.

Mr. Masters quickly tells me the story. Apparently the party was boring and Jenna wasn't feeling well, so we decided to leave early, several minutes before the attack, in fact. When everything went down, we were already on the bus, headed to go get coffee.

"But I hate coffee," I tell Mr. Masters.

The head of H.E.R.O. shakes his head. "Make it pancakes, then. Point is, you weren't there. When your parents hear the news, they will flip. It's your job to keep them calm." Mr. Masters glances at his watch. I can see the second hand clicking away. "Is everyone okay?"

I nod, still wondering how he could possibly know all this already. I want to ask him, but there's no time. Not now, anyway. I've got to hurry and get my mask back on.

"All right. Ten seconds. Smile. Act like nothing's happened."

Mr. Masters puts his hand back on my shoulder and stuffs his other hand into his pocket.

My mother finishes lifting herself up and walks toward us. My father takes a sip of tea.

"Yes, Andrew," Mr. Masters says to me, "how was that party?"

Only after Mr. Masters leaves do I learn that he was actually there to drop off some notebook that I apparently "left on my desk." I have no idea whose notebook it is sitting on the coffee table—it's certainly not mine—but I take it up to my room anyways. Inside, the pages are blank.

My parents don't find out about the attack until they are ready for bed and my father turns on the news. I can hear them furiously whispering about me through the walls: *"That's the second close call this week,"* and *"He could have been killed."* I'm not sure how much longer I can hide it from them, even with Mr. Masters's help. I make a note to do a better job of concealing my H.E.R.O. stuff, just in case they go snooping around my room. I listen for their footsteps in the hall. At one point I think I can hear my mother breathing right outside my door and I duck under my covers, pretending to snore. Then she goes away.

The news is twice as long that night. I know because my parents leave their television on and I lie in bed and listen. Once again, the Fox is the star of the show. By the time the cops and reporters flooded the room, the three of us were gone and two of the Jacks as well, leaving only the hero with her catch, pinned to the wall with a sword to his throat, his left eye cracked. Broken. No good to him anymore. Clubs and Spades had escaped the same way they had come, through the new skylight they had made in the ceiling. The mayor's three bodyguards were taken to the hospital along with four other guests, though none of the injuries were serious. Some witnesses reported seeing a rock man or a golem of some kind, but none of the OCs managed to get a picture of him. They were all too busy running for their lives. I lie in bed and wait for the mayor to say something, to call us out, but when he finally does give a little speech, he simply thanks the Fox "and all the other nameless heroes who helped to stop this vicious attack and bring the Jack of Diamonds to justice."

Sometime around midnight I get a message from Jenna. It says:

You were wonderful. Thanx.

And I fall asleep smiling for once. It was a terrible date, but for the moment I don't care. Because whether anybody knew it or not, we did something right.

And because even being a nameless hero is still better than being no hero at all.

H.E.R.O.'S END

It's Monday. Turkey burger day. With carrot sticks and applesauce. Edible, if you can stand applesauce that tastes like tin and turkey that tastes like mulch—or at least what I imagine mulch would taste like. Mike would say it's all about how much ketchup you put on a thing, but the truth is, some things just can't be covered up.

It's Monday, the day after the day after the day I narrowly escaped death again, and thus the day after the day my parents wouldn't let me out of the house. The event at the hotel, the break-in, my own strange behavior—it was all starting to add up. They were more than suspicious. They were paranoid. I couldn't blame them. I just don't know why they had to watch me brush my teeth or sit with me at the table until I finished my cereal.

So I spent my Sunday avoiding anything sidekick related

in the hopes of calming them down and preserving my identity. I did manage to sneak away and spend an hour on the computer. I took five minutes to answer my fan mail—one message from mikevanderB telling me I was "messed up" and that the whole thing on Saturday was "killer" and that the next time he hears about something like that through Eric via *Gavin*, he was going to show me what electroshock therapy must feel like—and then I spent the rest of the time reading various accounts of the mayor's rescue, looking for casual mentions of the three teenagers who had helped the Fox save the day, but there is little room in the spotlight next to Justicia's champion; the Fox soaks it all up. Still, that doesn't stop me from smiling when I step off the bus Monday morning.

I walk down the hall, listening to the clueless masses brag about their parties and their rock concerts, all the while thinking that I, for once, had a more exciting weekend than any of them. While they sat through another tweeny vampire movie, I—Andrew Macon Bean, Beanhead, the Beanie Baby, the kid most of them ignored and some of them unfortunately didn't—I had actually saved the mayor's butt. In fact, I *personally* dragged said mayoral butt through a veritable war zone, dodging laser blasts and flying clubs and falling chandeliers. If I was a full-fledged sidekick and out of the closet, I would probably be in costume right now, accepting a medal on the steps of city hall rather than stuck in English class, counting the syllables in sonnets. Still, medal or no, I feel different.

Special. Like I finally have a secret that's worth keeping. As I pass my fellow sidekicks in the halls, we high-five. Gavin and I nod and wink almost like we are friends. Just last week we were huddled in the school basement licking our wounds. Now we grin at each other stupidly. And for the first time in too long, I can't wait for fourth period to come.

I walk down the stairs into the school basement, thinking that our rescue of the mayor will earn us cool points or sticker stars or trips to Disney World or whatever it is that sidekicks get for saving elected officials from gangs of supervillains. I figure at the very least I'll get a reprieve from having to sniff test tubes and eavesdrop on teachers, that Mr. Masters will look at me a little differently from here on out. Maybe I'll get bumped up to ready reserve status or get to do more combat training with the rest of them. After all, I actually managed to not get stabbed two or three times. That has to count for something. I suspect Mr. Masters will be beaming. I'm almost positive there will be pizza.

Instead, we find a red-faced and sweating Masters, whose green-and-orange sweater vest looks like something a serial killer might wear, pacing in front of us like a preacher at a pulpit while we take our seats. I sit next to Jenna, who looks serious as always, but I see that Gavin has the same birthday-cake-eating expression I do.

"By circumstances that aren't entirely clear to me," Mr. Masters says in a voice that is both hoarse and harsh, "three of you were in attendance at the charity benefit to stamp out hunger when it came under assault by the Suits two days ago."

"We totally *rocked* that party," Gavin whispers to Jenna under his breath. I suddenly hope that if Gavin and I are ever fighting crime together and get interviewed by Eyewitness News, he lets me do the talking.

Mr. Masters holds on to both sides of the podium as if struggling to stay upright. I can see the blood vessels in his forehead throbbing. His nails are bitten down to the quick. He doesn't look like a man brimming with pride. "I understand that you three followed the Code to the best of your abilities, and I want you to know that I took that into account when considering your fate," he says.

Our fate? I look back over at Gavin, whose brow knits faster than my grandmother.

"You would think after the events of last Wednesday that I could count on you all to stay out of trouble, not go looking for it," Mr. Masters chides, taking me, Jenna, and Gavin in with one glance, making me suddenly wish that we didn't all sit next to each other.

"And this time," Mr. Masters adds, "there are consequences."

"Oh, this doesn't sound good," Mike groans, sinking down in his chair.

"This most recent encounter has only confirmed that you are all too involved. Had this confrontation gone differently, had the Fox not arrived in time for the rescue, H.E.R.O. might be answering for the lives of the mayor and any number of civilians. Worse still, I might be in your living rooms right

255

now, explaining to your parents why you didn't come home. In light of this and other events," Mr. Masters continues, "and in consultation with the Fox, I have decided that the current environment is simply too risky for further sidekick involvement."

I can see where this is headed. Mike is right. It's not good. Mr. Masters takes a deep breath, then drives the nail in.

"I have accepted the Fox's recommendation that the H.E.R.O. program be temporarily suspended."

"What?" the three of us say at the same time.

Eric spins around in his seat looking for confirmation, making sure he read Mr. Masters's lips right. Gavin looks like a little kid who's just caught his parents filling his stocking on Christmas Eve. Mr. Masters tries to calm us, but he might as well be trying to put out a forest fire with a water pistol. Gavin, Mike, and Nikki are spewing protests, and Eric is signing so fast no one can possibly follow him.

Only Jenna seems unfazed. I try to read her expression, but she's a sphinx, her lips pursed, her face fixed, as if someone had just sculpted her into the seat next to me.

"That doesn't make any sense," Gavin complains. "The Jack of Diamonds was captured. We helped save the mayor. You can't cancel the program."

Nikki follows right behind. "Yeah, so, like, now that some of us are actually in some serious danger, now that we have somebody to fight, *now* we are going to *stop* learning how to be Supers?"

Mr. Masters pounds on the podium to get our attention. "But you are *not* Supers," he says fiercely, then a little softer. "Not yet, anyway. And you did not capture the Jack of Diamonds. The Fox did. What *you* did was purposely put your lives in danger."

I look at Jenna. She was the one who invited me. What was I supposed to say, no? But even she couldn't have seen this coming. There's no way she would have done something to jeopardize H.E.R.O. Being a sidekick was her life. Jenna continues to stare stoically forward, not so much as a twitch.

"You simply aren't ready," Mr. Masters continues. "Most of you don't even have Supers to sidekick for. You have no one to look after you. I won't be responsible for losing one of you. Therefore, effective immediately, you are to suspend all sidekick-related activity."

"What about the Code?" Gavin protests, turning and pointing to the huge stone tablet in the back. "Are you telling us to just give up? What about Hotshot? And Cryos? What about the Dealer?"

Mr. Masters shakes his head. "There is too much at stake. Your identities have already been compromised. The Fox assures me that she is only days away from catching the remaining Jacks. I think it best if we just stay out of her way. Don't you agree, Jenna?"

Suddenly all eyes are on Jenna. She and Mr. Masters have locked onto each other, and I realize that it comes down to her. She's one of us. The best of us. I know that whatever she says, the rest of H.E.R.O. will follow, but the way they look at each other, it's almost as if they've already had this discussion, and the rest of us are coming to it secondhand.

"Yes," Jenna says softly. "I think it's better if we all stay out of it."

Something flashes between the two of them, a charged look, though I can't tell what all is behind it. Then Jenna folds her hands in her lap, and it's over.

H.E.R.O. is finished. United, we could have protested further, but as the only sidekick with an active Super, Jenna took away our right to veto.

"It's settled, then," Masters says. "No more H.E.R.O. until further notice. You'll just have to try to be normal."

I want to tell Mr. Masters that I don't know how to be normal. That even before I joined H.E.R.O. I never felt normal, and that some days, sitting in here with my fellow sidekicks was the most normal I ever got. But it's clear that the conversation is over. We aren't Supers, we aren't even really full-fledged sidekicks. We are still in training. Nikki's Super is still halfway around the world. Eric's, Gavin's, and Mike's are probably chained away in some secret dungeon somewhere, having their powers sucked out of them. And my Super . . . I have no idea where he is.

"I'm sorry," Mr. Masters says, looking at all of us. "But until the Dealer and the remaining Jacks are captured, I'm afraid there is nothing we can do."

He lets us finish out the session, circled together in the base-ment as he retreats back into his office. None of us dares to suggest a bright side—like the fact that we don't have to carry our costumes in our backpacks anymore or that this greatly decreases our chances of dying before we make it to high school. Gavin huddles next to Eric and writes some-thing in a notebook, and I wonder if they aren't thinking about striking out on their own. I hope not. They can't pos-sibly take on the Suits, even with the Jack of Diamonds out of the deck, not without authorization. Not without Supers or the support of Mr. Masters. Nikki sighs and says that at least it will free up more time for her love life. Mike sits cross-legged and practices shooting sparks back and forth from his fingertips. It isn't long before Jenna excuses herself, retreating to her training room and shutting the door behind her. Mr. Masters, pacing behind one closed door, and Jenna, sitting in the dark behind another. The rest of us somewhere in between.

The way back up the steps to the teachers' lounge at the end of the period is quiet as a funeral procession. No one but Mr. Masters says anything. "It's only temporary," he repeats over and over again. "We'll be back down here disarming bombs and flexing our spandex in no time." Jenna heads up the stairs without a word to anyone. With the mood she's in, I'm not brave enough to chase after her. In fact, I'm the last to leave again.

Which makes it easier for Mr. Masters to stop me on the way out. He smells like Vicks VapoRub. Standing right next to him, I can tell by the rattle in his chest that he is fighting something, something lodged inside that he can't choke down.

"Drew, I want you to know that I think you've handled yourself remarkably well the past couple of weeks," he begins. "I know things haven't quite worked out the way you wanted them to."

"Yeah, well, I guess it doesn't matter now, does it?" I say. It's not a question. Just an observation.

"I've decided that when this is all over, when the Suits are all put away and H.E.R.O. starts back up again, I'm going to work on finding you a new mentor. I think you deserve it."

"Oh," I say.

"Oh? That's all you have to say? I kind of thought you'd be happier."

He's right. I've been waiting for him to say this for weeks. Months. Probably since the day the Titan and I first met. But something about it doesn't feel right. All along he's told me to be patient, that the Titan will come around. And now he's telling me to give up. Just like he's giving up on H.E.R.O.

"No. You're right—it wasn't really working out."

Mr. Masters nods sympathetically. "It's for the best," he says. I let him nudge me up one step, but then I stop and turn to face him, now on eye level.

"He's still in danger, though," I say. Mr. Masters looks at me questioningly. "The Titan. Even with one Jack gone. He's in danger as long as the Dealer is still out there."

I can see him studying me. Planning what he's going to say next.

"If the Fox can be believed, then the Titan has nothing to worry about," he says.

"But you're not so sure?" I thought I heard a sliver of doubt in his voice. Just the slightest tremble.

"I'm sure that it's no longer your responsibility. H.E.R.O. is suspended, Drew. You're not a sidekick anymore. The Titan can take care of himself."

He wouldn't say that if he knew. If he had seen him the way I've seen him.

"Go on," Mr. Masters prods. "You're going to be late to your next class." He pushes me back up the stairs. Pushing me up and out.

I make it halfway before I stop and turn around again. I glance at the code on the back wall. I suppose it can't hurt telling now. It's probably nothing anyway.

"If it helps, I think he may be with someone named Red."

Mr. Masters blinks.

"Do you know that name?"

He appears to think for a moment, one eyebrow arched. "No, I don't think I do," he says finally. "But if you learn anything else, be sure to tell me."

Then Mr. Masters turns and heads back to his office. I listen to the sound of his loafers shuffling along the cement as I slowly climb the stairs to the teachers' lounge.

But I don't leave. I stop at the top and wait.

When someone is lying to you, there are a few things you watch for. Their face and hands sometimes lose color. Their lips tighten. Their foreheads scrunch. They will look down or squint. They tend to scratch something, an arm or an elbow. Their nostrils flare.

When I mentioned the name Red to Mr. Masters, none of those things happened. They wouldn't, of course. After all, Mr. Masters is the one who taught me what to watch for.

But his heartbeat did go up, nearly doubling, just for a moment. You could tell if you had a finger on his pulse. Or if he was hooked up to a monitor.

Or if you could hear it from three feet away.

Which is why I stop at the top of the stairs and listen. I hear him close his office door, but I know now what I'm capable of. I've done this before.

I move down a few steps and sit down, concentrating. I hear him grunt as he falls into his chair. Then he picks up the phone. I try to focus. The halls are emptying already for the next period, but I block all of it out. There is a moment of silence from Mr. Masters's office; then I hear his voice, urgent and annoyed.

"It's Nathan Masters. Answer the phone. I know you've been lying to me. We need to talk. I think you're in trouble."

Mr. Masters hangs up, and I sneak out the door and through the lounge, wondering who's been lying to him.

And what he's hiding from me.

And planning how to find out.

BREAKING IN

I can't concentrate. In history, Mr. Broadside is lecturing about the burning of Rome and promising to bring his fiddle to the next class and play for us, just like Nero. In Spanish I can't even manage to say "That skinny girl in the yellow dress is the winner" without flubbing it up. There is too much in my head.

H.E.R.O. is suspended.

Mr. Masters knows who Red is.

Jenna kissed me.

The Titan is in trouble.

A sidekick is sworn to accompany his Super in all acts of heroism.

Jenna kissed Gavin.

Gavin still has my suit coat.

Sworn to protect his Super when the occasion arises.

Mr. Masters is hiding something.

My coat is going to smell like Gavin's B.O.

I'm not the Titan's sidekick.

How do you say "skinny" in Spanish?

To walk in the path that his Super sets forth.

I'm not anyone's sidekick.

Flaga, flaca, flanco, flaccido?

Why doesn't Mr. Masters want me to be the Titan's sidekick anymore?

Why doesn't he want the members of H.E.R.O. involved?

Jenna's acting weird.

The Titan is still a hero.

Muy weird.

How do you say "Your rocky boyfriend stunk up my jacket" in Spanish?

How do I find out who Red is?

Su novio rocosa apestaba a mi chaqueta.

He's still my hero.

I've got to break into his office.

I need to talk to her. Figure out what's going on.

To trust in his Super above all else.

I've got to find him before it's too late.

Mrs. Muñoz puts her face in mine to get my attention. I tell the class that the flabby girl in the yellow dress is a cow and half of them laugh. The other half isn't paying attention.

"It's *flaca*, not *flaccido*," Mrs. Munoz says to me. "And *la chica en el vestido amarillo no le gustas tanto.*"

But the girl in the yellow dress is the least of my worries.

After Spanish is math, and it's the same thoughts cycling through, though by the end of the period I at least have a plan.

Mr. McClain asks if I would like to share what I'm thinking about with the rest of the class.

I tell him that that is not a good idea.

Getting in isn't a problem. All it takes is an empty teachers' lounge, sixty-five cents, and a willingness to waste a bag of pork rinds. Lucky for me, the teachers' lounge is deserted during last period. Any teachers who don't have a class to bore are gathering their papers, on the phone with parents, or driving away at breakneck speed. I pay the price, press the button, and hold my breath, listening intently for the sound of footsteps, papers shuffling, his voice, anything.

As far as I can tell, there's nobody down there. I take the steps slowly. The hall is empty. The practice rooms are empty. The screen is dark. The chairs are all lined up neatly. H.E.R.O. is officially closed for business.

Mr. Masters's office door is locked, of course, though I wonder why. Force of habit, I suppose. Jenna could just kick it in. Mike could melt it. Nikki could melt through it. But I have to go about it the old-fashioned way.

It's your standard pin tumbler. I rifle through my bag for my oversized pencil case, which happens to include three pens, a giant pink eraser (for really big mistakes, it says), a highlighter, and three paper clips. I could use the paper clips if I had to, but instead I depress the hidden lever, popping the bottom of the case free—the part containing my lockpick set. I take up my tension wrench and hook pick and needle them into the lock.

Turns out I'm a natural. Know how in the movies the burglar has a stethoscope pressed against the door of the safe so he can hear the tumblers in the lock drop? I've got built-in stethoscopes. I press my face flat against the door, as close to the lock as possible, and work the tumblers, listening for the click as each one drops into place and the cylinder turns.

I'm in.

The Jack of Diamonds would have just blasted his way in. The Jack of Spades would have ripped the door from its hinges. We all have our talents.

I flip on the light and look around. Unlike our training rooms, which are equipped with the latest technology, Mr. Masters's office looks like any of the ones you'd find upstairs. A desk. A phone. Some bookshelves. The shelves are mostly empty—only a few titles: *Michelson's Forensics*, 5th edition. *Riley's Catalog of Super Abilities and Their Origins*. *The Idiot's Guide to Bomb Disarmament. Teaching the Supremely Gifted Child*. That sort of thing. There is a stained coffee cup on the desk that says WORLD'S #1 TEACHER. The carpet is stained too. Nothing is spotless.

There is a clock perched on the wall behind the chair. I notice the hands aren't moving and am suddenly frozen with fear. Then I realize that I am still moving, still breathing, still beating. Time isn't frozen. The clock is just dead. And Mr. Masters's sense of time is so convoluted that he doesn't notice.

Below the clock is a bulletin board with newspaper clippings—all of them tracking the recent activities of the Suits and the Fox's attempts to capture them. I scan through the headlines, working back through the past two weeks. FOX POLISHES OFF DIAMOND, PROMISES OTHER JACKS ARE NEXT. SUPERHEROES AMBUSHED: FOX VOWS REVENGE. DEALER REVEALS HAND: JACKS ON A RAMPAGE. BACK FROM THE DEAD: DEALER RETURNS AND BREAKS OUT SUITS.

Some of them are older, though. One shows the Fox holding two burglars by the scruffs of their necks. JUSTICIA'S NEWEST SUPER SAVES DAY. Another shows her shaking hands with the mayor.

And then there's one of the Titan, looking young and fit, but lost somehow, standing in front of a microphone. The other members of the Legion of Justice stand behind him. Kid Caliber. Mantis. Corefire. Venus. The headline reads TITAN STEPS DOWN: FUTURE OF LEGION UNCERTAIN.

And one more, tacked in the bottom corner, showing the Legion of Justice standing in front of the smoking remains of the Suits' secret headquarters. I've seen this one before. I've got a commemorative copy of it stashed away at home somewhere. I know what the headline says before I even read it.

DEALER DEFEATED!

It's dated six years ago.

I touch the picture lightly, forgetting for a moment where

I'm at and that I shouldn't be touching anything. Then I turn and look at Mr. Masters's desk.

I sit down slowly, careful not to move anything. The desk is covered with file folders, all with names of superheroes on them, both old and new. Corefire. Kid Caliber. Cryos. Hotshot. Mantis. Miss Mindminer. The Rocket.

The Titan. Sitting right here at the top of the pile.

I take the folder and open it carefully, using my sleeve as a glove. The folder is stuffed. Bio sheets and copies of old mission reports. Photos of the Titan battling half a dozen different villains. Taking on a convoy of tanks. Leaping from rooftop to rooftop. Stealing away into the night. I flip through the pages, not sure what I'm looking for. Some mention of the name Red. Some clue as to what Mr. Masters is hiding from me. But I don't find anything. Only a copy of a letter stashed at the very back, dated well over a year ago. It's to Nathan Masters from Parker Kent at the Department of Homeland Security.

It's a request. For Mr. Masters to find the Titan and do whatever he needs to do to bring him back into the picture. To get him involved in the H.E.R.O. project perhaps.

To give him a sidekick.

I hear a noise, closer than the rest—the sound of someone opening the door to the teachers' lounge—and I shut the folder and hold my breath, forgetting that no one but me could possibly hear me breathing from that far away. I concentrate, listening to the sound of coffee being poured.

Someone—Mrs. Rattishburger—moans, "Is it four o'clock yet?" And then I hear the door close again.

I remember to breathe and then quickly shuffle through the remaining folders, looking for the name Red, but there's nothing, no mention of him anywhere. My eye catches the clock behind me. Time stands still still, it seems. But I know I don't have long. Once the last period is over, Mr. Masters might come back down here. I need to be gone. Then I remember the phone call.

I know you're lying to me.

I look at the phone. It's an untraceable line, I'm sure. The green display shows no record of past incoming calls.

But there *is* a redial button. It's a shot in the dark, but I've already come this far.

I scoot to the edge of Mr. Masters's chair and pull my sleeve back down around my hand before picking up the phone, then press redial using the tip of a pen from my pocket. It rings four times before voice mail picks up.

"Hey there. You've reached Jim Rediford. Unless this is an emergency, I don't want to talk to you. If it is an emergency, hang up and dial 911."

Jim Rediford.

Red.

I hang up, but I don't dial 911. This isn't that kind of emergency.

I look at the display, at the phone number that's listed there. Then quickly use my pen to write it on the back of my hand.

My palm is way too sweaty, and it smears a little.

So Mr. Masters did lie to me. But why? To protect me? Or to protect someone else? Maybe to protect himself.

I bend down to check the desk drawers when I hear a familiar voice. It's Ms. Canfield, my history teacher from last year. It's coming from right outside the teachers' lounge. "Aren't you supposed to be teaching this period?" she asks. I hear the door open. Then I hear another voice.

I freeze.

"Eighth grade has that convocation, remember?" Mr. Masters says. "Thought I'd hit the coffeepot early."

You've *got* to be kidding me.

I hear Mr. Masters's feet shuffle across the floor above me. I don't know his step as well as Jenna's, but I can still pick it out of a crowd. I think about the vending machine and my blood runs cold. It's short one bag of pork rinds. And if anyone would notice that, it's Mr. Masters.

I've got to get out of here, or at least hide. Maybe I can somehow sneak past him once he gets downstairs. If he finds me, he'll think I'm spying on him, which is technically true, I guess—but he'll also think that I'm up to something no good, which is only partly technically true.

As I'm backing up, I bump something from the corner of the desk. Another folder, one I somehow missed before. It spills out all over the floor, and I hiss something my mother begged me not to and bend down to gather the contents.

Something catches my eye. A blueprint for a hideout of some

kind, several rooms, including a garage, a hanger, a boat dock. There are symbols scrawled in the margins indicating entryways and secret passages. Arrows mark the presence of video cameras and infrared beams. There are notes scribbled at the top about possible ways to bypass security. For a moment I think I must be looking at the Dealer's secret lair. It's the only thing that makes sense.

I turn over the folder and look at the label.

THE FOX.

"What the heck?"

My mind races. Why would Mr. Masters have a layout of the Fox's den? Was this some other trap that the Fox was setting, and she needed Mr. Masters's help? Or was there something else going on? And why are all the security measures circled?

A half hour ago I was sitting in math class, thinking that I was in it up to my neck. Now I realize I'm in way over my head.

There is another sound. Mr. Masters taking a few more steps. I imagine him up there. Staring at the vending machine. Staring at the floor. Fingering the watch in his pocket. Wondering if he should take a minute. If he used the watch, I wouldn't know it until he was already down here, staring into my face. I'd be caught, crouching on the floor of his office with the Fox's folder in my lap.

I try to calm down. I'm overreacting. This is Mr. Masters. He might be hiding things from us, but that's the nature of the job. It doesn't mean he isn't on our side.

Does it?

I hear a coin drop, clink-clanking through the inner maze of the vending machine. Then another. And another. I have to move, to get out of here, but I can't seem to make my legs work.

Then I hear the springs working, and something heavy falls to the bottom of the machine. The rusted hinge of the door swinging open.

The vending machine door. Not the secret entrance to the basement.

The footsteps come again, moving away. Another door opens and then clicks closed.

He's gone.

I close my eyes and concentrate. Sifting through the noise, filtering through the voices in the hall, everything, trying to make sure the lounge is really empty. I think about all those hours Mr. Masters made me sit in my room and listen through the ceiling, up through the floors, targeting people and rooms and conversations, weeding through one after another. "What's Mrs. Cavendish saying?" "Who's in the boys' bathroom?" "What are the lunch ladies talking about today?" I always thought it was kind of a waste of time. Who knew I would one day use it to hide from him? After another minute, I decide it's safe. Now's my chance.

I put the folder back together, then make sure everything is still just the same as when I found it before slipping back through the office door and up the stairs. The room is empty. So is the coffeepot.

There are still two bags of pork rinds left.

I look at the clock in the hall. This one, at least, is working. The last period is almost over. I head down the hall to the boys' bathroom, staring at the phone number written on my hand, committing it to memory. I scrub it off in the sink, then I check all the stalls to make sure they are empty.

Most Supers have top-secret lairs that they operate out of, complete with forensics labs and sophisticated computer systems and weapons testing facilities.

I've got the second stall from the right. I'm sitting on the john with my cell phone in my hand, trying to figure out what to say. This Jim Rediford, whoever he is, was clearly not interested in talking to anyone, not even Mr. Masters. Why would he possibly want to talk to me? Even if he knows where the Titan is, what can I say that will possibly convince him to tell me?

Then again, what do I have to lose?

It rings four times again. "Hey there. You've reached Jim Rediford. Unless this is an emergency, I don't want to talk to you. If it is an emergency, hang up and dial 911."

I clear my throat. "Hi, hey, there . . . Mr. Rediford. This is . . . um . . . Drew, I mean Andrew . . . um . . . Bean. You probably don't know me, and I really don't know you, but we both know somebody . . . at least I think you know him, and, see, I was wondering . . . "

There is another long beep, and the line cuts off.

I curse under my breath and dial again.

"Hey there. You've reached Jim Rediford. Unless this is an emergency, I don't want to talk to you. If it is an emergency, hang up and dial 911."

"Right. Drew . . . Andrew, again. Bean. Sorry, the last message got cut off. What I wanted to say was that I think maybe you and I know someone who might be in trouble, and even though you're probably not supposed to know this, I feel like I should tell you that this guy—"

I'm cut off again.

"Hey there. You've reached Jim Rediford. Unless this is an emergency, I don't want to talk to you. If it is an emergency, hang up and dial 911."

"Right. So, here goes. This is Drew. I need to talk to George. That's the guy. It's really important. If he's there, call me back. If you have no idea who I am or what I'm talking about, then just ignore this message. Um. . . Thanks. I really . . . " Beep.

I sit there on the toilet, elbows on my knees, staring at the phone. This is stupid. This bathroom stinks. There's no way this phone is going to ring. Then I realize I didn't even bother to leave my number. Jim Redford doesn't even know how to contact me. I go to press redial.

And then my finger lights up like E.T.'s.

RED

By the time the bell rings I'm already standing by Jenna's locker. I smell her before I see her, the purple passion still a dead giveaway. When she sees me, her face darkens for a moment, almost as if she can sense what I've been up to.

"I think I know where the Titan is," I whisper as she jerks her locker open. She has a mirror magnetized to the inside, and I look to see I've grown a brand-new zit nestled right above my eyebrow. Marvelous.

Jenna bites her lip and studies me. "The Titan? How? You told me he disappeared. That you didn't know where to find him."

I point to my fingernail. Then I tell her about the message I got while sitting in the boys' bathroom, projected in green light against the back of the stall door, underneath MICHELLE

M. SUCKS and PRINCIPAL BUCHANAN SUCKS MORE. Jenna knows what it means. Communications go both ways. A click of my fingernail activates the Titan's ring, but he can use that same ring to send messages to me.

This was the first one I'd ever gotten.

It gave me an address and simple directions.

Have something for you, it said. Come alone.

"That's what it said? 'Come alone'?"

I nod.

"And now you're asking me to join you?"

"I'm not very good at following directions," I tell her.

"Yeah, I guess not," she says. She grabs her jacket and slams the door shut.

"So does that mean you're not coming?" I ask her.

"I'm not good at following them either," she says, then grabs me by the elbow and pulls me down the hall and out the door.

It's a five-minute walk to the nearest city bus stop, and then another five minutes for us to plan the route. The address that I copied onto a slip of paper is about thirty blocks away, right in the middle of one of the oldest parts of town, full of abandoned apartment buildings and boarded-up restaurants that have been out of business for years. It's just the kind of place a criminal might go to lay low.

Or anyone, for that matter.

On the bus ride over, I tell Jenna everything. Or almost

everything, at least. About sneaking into Mr. Masters's office. About the news clippings and the letter in the Titan's folder. And the files of all the other Supers. Then I tell her about the plans for the Fox's lair. She frowns and turns to look out the window.

"You don't know of anything going on between Mr. Masters and the Fox, do you?" I whisper. The bus is mostly empty, but it doesn't hurt to be cautious.

Jenna shakes her head. "She doesn't tell me everything, Drew."

"Did she tell you about last Saturday? Did she tell you it was a trap? Did she know the Jacks were coming?"

"She told me to keep an eye out. Just in case."

"And she told you to invite us?"

"She told me to bring a guest," Jenna says. "I brought two, just in case."

I know she's still holding something back. But the bus stops before I can press her on it.

"But if you could only bring one," I say, but she's already in the aisle, leaving me behind.

I follow her down the aisle and off the bus and we study the street signs together, walking two blocks to the address in my hand.

"This place is a dump," she says.

I can't disagree. Thirty-seven fifty-six East Fifty-fourth is an ancient apartment building. Its red brick is cracked, and a third of its black shingles are ripped or missing. The grass is cut short, and the paint on the trim is peeling through all three layers, exposing the wood at its core. One block down is what appears to be a rundown park with rusted swings. Still, this is the address. *I have something for you.* The row of mailboxes in the hall shows five vacancies and only one occupant.

J. Rediford.

I head for the stairs when Jenna's hand stops me.

"It could be a trap, you know," she says.

"Why do you think I brought you?" I tell her.

The door to the second-story apartment only tells us it is apartment 2–B. No gold R or "Lord Bless Our Home." No doormat that says SUPERHEROES WELCOME. No fancy fingertip-scanning entry device. Just a brass knocker, which I hit three times. Through the door I can hear the shuffle of feet. Then an old man's voice that tells us to go the hell away.

I look at Jenna. She shrugs.

"My name is Andrew Bean," I say. "I called earlier and left a message."

There is a pause. "You said you had something for me," I add, then wait again, listening close. I can hear breathing on the other side of the door. Jenna points to her foot as if offering to kick it, but then it opens a crack and a man with more hair in his ears than on his head peers through.

He is wearing thick glasses that make his eyes look luminous and large, and his shaggy eyebrows are pressed close together, almost connected. He is dressed in an old gray turtlenecck sweater and baggy brown pants that barely reach his argyle socks. His feet are tucked into slippers made to look like frogs. One of the frogs' eyes is missing. The guy's face looks familiar to me, but I can't place it.

He looks at me, then at Jenna, then back at me.

"Andrew Bean?"

I nod twice. His eyes narrow, and he presses his face farther through the crack in the door. He looks down the hall, down the stairs, then back at me. "Prove it," he says.

I guess I should have expected this. I reach for my back pocket, for my wallet that has my school ID in it.

"I don't need to see a picture of you. I can see you standin' right there. I said, 'prove it.'"

Then I realize what he's asking.

I close my eyes and take a whiff. My heart skips.

He's here. The Titan is here. In the back room. I can smell him. Which means this crotchety old man, whoever he is, is an ally or at least someone the Titan trusts.

"Come on, son, show me what you've got," the old man says.

I take another whiff. "All right. You had a bagel with cream cheese for breakfast, followed by a glass of iced tea. You use lemon-scented soap when you wash your dishes and you've got a fondness for pickles. Also you have an irregular heartbeat and a little indigestion this afternoon."

The old man looks down at his stomach, then grunts.

"That's all you've got?" he says.

I smile. "And one more thing. There's a man sleeping in your back bedroom. His name is George Weiss, though you and I know him better as somebody else."

Jim Rediford shakes his head. Then he nods at Jenna. "And who's she?"

"She's with me," I say. "She's . . . another friend."

Jenna and the old man contemplate each other. If he's the least bit intimidated by her, he doesn't show it.

"You were told to come alone," he says at last. "You don't listen very well."

"Yeah, I get that a lot," I say. For a moment I think he's not going to let us in and I'll have to let Jenna have her way with the door. Then Jim Rediford says, "Hrumph," and steps aside.

"Welcome," he says, "to my secret lair."

It isn't much to look at. A two-bedroom apartment, neat but sparsely decorated. An old, boxy television sits silent in one corner of a living room. A bookshelf holds several torn mystery novels and a couple of bent-boxed board games: battleship and backgammon—the kind only playable by two. The sink is full of coffee mugs. A small circular table sits in the corner. There are no posters of superheroes on the wall.

As Jenna and I enter, Red closes and locks the door behind us. Force of habit.

"You're a little taller than I thought you'd be," he says.

"From how George described you, I thought maybe you were a midget."

I'm not sure what to say to that, so instead I turn and look down the hall to the last door on the right. I can hear the Titan breathing, slowly and steadily. "He sent me a message," I say. "Said he had something for me."

Out of the corner of my eye, I see Jim Rediford shake his head. "He didn't send you that message," he says. "I did."

I turn back around to get a good look at the old man, trying to gauge just how much he knows. About the Titan, about me, about what's going on.

Jim Rediford points to the empty chairs at the table. I sit, but Jenna starts pacing, moving through the living room as if making a mental picture of the place. Finally she stops and hovers over a glass case with an antique-looking pistol inside. The old man watches her through his thick glasses.

"It was my granddaddy's," Red says, taking a seat across from me. "Smith and Wesson, 1902, one of the first hand ejector models they ever produced, before John Browning came along and put revolvers outa style. Never fired it myself. Darned thing blew up in Granddaddy's face and took two of his fingers with it. It's just for lookin' at now."

"You know a lot about guns too," Jenna says, and the old man gets a funny look on his face.

And then it hits me: where I've seen him before. How Mr. Masters knew him. How he knew how to send me a message.

Why he called this ramshackle hole in the wall his secret headquarters.

And why, of all the people in the world, it was him the Titan trusted.

I saw his face just this afternoon, in fact, on the front page of a six-year-old newspaper.

"Kid Caliber," I whisper. Behind me, I hear Jenna's heart race for a moment, then calm again.

The old man rubs the stubble of his chin. "Maybe once," he says. "I'm just Red now. Kid Caliber's been gone awhile, and he ain't comin' back." The man sitting across from me, with his wisps of hair and his sagging cheeks, looks twenty years older than the picture in the paper, not six.

"But you *are* him," I say. "I mean, you were."

Red points to the glasses on his face. "Son, Kid Caliber was the sharpest shot with any firearm this side of the Milky Way. He could hit the backside of a bumblebee from forty yards out in the middle of a hailstorm. He was a tried-and-true member of the Legion of Justice and a menace to villains everywhere. That ain't me." He points to the thick Coke-bottle bottoms pinching his nose. "I'm 'fraid I couldn't hit the broad side of a barn with a bazooka if I was sittin' right beside it."

Jenna comes and takes the chair opposite me, both of us flanking the former Super, whose right hand shakes as he lifts his cup of coffee.

"How have you managed to stay hidden all this time?

Everyone thought you had vanished," she says.

"Or died," I add.

Red laughs. "Not dead. Not yet, anyway. And it's easy to stay hidden when nobody's looking for ya."

"We found you," Jenna says.

"Only because I wanted you to," the former Super and member of the Legion of Justice says. "Or wanted him to, at least," he says, pointing a crooked thumb at me. "Just because the TV's broke don't mean I don't know what's going on. I know why you called. And what you're hopin' to do by showin' up here. But I also know it's not gonna work. Which is what I wanted to tell you."

"Tell me?"

"Tell you why. Why you won't convince him to join you. Why he ain't there when you need him. Why you're better off just lettin' him go."

Red takes off his glasses and sets them on the table, and I can see him for who he was. He still looks nothing like his collector's card, but I can at least picture him in the pose, guns drawn, one eyebrow cocked, daring crooks to make a move. "Back when they could still find me, people'd ask me why he did it. Why the most powerful Super and leader of the Legion hung up his tights after takin' down one of the most notorious criminals around. And I'd always tell 'em it was complicated, but that was a lie. Nothin' in the Code about lying, you know, and it wasn't my secret to spill. But you got a right to know, if only so that you'll finally give up and leave him be. The reason he quit's simple enough. He quit 'cause he killed her."

I look over at Jenna, but she's actually staring out the window, as if waiting for something. Or someone . . .

"Killed her? Killed who?"

"Who do you think?" Jim Rediford, aka Kid Caliber, says with a snort. "The Jack of Hearts herself. The Dealer's very own daughter."

THE BROKEN HEART

"She wasn't much older than you, two, I guess. Taller, maybe, a little skinnier. Blond hair cut short. Like her father, she always wore a mask that covered everything but her eyes. None of us knew, not till the end. Even the other Jacks didn't know. It was the Dealer's best-kept secret—the card he never played. We didn't even know the Jack of Hearts was a she till the mask came off, and only a handful of people know that. All the papers, the books, the stories, they all got it wrong, assumed she was just another one of the Dealer's hired goons. Never guessed it was his own flesh and blood.

"You're about to call me a liar, of course. Surely we woulda noticed somethin'. But when you're dodgin' a sword deter-mined to separate your noodle from your neck, you don't worry so much about who's swingin' it. We only knew that she was powerful. Probably more powerful than the three other Jacks combined. When it was all over, when they were all captured, then we'd be able to take off the masks and get her whole life story.

"But we never got the chance. We tracked the Suits all the way back to their hideout, a little compound on some god-forsaken island in the middle of nowhere. No caverns or craters or volcanoes or anything, just a couple of square steel buildings tucked away in the middle of some mosquito-infested jungle. It was an even fight, five on five, but somewhere along the line we got split up. Corefire, Venus, and Mantis took on three of the Jacks, while the Titan and I chased the Jack of Hearts and the Dealer into a laboratory of some kind. He had been hard at work on somethin', you could tell. Rows of computers and two or three huge tubes, like glass coffins sittin' upright, all connected with cables like a scene straight outa Frankenstein.

"So we barge in blazin', the Titan crushin' everything in his path and me blastin' away with both barrels. The Suits had slipped through our fingers on a half dozen occasions before, the Dealer always one step ahead. But not this time. This time we knew we had him cornered. We get inside and see him workin' the controls of some machine. Lights are blinkin' red, there's a hum of electricity, there's smoke comin' out of pipes. I'm thinkin' maybe I shot somethin' I wasn't s'pposed to and figure the whole place is about to come apart. The Titan sees the Dealer and goes to grab him when the Jack of Hearts jumps us from behind.

"I didn't even see her comin'. That's how good she was. She sneaks in behind me, and next thing I know I'm on the ground, both my legs crushed, my guns out of reach. I tried to crawl after 'em, but it was everything I could do just to keep from blackin' out. Then it's just her and the Titan, head-to-head, smashin' everything around them, calling down the thunder and lightning. Fists flying, glass shattering, the whole room electrified. The Titan's in his prime, mind, yet the Jack of Hearts keeps step with him, blow for blow, almost like they're dancin'. And for a moment, I think maybe he's met his match.

"Then it happens. I didn't see it, only caught the look on the Dealer's face when she hit the ground. Just dropped like a sack of flour, falling outa the Titan's hands.

"When the Dealer saw her fall, he let out the kinda cry that squeezes your gut so hard you can't breathe, and he crawls over to her on hands and knees and rips her mask off, and we both see what she is at last, just a girl. A teenage girl. And the Titan's lookin' at her and at his own giant hands and he don't even care that the Dealer himself—the man he's been chasin' for years—is kneelin' right there in front of him. We've won. But the Dealer looks up, his eyes burning through that gray mask of his, and tells the Titan he killed her, killed his only daughter.

"And then the alarms start blaring and some voice from the computer says something about a power overload. The room

288

shakes, and fires pop up all around us. And the Titan finally snaps outa it and says it's time to go. But the Dealer just drags his daughter by the shoulders to one of them giant glass tubes and places her inside, like Snow White. And I'm yellin' that we probably got less than a minute left to get out, but the Titan's just standing there watchin' his nemesis laying this dead girl in that glass coffin, kissin' her once before sealin' it tight.

"The next thing I know, the whole room is full of smoke and the Titan's liftin' me up and throwin' me over his shoulder and we're runnin' through that place as it's comin' down on top of us. And I look back to see the Dealer standing in front of his daughter as the ceiling collapses around him. That was the last I ever seen of him. Of either of them."

Red finishes the last of his coffee and puts his glasses back on. "We barely make it out to find the rest of the Legion waiting for us, the other three Jacks captured. One of 'em, Mantis, I think, he looks at the Titan and asks him what happened, where the Dealer is and the Jack of Hearts, but all he says is 'I did it' over and over again. 'I did it.'"

The old gunslinger holds his empty mug out in front of him, as if he's waiting on it to fill itself. "Code says that all life is precious. That everyone deserves a chance at redemption. The Titan believed it, as much as any of us. But it ain't always that easy. You can't always pull your punches, especially when you punch like him. I tried to tell him it wasn't his fault. That there is good and there is bad and there's no in-between, and that as soon as you start thinkin' there is, that's when you need to hang up the cape. But I guess that was the wrong thing to say.

"Two or three weeks later, he stepped down as head of the Legion. Within the year he was pretty much done. I tried to take him out on patrol, easy stuff. Armed robbery. Kidnapping. Couple of car thieves. But I could see his heart just wasn't in it. Somethin' snapped that day, though maybe it was splintered already."

Red leans back in his chair, staring into his cup as if wishing it full again.

"It's funny," he says. "You look at the Dealer, and all you see is a villain in a mask. But the Titan saw something else. Something worth saving. He tried. Tried to hold on. But he ended up squeezin' too tight.

"And he ain't never been the same since."

WITH THIS RING

When Red finishes, I stand up from the table, pushing my chair back.

"I need to talk to him."

"I don't think that's a good idea," Red says. "Weren't you listening? Six years and he hasn't gotten over it. Six years, and he hasn't saved a single soul, yours included."

"Mine especially," I say. "Which is exactly why I need to talk to him."

Red—Kid Caliber—looks like he's going to protest further, then gives up with a shake of his head. "He hasn't had a drink in three days . . . just so you know," he warns.

I look over at Jenna. "Do you want me to come?" she asks. I can see in her eyes she thinks maybe he's dangerous still. She hasn't seen him. She doesn't know.

No, I tell her, giving her hand a squeeze. "Remember, I'm

always only in danger whenever the Titan's *not* around."

I leave her standing by the window and Red sitting at the table and walk down the hall. I stand at the back bedroom door and listen. His breathing is regular. So is his heartbeat. I figure he's still asleep and decide just to peek in, but when I open the door, I see him sitting on the edge of the bed, arms on his knees, staring at a mirror on the dresser in front of him. He doesn't bother to turn and look at me, but from where I am, I can see most of his face in the mirror anyway.

He looks better than the last time. He's wearing a new shirt and new pants, at least. He must have showered since I saw him last. He's not wearing his sunglasses, and I realize it's the first time I've ever seen the man's eyes. They are light gray, a kind of milky hue, and they make him look inhuman, almost. They don't look my way, just keep staring blankly into the mirror.

I clear my throat. The Titan still doesn't move. I take a few steps so that I'm standing near the corner of the bed, only three feet away. I can count the scars on his face. I forgot there were so many.

"I know what happened," I say.

He still doesn't budge. Not even the slightest twitch. As if he's frozen in place. Like in a Mr. Masters minute. I move closer and take a seat on the corner of the bed, careful not to touch him.

"It's the same with me sometimes," I say. "I see things. And hear things. From miles away. I know they're coming, and it pisses me off because I know I can't do anything about them."

292

The Titan's hands are folded in his lap. So large. I think about every thug, minion, and villain he's captured with those hands. Think about them wrapped around the Jack of Hearts, crushing the life out of her. Think about his hand holding my own outside the bowling alley, squeezing just tight enough. He tried to warn me, even then. But I wouldn't listen.

"You can't save everybody," I continue. "As much as you'd like to. It's just not possible. I know that. But that doesn't mean you stop trying. The city is in danger. You're in danger. The Code says I'm supposed to stand beside you. To follow you. But I can't stand by you if you won't get up."

I stand back up and look at him. Not at the reflection, but at the man himself.

"You told me to go save myself for a change. Now I'm asking you to do the same."

That's it. That's the big speech.

I stand there. Five seconds. Ten. Twenty. Waiting. Breathless. This is the moment in the movies where the music swells. The camera pans to the feet, starting to twitch. Maybe the hero clenches those giant fingers of his into a fist. The camera zooms in on a narrowing of the eyes, the look of determination surfacing as he rises up at last to the crescendo of trumpets blaring.

But there's nothing.

The Titan doesn't move.

And all of a sudden I want to scream at him. To get behind him and kick him off the bed. To grab his face and force him to look at me, to apologize, to admit that anything he might have done in the past doesn't compare to what he's doing now by abandoning his friends, his city, his sidekick, his Code. But I don't.

Because I just can't make myelf believe anymore.

"Drew?"

I turn and see Jenna standing in the doorway. I don't know how long she's been watching.

"Let's go," I say.

Jenna puts an arm around my shoulders and leads me out, but I can sense her own muscles tense as she looks back into the room at George Raymond Washington Weiss.

"Hardly worth it," she says, then turns and follows me through the hall.

Red is waiting for us with the front door open, eager, it seems, to usher us out.

"Hate to say I told you so," he says. "I mean, really. I would have liked it to have gone the other way."

"You could leave, you know," I say. "Get away. Take him with you. It's too dangerous here. The Dealer is still out there, and he's taking revenge on anyone who has ever worn a cape. He won't have forgotten. He will find you eventually."

"Son," Red says, "I once stared down a mechanical bull that had fifty-caliber machine guns for horns and hand grenades for poop. I ain't afraid of the Dealer or his Jacks. Besides, I've managed to say hidden this long, so unless one of you decides to break the Code and start spilling secrets, I'm guessin' I can hold out here a little while longer."

Red holds out his hand, and I take it. It's a lot smaller than the Titan's, but the grip is still firm. His other hand holds an envelope. "This is what I wanted to give you," he says, holding it out to me.

I already know what it is. I can trace the shape through the paper. It's the Titan's ring. The one he's supposed to use to track me down. The one he's supposed to use to save me. The one Red used to contact me, to bring me here, only so that he could push me away.

"He says to give it to someone who deserves it."

I steal a look at Jenna. I can't help it. It's an unconscious move. But she doesn't notice. She's not looking at me. She's looking over her shoulder and down the hall.

"You were never here," Red says, eyeing us both." Either of you."

"I understand," I say, taking Jenna's hand and pulling her after me.

Red stands in the doorway, watching us go down the stairs. Then I hear him lock the door.

The bus ride back is quiet. I sit on the inside, staring out the window. Jenna sits noticeably apart from me, studying the back of the seat in front of us. Neither of us knows what to say, I guess. I keep one hand in my pocket, playing with the Titan's ring, turning it over and over in my hand. It has our names engraved on the inside, Titan and Sensationalist, one beside the other.

"You don't need him," Jenna tells me again, though this time I really can't argue with her. "Nobody does." I drop the ring into my pocket.

When the bus drops Jenna off at her house, she puts her arms around me and tells me not to worry. "It will all be over soon," she says. "Then everything will be better, I promise."

I ask her how she can be so sure, given everything that's happened. "He was the best of them," I tell her.

"Not anymore," she says.

Then she squeezes me again, and I can smell the lilac from her shampoo underneath the haze of the body spray, and trace the lightning-bolt part of her hair, and feel the heave of her chest against mine, and I squeeze back as hard as I can, afraid she might let go.

JUST YOU AND ME

She's right, of course.

That night, the Fox strikes a major blow to the Dealer, emptying his hand in one fell swoop.

I find out about it the same way everyone else does—well after the fact. Mike calls me at midnight and asks if I'm watching the news, that he can't believe what he's seeing. I sneak downstairs and turn the TV on, turning it down so low that only I can hear. I find a place on the couch, and Mike and I watch together. At first all I can see is fire. Then from the smoke and ash, I see her emerge, like the phoenix. The reporter is practically shouting to be heard above the sounds of sirens and the helicopters.

"We're coming at you live from this abandoned boathouse on the lake, and you can see it's absolute chaos. Some fishermen who had been on the water after dark said they heard several explosions and called 911. We arrived just in time to see the whole place go up in flames and our city's savior emerge," the reporter says.

The Fox stands before the camera: flaming red hair, tight white bodysuit, samurai sword slung across her back. She has dragged two bodies out of the burning building, both limp, unconscious, dressed in black suits ripped to shreds. One of the bodies is average size, but the other is enormous, probably the biggest catch anyone at the pier has ever seen. She pulls the two Jacks out of the smoke and drops them at the feet of the authorities, who take several steps back instinctively.

The camera zooms in on the Fox, the Jacks of Spades and Clubs crumpled at her feet. She is alone.

Mike gushes. "Just look at her, man. She is so hot. I wish I could have been there—you know, not to do anything, of course, just to watch. Do you think she did that thing where she claps her hands together and creates a sonic boom? They must not have even seen her coming. I mean, did you see them? Those guys were out cold. And she took 'em down solo. There's no way the Rocket could have done that."

"I wonder how she even knew where to find them," I say. It wasn't like the night of the party. There was no mayor to dangle as bait. Was it just an old-fashioned throwdown? Did the Fox leave them a note somewhere—Meet me behind playground after school? Did she somehow set them up?

"Who cares?" Mike says. "Don't you get it? That's all three Jacks. It's just the Dealer and the Fox now, mano a foxo."

I tell him "fox" in Spanish is *zorro*. Which is pretty cool, given the sword and all.

"Seriously? That is so awesome. I can't even imagine what Jenna must be thinking right now. To have H.E.R.O. shut down the very same day that her Super beats the bad guys. That really sucks."

Jenna.

"Right. Listen, I'll call you back," I whisper.

"What?"

"You just keep drooling. I'll call you later."

I somehow manage to get off the phone with Mike and immediately call Jenna, but she doesn't pick up, so I text her instead. On the news, the Fox stares into the camera. "I'm coming for you, Dealer," she purrs, which from anyone else would have been cheesy, but coming from the Fox it gives me chills. She leaps over the reporters who are desperately trying to interview her and the cops who are trying to question her and the groupies who are trying to fawn over her and disappears into the shadow of night.

"There you have it," the reporter says, visibly shivering despite the fire raging behind her. "The city's true champion. Triumphant once again. And a firm message to the Dealer—that wherever you are, whatever you're up to . . . the Fox is on the prowl."

My phone rings and I answer it instantly, but it's just Mike again.

"She did it. That thing with her eyes? Did you see it? Just

299

then? I swear they change colors. It's wicked. God, what I wouldn't give to be her sidekick. Do you think she'd let me hold her sword?"

"You'd probably just cut your other arm off," I say. The camera zooms in on the bodies of the two Jacks. The same guys who took out Cryos and Hotshot. And yet she somehow managed to take them both on at once.

"She makes it look so easy," Mike marvels.

I can't argue with him. It's almost as if she was waiting until this very moment to make her move, waiting until she was practically the only one left who could stop them, to stop them.

"Don't you think—" I start to say, but before I can finish the thought, my phone buzzes. "Mike, I gotta go. See you tomorrow, 'kay?" I hang up before he can protest.

"Hey," Jenna says. "You called?" She sounds distracted.

"Hey," I say. "I didn't know if you'd be home. I thought maybe you'd be, you know . . ."

"Out?" she says.

"Busy," I say.

On the television, the fire trucks have arrived and have unleashed three hoses on the hollowed-out remains of the building. The unconscious villains have been strapped down and loaded into bulletproof vans, surrounded by a dozen armed officers.

"I just thought, when you didn't answer—"

"H.E.R.O.'s suspended," she says curtly. "We aren't side-kicks anymore. You were there. Remember?"

"I know, but I thought . . ."

"That the Fox would make an exception? That things were different between us? I'm not a Super, Drew, any more than you are."

I'm not sure how I'm supposed to take this. "What's that supposed to mean?"

"It just means that you and I aren't that different."

"Hardly. Your Super just collared the last two Suits single-handedly," I say. "Mine is a lump on the edge of the bed in a rundown apartment in the middle of nowhere. You were there. Remember?"

"And here we are, both sitting at home, watching it on tele-vision," she says, her voice sharp.

And I get it. Why she's miffed.

I stare at the television screen, picturing the Silver Lynx in place of the Fox. Seeing Jenna up there instead. It's what she's always wanted.

"One day you're going to be the one everybody's talking about," I tell her.

"Really?"

"Are you kidding? Kids around the world will worship you. You'll have trading cards and posters and action figures and documentaries and your face on the cover of every magazine. And I'll be able to say that I knew you back when you were just a sidekick, waiting for your shot."

When she speaks again her voice is softer. Guarded.

"Drew. I have something to tell you."

I switch the phone to my other ear and sit up. Anytime somebody says they have something to tell you, it's either really good or really bad. It's never "I have something to tell you . . . we are having burritos for dinner."

"Don't be mad," she says.

Then they say that, and you know it's the bad thing.

"I told the Fox what you told me . . . about Mr. Masters. About breaking into his office."

I swallow hard. She's right. This isn't good. Somehow this is going to get back to me, I know it. I shouldn't have said anything.

"And what did she say?"

"She said that she'd look into it, but in the meantime I should maybe keep my distance. And maybe you should too."

"Keep our distance?" From Mr. Masters? "She doesn't think he's dangerous or anything, does she?"

Jenna doesn't even have to think about it.

"We're all dangerous," she says.

Then she says it's getting late and she will see me sometime tomorrow. "Everything will be better," she says, though she doesn't say when, or why, or how. And I don't question it. It's Jenna. I just say, "Okay."

Then she hangs up.

I sit there for a few minutes, watching the flames turn to ash. Then I sneak up to my room and close the door as far as it will go—it's still not fixed—and pull out my backpack. I take out *Julius Caesar* and toss it in the pile. We are done with it, finally. Cassius is dead, Brutus has kabobed himself, and Caesar is avenged. The forces of goodness and light prevail. As I reach into the bottom of the bag, my hand closes around something soft.

I pull out my mask and just stare at it, thinking about the last time I wore it. Back when this whole mess started. Hanging there next to Jenna, wanting things to be different.

I just hold it, crumpled up in a ball. H.E.R.O.'s suspended. My Super is beyond help. The Jacks are beaten, and the Fox has the Dealer on his heels. Pretty soon it will all be over.

No need for the Sensationalist.

But I can't help myself.

I put it on anyway.

PART FOUR

IN WHICH
SOMEBODY
FINALLY DIES

HOT-WIRED

t's Tuesday.

Exactly two weeks since I found myself hanging above the Justicia community pool, waiting to be dissolved.

Nearly one week since I found myself huddled in my bedroom, waiting to be bludgeoned.

About six months since I first met my Super outside of Bob's Bowlarama and was told I should find somebody else.

About a year since my best friend bloodied my nose.

I'm beginning to hate Tuesdays.

It's Tuesday. Salad day, because after numerous letters to the school board, Highview is implementing a new dietary policy, which basically involves picking two days a week to feed us like guinea pigs. What they don't anticipate is that most of the kids will just dip their croutons in the ranch dressing and toss anything remotely green in the trash. I have a granola bar and an apple in my backpack, right above my Taser and my sleeping gas grenades. I know I don't need my utility belt anymore, but the Dealer is still out there somewhere, and having a customized X26 electroshock personal defense weapon snuggled underneath my Darth Vader lunch box makes me feel better about myself. The Dealer apparently knows who I am and doesn't care that H.E.R.O. has been canceled or that I'm supposedly "being normal," whatever that means.

It's Tuesday, and everyone is wired. The whole school is talking about last night. I count at least sixteen Fox T-shirts, white with two burning sapphire eyes. Some of the blondes have dyed their hair orange to match hers. One of the cheer-leaders has even come to school dressed in a white bodysuit with a plastic sword strapped to her back. The principal takes the sword away—even plastic, it could still be considered a weapon. I just hope he never looks in my bag.

It's Tuesday, and I haven't seen Jenna yet this morning. She didn't wait for me outside the music room like she usually does after first period, and she wasn't in English class. When Ms. Malloy asked me if I knew where she was, I actually stopped and listened for her—*really* listened, hoping I could catch the sound of her voice anywhere in the school, but there was way too much to sift through, and Ms. M was looking at me strangely, so I just shook my head.

Still, I'm a little worried.

Because it's a Tuesday. And the Dealer *is* still out there. He still has most of Justicia's Supers locked away somewhere and only has one more standing in his way.

After English, I run into Gavin. "Have you seen Jenna?"

"Yeah, saw her this morning before school," he says. "She was talking to Mr. Masters out in the parking lot."

Mr. Masters.

Now I'm more than a little worried.

"What do you mean, she was talking to Mr. Masters? What were they talking about?"

"Gosh, Bean, let's see, their favorite episode of *iCarly*—I don't know. Do I look like I have super hearing?"

"Well, did they look upset or anything? Did they go some-where together?"

Gavin shakes his head at me and starts talking to me slowly, as if I were a toddler. "I . . . don't . . . know. They spoke for a little bit, then they started walking toward the parking lot. I didn't think anything of it. Then a bus passed between us, and next thing I knew, they were gone."

I've heard too many people use the phrase "next thing I knew" right after the phrase "I was talking with Mr. Masters."

"Did you notice anything strange? Did you feel funny at all, like maybe you missed something, or that time had passed you by somehow?"

"No. I don't think so. Why? What's going on, Drew? Is Jenna okay? Is there something I should know about?"

I look at Gavin, who's staring at me like I'm insane, but like "you're insane and I'm a little worried about you," which is better than the "you're insane *and* a total dweeb" look he used to give me.

"No. Nothing," I lie. "I'll see you at lunch, all right?"

I take off, heading for the office, leaving Gavin with his hands in the air.

On the way to the office I run into Mike and pull him by the cast, jumping at the shock I get.

"What the heck? Dude, that arm is broken, in case you haven't noticed. And how come you never called me back last night?"

"Have you seen Jenna?"

"No, why?"

"Have you seen Mr. Masters?"

"No. Was there some kind of meeting? Is H.E.R.O. back on already?"

"No. I don't know. Something's weird. Come on," I say, pulling him along with me to the front desk, ignoring all his protests. I catch my breath and very calmly ask the front secretary if she knows where Mr. Masters is this period.

"I'm sorry," Mrs. Beal tells me. "Mr. Masters is out for the day. He called in this morning. Is there something I can help you with?"

"Did he say he was sick or something?"

"He said he had an urgent appointment, not that it's any of your business. Are you even a student of his? What class are you in?"

"Sorry. Forget about it. Thanks," I say.

When we are out of the office, I grab Mike somewhat forcefully by the shoulders. The look in his eyes says he is actually a little scared of me. It's the first time I've had that effect on someone.

"Can you hot-wire a car?"

"What?"

"You know." I bring my fingers together. "Bzzt, bzzt, zappity, zap." I can practically smell the voltage crackling inside him. The hair on my own neck is standing on end.

Mike shrugs my hands off. "Yeah, I guess so. I once jump-started a lawn mower. Why? What are you thinking?"

I don't answer. Instead I drag him to the end of the hall, to the exit leading out to the staff parking lot. I shush him with one finger and look around. The bell for next period rings, and we are out the door.

"Dude, where are we going?"

"Out," I say.

I pull Mike along, thinking we'll just take the first car we see, but that turns out to be an Escort that rolled off the factory floor back when Henry Ford himself was still managing it. In fact, the next four cars in the line are all beaters or hatchbacks, most of them rusted and dented. I was hoping for something a little sturdier. After all, I'm only thirteen. I have no idea what I'm about to do.

This school needs to pay its teachers more, I think to myself, passing by two more compact cars before we get to a Suburban.

"Finally." I try the door, but of course it's locked.

"Hand me that rock over there."

"Are you nuts? What are you doing? Are we going to steal that thing?"

I hope my grabbing the rock myself and smashing in the driver's side window is enough of an answer. The Suburban smells like cappuccino and cigarettes. I'm guessing it's the French teacher's.

"You could have picked that, you know."

I hadn't thought about that. Too late now. I brush the glass off the seat with the sleeve of my coat and slide in behind the wheel, then motion for Mike to get in on the other side. He obeys, but not without protest.

"You're crazy. You are totally flippin' crazy. All those little voices you hear all the time have finally gotten to you. What the heck is going on?"

"I think Jenna's in danger," I say. "And I think Mr. Masters is involved."

Mike gives me the raised eyebrow. "What?"

"I don't know. But when I broke into his office and saw the plans for the Fox's lair, and then yesterday I took Jenna to see the Titan and Kid Caliber—"

"Kid Caliber? Wait a minute—I thought he was dead or something, and what do you mean you broke into Mr. Masters's office? Are you insane?"

I ignore his questions. "And last night, she said to stay away from him, and just this morning the two of them were seen

312

together, and I'm not sure, but I think maybe Mr. Masters kidnapped her."

Mike shakes his head. "Kidnapped her? What? Why?"

"To get to the last two superheroes who have a snowball's chance in hell of stopping the Dealer. . . . Or something."

I admit. It sounds even more nutzoid when I say it. I look at Mike. Every hair is raised. Even his eyelashes are rigid.

"Yeah, forget this," he says, reaching for the door.

I reach out and grab his arm. The broken one.

"All right. Maybe not kidnapped. But I think Jenna needs us. You just have to trust me. Please, just get this thing started and I'll tell you everything on the way."

Mike shakes his head and mutters, "I can't believe I'm doing this," but he leans over me, placing his fingers around the ignition anyways.

"I'm not sure this is going to work."

"Just do it."

"I haven't tried anything like this since the accident," he says.

"I believe in you," I say. I mostly do.

"I'm just saying there is a very small but not statistically insignificant chance that this car could explode."

"Mike!"

"Fine!"

There is a jolt of electricity that encircles the ignition and then dances its way across the console. Suddenly the overhead light explodes, shattering the plastic covering, and the radio comes on really, really loud. We both shield our heads with our hands, then look at each other to make sure we are intact.

> *"I need a hero.*
> *I'm holding out for a hero till the end of the night."*

I reach over and start mashing buttons on the stereo. The windshield wipers suddenly kick on at hyper speed. Mike is trying to cover his ears with his hands, but one hand just won't reach because of the cast.

Finally I find the off button.

"God, I hate that song," I say, buckling myself in and trying to get my bearings.

"This is insane," Mike says. "The last time we rode *bikes* together you nearly ran over a dog."

"He was chasing me. Besides, even high school dropouts can drive a car. How difficult can it be?"

I step on the gas and the Suburban jumps forward over the sidewalk onto the grass, nearly knocking over a sculpture of a bronze eagle—the Highview mascot.

"Reverse," Mike spits out.

"Right. Reverse."

I throw it into reverse and nearly crunch the car behind us. I notice that Mike has his eyes shut. "I'm going to pee myself, just so you know," he says.

"Just hang on. I know what I'm doing."

"And what is that, exactly?"

"Saving the day . . . I think."

I gun the engine and we shoot out of the parking lot at something that feels pretty close to light speed.

"I just hope we aren't too late."

WE ARE TOO LATE

Driving is easy.

Not hitting stuff proves to be the difficult part.

I do pretty well, actually, seeing as how it is my first time, I am going way too fast, I'm having a little bit of difficulty seeing over the wheel because I didn't bother to adjust the seat, and I have to stretch some to reach the pedals. We rub against a few cars parked along the side of the road, not hitting them so much as flirting with them, though we do lose the passenger-side mirror to a light post when I almost miss my turn, nearly giving Mike a heart attack. I can tell he's nervous because every time we hit something—a little bump or the median or a mailbox—the radio shoots back on and the dashboard blinks on and off. The check engine light is glaring at me, but I don't know if that's something I've done or Mike's nervous discharge. I don't care. All I care about is getting to that apartment.

"Wait a minute," Mike says. "You're telling me that Mr. Masters is working for the *Dealer*?"

I shake my head. Then nod. Then bump another parked car. Then shake my head again.

"I don't know. All I know is that someone with ties to H.E.R.O. has been helping the Dealer. It's the only possible explanation for everything that has happened—leaking our identities, our connection to our Supers, everything. And Mr. Masters has been trying to locate the Titan. And because of me, Jenna knows where he is. And now she has disappeared with him. Besides, haven't you noticed anything strange about Mr. Masters lately?"

"I've noticed several things strange about you in the last ten minutes," Mike says.

I can't argue with him. He doesn't believe me, and I don't blame him. It's pretty far-fetched. But then I tell him about Red, and Mr. Masters lying to me, and the plans for the Fox's secret headquarters with all the security devices and entrances marked out. I remind him that Mr. Masters has access to secret information. Information the Dealer could use to, say, take Supers down one by one.

"And maybe, I don't know, maybe we were getting too close. Maybe he was afraid we would find out and that's why he shut H.E.R.O. down. To get the rest of us out of the way."

Beside me, Mike throws his hands in the air and stares at me with bug eyes.

"Drew . . . this is Mr. Masters you're talking about. He's like our ugly-sweater-vest-wearing second dad. There's no way he's working the other side," he says. "Probably he and Jenna went to get doughnuts or something, if they went anywhere at all. Or maybe you're just pissed off because your Super is a loser so you've concocted some harebrained, cockamamie scheme to give you an excuse to steal a freakin' car and pretend to play hero when there's absolutely no one out there who needs saving, except for your incredibly freaked out friend who you dragged into this mess who is now going to be arrested for grand theft auto!"

Mike pounds on the dashboard, and both headlights explode.

"Sorry," he says. "I'm under a lot of stress right now."

Maybe he's right. Maybe I am just being paranoid. Maybe we will pull up to the apartment and everything will be fine. Kid Caliber and the Titan will still be tucked away, and we will drive back to school in our stolen car to find Jenna waiting for us outside with news that the Fox has finally captured the Dealer and the whole thing is over.

Suddenly I slam to a stop, and Mike nearly breaks his other arm trying to keep himself from chewing on the dashboard.

"Then again," Mike says.

There, ahead of us, is Kid Caliber's apartment complex. Or what's left of it. There is a hole in the second-floor wall, and I can smell smoke.

"Do you hear that?" I ask.

"Hear what?"

Mike doesn't hear the sirens. Only I can hear them. They're still far away.

"Hand me my bag."

Mike reaches behind him and grabs my backpack. I dig through it and pull out my costume, slipping the mask over my face, clicking the belt into place. I look at the Sensational-ist in the rearview mirror.

Mike shakes his head. "What are you going to do? You're not going *in* there, are you?"

"Not me," I say. "Us."

It is way too quiet, and that means a lot coming from me. The door to Red's apartment has been blasted off its hinges and lies, a smoldering slab, on the carpet inside.

"Come on," I say, "the coast is clear."

The Sensationalist says things like that, I've decided.

"I shouldn't go in there." Mike points to the shaggy carpet stretching out from the door. His house is all hardwood floors.

"I think a little static electricity is the least of our worries," I tell him.

One look inside, and I know we've missed something big. There is a confusion of smells—hard to pinpoint through the smoke. The acrid tang of gunpowder is overwhelming, though. "There was a shootout," I say, sniffing.

Mike points to the holes riddling the walls. "What gave it away, Sherlock?"

By the kitchen lie a couple of spent machine guns, their

muzzles black. I have a good guess who they belong to. The television is shot out, twice broken now. There are scorch marks along the walls. The recliner looks like maybe it was split in half by a chain saw. There's glass everywhere, but no bodies. I look down the hall to the room at the end.

Outside, the sirens are getting louder. We don't have a lot of time. I reach down to my belt and pull out my stun gun, holding it out in front of me as we pass by the bathroom to the end of the hall. I realize the little bit of voltage I'm carrying is nothing compared to the human Taser walking beside me, but it helps to have something in my hand.

"Drew," Mike says. The hair on his head is standing at attention.

"Quiet."

Nothing. No sound. No movement coming from inside.

The Sensationalist stands at the door—I stand at the door. The same one I stood at yesterday. I give it a push.

This room looks normal, untouched. The bed's even made. I can still smell him, though. "They got him," I say. And then I catch another scent, lighter than the first but distinct. I close my eyes, zeroing in on it, dissecting through the layers to concentrate on the few molecules of it still lingering in the air. My feet suddenly grow numb. There is no mistaking that smell.

"Purple Passion," I whisper.

"What?"

"It's Jenna."

He took her too. The Dealer scooped up the two has-been

Supers and kidnapped Jenna on the side. And Mr. Masters helped. He must have. There's no other explanation. I can still catch a trace of his VapoRub as well. They were all here.

"Drew."

Mr. Masters must have somehow contacted the Dealer and then led Jenna into a trap. She probably knew too much. Maybe she had already confronted him. Maybe that's why she told me not to trust him, to stay away. To protect me.

"Drew."

And now the Dealer had her. His ticket to the last Super who still posed a threat to him. Somewhere Jenna was probably dangling from a hook or staring down a death ray with the Dealer at the trigger, waiting for the Fox to arrive. Capture her, and there would be no Supers left. He would have his revenge, and Justicia would be his for the taking.

"Drew, I think you should take a look at this."

I shake my head to clear it and then step back into the hall. The sirens are only blocks away; I'm sure even Mike can hear them. I grab Mike to push him out the door when I see what he has in his hand. Actually, had I been concentrating on sounds instead of smells, I would have heard it.

An old rail conductor's watch, gold plated but tarnished with age. A crack runs down its face.

"I don't think Mr. Masters would have just left this behind," Mike says.

I take the watch in my hand, trace the jagged lightning bolt along the glass.

"No. I guess not," I say. The wind sneaks through the hole in the wall of the apartment.

In that wind I can still smell her.

Then we both hear the voices coming from outside.

"This is the Justicia police. We know there is someone in there. Come out with your hands on your head."

Mike looks at the cast on his arm.

"I don't think I even *can*," he moans.

I look at Mr. Masters's watch. This is getting worse by the minute.

HELP IS ON THE WAY

Mike is having a panic attack. Little jolts of electricity are literally weaving their way in and out of his hair; he looks like one of those trolls people used to stick on top of their pencils.

"Oh. Fantastic! Because stealing a car wasn't enough, now we can add breaking and entering!"

"Just entering," I say, peering through the window. "The door was busted down when we got here."

"You're hilarious."

That's what the Sensationalist does, I decide. He makes jokes to help defuse the tension of the dangerous circumstances he always seems to find himself in. I take a peek outside.

There are only two squad cars, though I can hear other sirens in the distance. Fire. Ambulance. Who knows, maybe the National Guard. Justicia's already on high alert, and I'm sure the guys in costume outside the apartment are just as antsy as we are. The cops don't have their guns drawn yet, though their hands are ready at their sides. Behind me Mike is spinning around in circles, looking for some kind of secret escape route—a slide or a pole that leads to an underground passage, perhaps. I look at the watch again. The crack runs straight down the middle, but the hands are moving. I wonder if it still works.

I concentrate on the Purple Passion again, focusing in on it the way Mr. Masters taught me. It's just strong enough to pin down. I think this will work. I hope it will.

"We are only going to have one minute," I tell Mike as I adjust my mask and belt and stand by the doorway.

"What?"

"You take the SUV."

"*What?*"

"I'll take one of the cop cars."

"*WHAT*? You're stealing a cop car? Don't you know they can hang you for that?"

"Go get help. I don't care who. Find someone."

"I don't need to go get help. Help is outside, about ready to blast my head off."

"Yeah—I think we're going to need bigger help than that. Besides," I say, pointing to my mask, then gesturing toward the trashed living room with the bullet holes and smashed furniture, "this would take more explaining than we have time for."

"How am I supposed to drive with only one arm?"

"You'll figure it out. I'm going to find Jenna," I say. "Take this."

I dig in my pocket and pull out my ring. The Titan's ring, the one that led me here the first time around.

"What is this? Are you proposing?"

"It's my SLD. You can use it to find me."

"Find you? Find you where?"

I give an exaggerated sniff. "I don't know, wherever Jenna leads me. If I had to guess, I'd say the Dealer's secret hideout." Mike just shakes his head.

"This is the Justicia police," repeats the voice outside. "Come out with your hands on your head. You have thirty seconds to comply."

Mike takes my ring and slips it into his pocket. It wasn't designed for his skinny fingers and would just fall off—besides, we'd both feel a little weird if he actually wore it. "My mother is going to kill me if I get arrested," he says.

"She might not get the chance," I say.

I grab Mike's hand and then press the button on Mr. Masters's watch. The world is instantly silent. It still works.

Sixty seconds.

We careen down the stairs and throw our backs against either side of the hallway door leading outside. I take just one second to listen, just to be sure, then throw it open.

Outside the apartment, three cops are lined up, pistols at their sides, ready to storm the building. A fourth is sitting on the driver's side of one of the squad cars. Just down the street, an ambulance is turning a corner. Above us, three birds have just launched from an electrical wire. They are all frozen. Everything is. I hand Mike the watch. "Take it," I say.

"No, you take it," he says, pushing it back.

We have forty seconds left. This is no time to argue.

"You're going in alone. You're going to need it," he insists.

"Yeah, but it's me, remember? I can sense danger coming from a mile away."

Probably to end the argument before the cops come unstuck, Mike takes the watch, then heads to the Suburban. I run over to the nearest squad car, which is, unfortunately, the one with the cop sitting in it. Thankfully the keys are in the ignition. I have about twenty seconds left.

I pull the cop free, with some effort, and then take an extra five seconds to unholster his gun and throw it in the bushes by the apartment. Cop cars are significantly different from Suburbans. There are a lot more distractions. Still, the basic mechanics are the same. With two seconds left, I throw the car into gear.

Time thaws instantly, and I turn to stare at the face of a police officer who just a second ago was sitting where I am now. He looks completely bewildered as I throw the car into gear. As I screech away, I see him reach to his side for the gun that isn't there.

Up ahead I see Mike tearing down the street in the bor-rowed Chevy, making trophies of other cars' taillights as he careens back and forth, trying to drive for the first time in his life and with only one good hand. On the police radio, someone is asking me to report in. I figure that's a bad idea. After all, this is the second car I've stolen in less than an hour. Mike is right. I'm probably going to hang for this.

Provided I don't die first.

THE JACK OF HEARTS

It is said that a bloodhound's sense of smell is fifty million times better than a human's. Bloodhounds can track a scent several days old. They can pick up a whiff of a lost girl from one of her mittens and track her through miles and miles of forest, using their big floppy ears as shields to block out other smells.

But can a bloodhound steal a patrol car and drive with its head hanging out the window, following a faint trail of Purple Passion body spray through the streets of town at sixty miles an hour?

I've been training for this moment.

I can still hear sirens, and I'm guessing several of them are probably headed my direction. I've turned off the constant chatter of the police radio so I can concentrate on Jenna. I don't care about anything else right now. How goofy I look with my mask on and my head sticking out of the car, how much trouble I'll be in from the cops, how much trouble I'll be in from my parents. How there's no way I'll be able to keep my secret any longer. How I'm not even sure that I want to. As long as I find her. As long as she's okay.

I follow Jenna's scent for several miles, to the outskirts of town, past a series of warehouses to an old abandoned factory situated next to a lumberyard. It smells like rotten wood and rusted iron. The factory looks like it hasn't been used for decades. It's the kind of place you see in gangster movies when they tell the snitch who ratted them out that he is "going for a ride." Even if I couldn't still sense her, I'd know I was in the right place.

I can't hear any sirens anymore, which actually makes me nervous. Surely there is some GPS locator or something that will allow them to track this car down. The cavalry will arrive. And Mike should have gotten help as well by now. Maybe he's even using Mr. Masters's watch to buy us all some extra time without me even knowing it.

Mr. Masters.

Maybe I was wrong about him. Or maybe the Dealer betrayed him, just as he betrayed us. Hopefully I will find him here too.

The huge sliding doors to the factory are all sealed tight, leaving just one entrance on the side, protected by a complicated-looking electronic lock—not something I can pick easily. I reach down to my belt and pull out a canister of concentrated liquid nitrogen—the advantages of a strong background in chemistry. In a matter of moments, the lock is just a block of solid ice. A nearby rock serves as a decent hammer, and the lock shatters in three blows. The door swings open.

Now *this* is breaking and entering.

The air is thick with dust, but Jenna's trail comes back to me. It is stronger than it was outside, and I catch it without even trying. I'll find her first, then together we will find the Titan and the others. I listen for voices, but the place is massive and the walls thick cement. I catch a sound other than the buzzing of the fluorescent lights above me and follow it, taking shallow breaths and keeping my feet from shuffling on the cold cement floor. Every beat of my own heart sounds like a gunshot, giving me away.

The sound I'm following gets clearer, and I press my ear up against the wall. They are voices, muffled through the thick stone that separates us, but I recognize one of them immediately.

"You won't get away with this," it says.

They are the first words I've heard him say since that day at the bar.

And if he's saying that, it means things are really bad. Supers only say somebody won't get away with something when that somebody is right on the cusp of getting away with everything.

I keep my right ear against the wall as I walk, turning a

corner, looking for an entry, but this place is a labyrinth, and the voices are like echoes. As I get closer, I can start to make out the other voice more clearly, and though I've never met the Dealer, never even heard him speak, his voice seems strangely familiar.

"You say that, but all the Supers who had even a chance of stopping me are already my prisoners," the voice says. "There's no one left to save you."

I see a door up ahead and crouch down. From inside I hear the Titan coughing, his voice hoarse, barely a whisper. The other's voice is cool and confident, much younger than I would have expected for someone who's been dead for the last six years. It's a soft growl. Almost sultry. "You were the last piece of the puzzle," it says. "The last on either side, in fact. The Suits are back in prison. All the other Supers are out of the picture. Even that meddlesome watchman is taken care of. The Fox is the only one who can save the day, though I'm afraid she won't arrive in time to save you. You will sink into oblivion as the whole place goes up in flames. When the smoke clears, I will emerge victorious, and you will be forgotten."

"Then I guess you've thought of everything," the Titan says.

I stand at the door, trying to understand what I'm hearing, but none of it makes any sense. I'm not even sure who all is in there. I hear the Titan mumble something, and even I have to strain to make it out.

"Killing me won't bring you justice."

The other voice laughs. "Justice? I'll worry about justice later, when I'm the only hero left who's worth a damn. I'll give new meaning to the word and mete it out, wherever and whenever I see fit. But that's after you pay for what you've done."

That's it. I've heard enough. I reach for the door with one hand, dropping the other to my belt and grabbing a smoke grenade, hoping that it might buy me enough time to sneak in, maybe even get the Titan free before the Dealer—or whoever it is—even knows what's happened.

Then I catch the scent that brought me here, suddenly intense, and turn to see just the girl I'd been hoping to run into again.

"Thank god it's you," I whisper. "Where have you been?"

She is in costume. Her hair falls down around her shoulders. Her green eyes glow. The silver shimmer of her outfit reflects the glare from the overhead lights. I expect her to be surprised to see me. Or relieved. She looks neither. She looks irritated.

"What are you doing here?" she hisses, taking two steps closer to me so that we are within arm's reach.

"I came to rescue you," I say, then realize how ridiculous that must sound coming from me. "I thought Mr. Masters kidnapped you. I tracked you from the apartment."

If any of this comes as a shock, she doesn't show it.

"The Titan," I say, pointing to the door. "The Dealer's going to kill him. At least I think it's the Dealer, but it sounds an awful lot like . . ."

I don't finish the thought because something suddenly occurs to me. Jenna is here. The Silver Lynx is here. But she is alone; her Super isn't by her side. And the voice on the other side of the door sounds just like . . . I try to clear my head. It's impossible. There's no way the Dealer and the Fox could be working together. Could they? Surely somebody would have known. Mr. Masters. Or one of the other Supers. Or . . .

"Jenna?"

Something's wrong. Something in the cold, calculating tone of her voice. It makes me shudder as she takes another step closer.

"I'm sorry, Drew," she says. "This wasn't how it was supposed to go."

"Jenna, what are you even talking about?" I want to reach out for her, but I don't. I'm afraid. She is so close I can feel her breath.

"It's messed up. I know," she says. "But I'm going to fix it. Everything will be all right. It's all part of the plan." Instead she's the one reaching out for me. "I just want you to know that I never meant to hurt you," she says.

And then I hear a click and look down to see one of my own sleep grenades in her hand.

"I'm so sorry," she says again.

Then she hits me.

Jenna Jaden. The Silver Lynx. The girl who bloodied my nose and promised to always be friends. Who taught me how to do yoga and introduced me to banana milk shakes, who sat next to me in H.E.R.O. three days a week and recited the Code that we both swore to live by. The girl who leaned in close on the bleachers of the baseball diamond and in only a few seconds, screwed up my life forever. That girl chops me hard across the base of my neck, hitting a nerve that I didn't even know existed, sending me to the ground, right next to the sleep canister that she activates and drops down beside me. The ether seeps into my lungs, instantly making me dizzy. I try to push it away, but whatever she did paralyzed me and I can't move.

I see three Jennas hovering over me, and suddenly I realize what I didn't before: that she's needed me to save her for a while now. Ever since that day at the bleachers. Probably even before that. I want to tell her to stop. That whatever she's done, we can fix it, together. But I can't—in part because I can't even feel my lips anymore—but also because she's not Jenna. She's not even the Silver Lynx.

She's the new Jack of Hearts.

And I'm a fool.

JUST HANGING WITH
MY SUPER

So it's Tuesday.

Salad day, as I think I might have mentioned, though you can get the salad with a vacuum-sealed Baggie of ham cubes that look as if they might be made out of used pencil erasers. I have an apple and a granola bar in my bag, which is probably still in a Chevy Suburban somewhere, hopefully being sat on by a group of vigilante ninjas or a team of Navy SEALS, or whoever Mike could scrounge up to come rescue me. It's Tuesday and I'm in costume, for what it's worth, though my gadget belt is stashed away in a corner of this great big hall that I find myself in, thrown there, no doubt, while I was unconscious. Not that I would do much with it anyway. The last thing taken from that belt was used by my very best friend to knock me unconscious. I should never have shown her how to use those things.

It's Tuesday—first week of October—and I'm dangling (again) over a giant pit in the floor of some evil mastermind's secret lair, hidden in an abandoned factory on the outskirts of town. Unlike the other rooms in the factory, which are all dust and rust, this room sparkles with tech, the far wall bulging with computer monitors, sensors, and gadgets. It reminds me a lot of our school basement. How long this place has been here I don't know, but I have a good guess where the money came from to furnish it—a generous donation from Kaden Enterprises, those costs easily recouped by a few knocked-over banks. After all, being a Super is expensive. I can only assume that being a villain is too.

Now imagine being both.

Because that's what I finally realize. It's not that the Fox and the Dealer are working *together*. *That* would be bad enough. But this is even worse. I think I realized it the moment I heard her voice, but I simply couldn't bring myself to believe it. I had to see it with my own eyes. That they are actually one and the same.

It's Tuesday and I'm dangling above a pit, my hands in cuffs, suspended here by a supervillain known as the Dealer, who also happens to be a superhero known as the Fox, who also happens to be the former Jack of Hearts who my Super supposedly killed so many years ago. The Fox—so good at hiding behind the mask.

And though I'm not one hundred percent positive, I'm pretty certain the pit is steadily filling with wet cement.

Seriously. Wet cement, which is actually very practical, all things considered. Much easier to get ahold of five hundred gallons of wet cement than seven hundred electric eels or two hundred poisonous snakes, and I take a miniscule measure of consolation in the fact that drowning in cement is marginally preferable to being dissolved by acid. Something at the bottom of the pit is slowly churning the bubbling gray mixture, making sure it doesn't set yet, though I have a feeling it won't be long. The fumes are dizzying and burn my lungs. Or maybe I'm just having a heart attack.

After all, it's Tuesday and I'm suspended by my wrists above this pool of cement, feet dangling below me in my cracked, weather-worn Pumas, and all I can think about is how stupid I was not to see this coming. Not the whole "the Dealer is really the Fox who was once the Jack of Hearts who was really the real Dealer's supposedly dead daughter" thing. That's still too much to wrap my head around. I mean, really. How was I supposed to get that?

No, I mean the girl in the silver outfit with her emerald eyes and her wavy blond hair, huddled over there in the corner, looking back and forth from me to her own Super, wiping the blood from her nose on her sleeve.

I should have known because the truth is, guys like me never get the girl. Other guys get the girl. Or maybe she goes off to boarding school. Or maybe she throws in her lot with a notorious villain bent on revenge and is forced to turn on her friends and see them swallowed up in a pit of quick-drying cement. Pick your ending, they're pretty much the same.

And that's why I'm hanging here. Because of her.

I *should* have seen it coming. But I didn't. Probably because I love her. Or love some version of her. Or *loved* some version of her. I'm not really sure anymore. I should hate her, of course, but I can't. Because I know that somewhere there might be that version of her that maybe feels the same way about me.

I know because I heard her begging for my life only moments ago. When I started coming out of my ether-induced stupor and found myself chained to the ceiling, looking through blurry eyes at a Super and her sidekick arguing. The Fox was dressed in her customary attire, the white suit, sword included, though she was no longer wearing her mask, and I could see the face of Kyla Kaden clearly in the harsh fluorescent light. Jenna was waving her hands, talking quickly, breathlessly. She does that. I could tell by the motions that she was thoroughly ticked off, more angry than I've ever seen her before. They were speaking in whispers, easy enough for me to hear.

"You said he'd be safe."

"That's before you led him here. We only needed him to draw out the Titan. Now he knows too much."

That's when I figured out they were talking about me. I wanted to say that I actually knew a whole lot less than I thought I did yesterday or even an hour ago, but my voice hadn't come back to me yet.

"But you told me no one else would get hurt. This wasn't part of the plan."

"Everything has a cost," the Fox snarled. "Power requires sacrifice. And look at it this way—he will die a hero. You can make up whatever story about him you want. Say that he went down fighting. If you'd like, you can even say he was instrumental in the Dealer's demise."

I saw Jenna, or the Silver Lynx, or the Jack of Hearts, or whoever she is, shake her head. "But he hasn't done anything," she pleaded, which was kind of true, when you think about it.

And then the Fox hit her, not as hard as she could, but hard enough to end the discussion. Jenna brought her hand to her face and stared at her own red, wet fingers. The Fox just glared at her.

"You made your choice," she said. "These are the consequences. Turn on me now, and it will be the *last* thing you do."

Jenna wiped the blood on her sleeve and turned to look at me, and I wanted to say something, but there was no way to keep the Fox from hearing as well. Then Jenna looked beside me.

And that's when I noticed the man hanging next to me. In a T-shirt and blue jeans. His feet bare. His massive frame just hanging there like a huge slab of beef.

The Titan and the Sensationalist. Together at last.

Which brings me to this moment. Hanging with my Super. Though he isn't saying or doing anything, doesn't acknowledge me in any way, just dangles there with that look of stupid resignation on his face, as if this was all to be expected. Almost as if he deserved it. And I can't help but feel that his dead weight is going to make me sink even faster. Jenna and the Fox are no longer speaking to each other. Jenna has retreated into the corner. The Fox stands at the computer terminals, punching buttons. I turn to the Titan, twisting around in my cuffs as much as I'm able.

"Okay. See?" I whisper. "This is exactly what I'm talking about. If you and I had spent even a little time together, we might have some really great plan for getting out of here."

But the Titan ignores me. I look at the bank of video monitors showing the grounds outside the factory. No doubt the Fox saw me coming. I didn't even think to look for cameras. Mr. Masters would be disappointed—though I'm guessing he's got bigger problems as well, wherever he is. The monitors reveal nothing. There's no one else out there. Reinforcements have yet to arrive. I try to wiggle around, see if there is any way I can free my wrists, but I'm cuffed too tight.

The woman at the console, I don't know what to call her anymore, speaks to us without even turning around.

"Don't bother struggling," she says over her shoulder. "Those bindings are made from an experimental alloy that my father created with you in mind. They're nearly unbreakable. Maybe in your prime you might have stood a chance."

She's obviously talking to the Titan. At the rate I'm going, I'm not sure I'll even have a prime. The warning is unnecessary, though. The Titan doesn't struggle. He barely keeps his head up.

"He thought of everything, my father," the Fox-Dealer-Kyla-former Jack of Hearts says. I look over at Jenna, but she just stares at her Super, still on her knees, blood caked on her lip. "Even the day you killed him. He knew he couldn't defeat you, so he played to your weakness. Your big, soft heart." Kyla turns around and stares at us. The Titan doesn't say a word. It's as if he can't even hear her. "It's in the Code, isn't it—the sanctity of life, the idea that everyone is worth saving? He knew exactly how you'd react.

"So I played dead, you took the bait, and he saved me. Those glass tubes led to tunnels that traveled to the other side of the island. Unfortunately, only I managed to get out in time. My father wasn't so fortunate. But you knew that—you watched as the whole place came down around him." Beside me, the Titan takes a long, deep breath, though he still makes no move to free himself. Kyla draws her sword and runs her finger along the blade. Even from here I can see how sharp it is.

"I wanted to kill you immediately, of course, but I knew I needed to be stronger. So I trained, spent some time on both sides, working for whoever would pay me, making the most of my father's gifts, waiting for this moment. But by the time I got here, you had all but disappeared. The Titan—leader of the Legion of Justice. Gone. That's when I realized the best way to find you was to become you."

"Your father would be proud," the Titan grunts, the first words he's spoken since I found him dangling beside me.

The Fox glares at him. "He actually admired you, you know. Not for your heroics, all those lies about truth and justice and peace on earth. No. It was your tenacity. Your determination. You would have hunted him to the ends of the earth."

"I never meant to kill him," the Titan says.

"Don't be so certain." The Fox turns and looks at Jenna, who quickly looks away. "We are all capable of more than we think. I became a Super so that I could more easily hunt you down and destroy you. But then, somewhere along the line I developed a taste for it. The adoration. The fawning, gape-mouthed bystanders. My statue in the courthouse. A villain is only ever feared. But a Super is feared and loved. And that's when I realized what I wanted most of all. Not just to be the one who defeated the Titan. But to be the only one who mattered. To be the last one standing."

"Pretty ambitious," the Titan says.

"I needed help, of course," Kyla continues. "A villain to frighten the masses. Some henchmen to sweep away the opposition. And someone who could help me put all the pieces in place. Someone I could teach the way my father taught me."

I look over at Jenna again, hoping to get her attention, but she still refuses to look up.

"When all is said and done, they will be chanting my name in the streets."

"You'll be a real hero," the Titan spits.

The Fox turns her back on us again.

"Both of us know there's no such thing," she says. "There's no good or evil. There are just those with power and those without. You and your Legion never understood this. My father didn't even understand this. Your Codes and your rules and your tiresome, outdated beliefs. Your epic battles for one truth or another. Such a waste. And I'm about to put an end to it all."

Suddenly one of the screens in the bank of monitors jumps to life, and I watch a Chevy Suburban gallop over three parking barriers and then skid to a halt just outside the factory's front gates. The doors open, and the reinforcements pile out. Mike, Nikki, Eric. Gavin emerges from the driver's side. H.E.R.O. has arrived. I told Mike to go get help. I should have been more specific. Still, the sight of my friends piling out of the car, all in costume, offers a sprinkling of hope on top of the big cement cake of doom I'm facing.

The Fox watches the monitor for a moment, then spins on Jenna.

"Are there any of your friends you didn't invite?"

Jenna finally glances up at the screen with a look of concern. Her arms are wrapped around her knees. The Fox turns back to the controls and presses a few buttons. Onscreen I see a couple of metal spheres hurtling toward the other members of H.E.R.O. Attack robots. I've seen them before, in the training simulations back at school, though those were only for practice, their weapons systems offline. This doesn't look like practice.

"You'd better hope that keeps them busy," the Fox snaps at Jenna. "I think one dead sidekick on your conscience is enough, don't you?"

"Actually I think one is overdoing it," I mutter, but nobody pays any attention. Kyla brushes the red hair from her face and takes a deep breath, regaining her composure. She walks to the edge of the pit and looks up at us, looks up at him. "We now have exactly fifteen minutes before this whole place explodes. Of course, you won't feel a thing," she adds, nodding toward the cement still pumping away beneath us. "To be honest, I really thought you'd put up more of a fight."

"That makes two of us," I say.

"Sorry to disappoint you," the Titan says—to her or me, I'm not sure. Still, I look at him and I can start to see something in his eyes. He isn't looking at me or the cement already starting to thicken beneath us. He is looking at her, at the woman who spent the last several years planning her revenge, preparing for this very moment. And then I see his muscles tense, as if testing, for the first time, just how strong the cuffs really are.

And then I hear something. A whisper.

But it's not him.

It's Jenna.

"Listen," she says under her breath.

I look over at her, and she catches my eye. When she speaks her lips barely move.

"The control panel is down and on your right."

344

I twist a little. There it is. Five buttons. OPEN. CLOSE. RAISE. LOWER. RELEASE. I nod.

"If his hands were free, do you think he could catch you?"

I take another look at the Titan. He is still staring at Kyla, who is busy putting on her mask, getting back into character, ready to save the world. She probably has some grand story for how she and the Dealer battled to the death, how she almost saved the Titan and his helpless, unknown sidekick and Cryos and Hotshot and all the rest of Justicia's Supers but was just too late. She will be the only one left, and she will be unstoppable.

I study the man hanging next to me. *Could* he catch me? Probably. *Will* he is the question.

"I'm going to count from five," Jenna hisses through gritted teeth.

I lean in as close as I can to the Titan and whisper, "In a moment your hands will be free."

He doesn't respond. His eyes are bloodshot, unblinking, staring at the Fox.

"We *will* fall," I add, though I'm not sure this bears stating.

He still doesn't say anything.

"I . . . don't . . . want . . . to . . . die," I say, very slowly, so that he can fully appreciate the sentiment.

Finally, at last, he turns to me. The first time he's ever looked me in the eyes.

"You won't," he says.

The Fox finishes adjusting her mask and turns back to the

bank of monitors. I watch as Silent Death leaps up and kicks one of those little metal spheres out of the sky and Stonewall crushes one beneath his fist. Keeping the trash off the streets. I wish Mr. Masters were here to see this. Or at least to see them. I'm kind of glad he's not here to see me right now. A voice over the intercom casually informs us that we have ten minutes to evacuate the building.

"If there's one thing I learned from our last battle," the Fox says over her shoulder, "it's that there's nothing like a good old-fashioned explosion to cover your tracks." She turns to Jenna. "Stop sniveling and stand up. It's time to go play hero," she says with a soft smile, almost motherly. Then she adds, with more force, "Unless you'd prefer me to just leave you *all* here." Jenna nods and straightens up. She wipes her nose one last time. She looks at me and speaks through still clenched teeth.

"Five," she says.

I feel the muscles in my legs tense. The Fox scans the video monitors one last time before shutting them off. The members of H.E.R.O.—caught in a fierce battle against spinning, buzzing robots—disappear as the screen goes dark.

"Four."

Jenna walks past the controls. Beside me, the Titan's biceps bulge. Gavin has nothing on him.

"Three."

She stops and turns.

"Two."

The Fox looks over just in time to see Jenna with her hand over the button. Even with her mask on, I can see her face is creased into a frown.

"Whatever you are thinking of doing, I would consider it very carefully," Jenna's Super says coldly. "We will be the greatest heroes the world has ever known."

Jenna looks at me, looks back at the Fox.

"You said yourself, there's no such thing."

And once again I am falling to my death.

THE END JUSTIFIES
THE MEANS

The Superhero Sidekick Code of Conduct has four rules. They are designed to guide us in our battle against evil, to help us walk in the path of goodness and light, and to protect Super, sidekick, and OC alike.

There is, of course, the main rule about upholding the virtues of justice and rightness and honor and all things sweet, rainbowy, and good, which I still insist doesn't say a thing *specifically* about math tests and is somewhat open to interpretation.

There is the rule about not betraying your Super's secrets, including his whereabouts and identity, even to the girl who isn't your girlfriend but who you kind of wish *was* your girlfriend, even if she does turn out to be a traitor, which, in retrospect, I guess *I* kind of dropped the ball on.

There is a rule about never endangering lives, which maybe I broke when I was doing sixty in a forty in a stolen cop car down the streets of Justicia with my head hanging out the window, though I swear I didn't hit anything living.

Then there is that rule about trusting your Super, above all else. Following his plan to the end. Believing in him. Even when the odds are stacked against you. Even when you are falling to your death. Of all of them, I think this rule is the hardest to follow.

There is no rule about screaming like a ninny while you are falling to your death. So I'm not doing anything wrong when the bindings around my wrists suddenly come loose and I shriek like a little girl with a bee in her hair.

Then a hand catches my own and squeezes just hard enough that I get the message. I look up to see the Titan, one hand holding on to the chain above him, the other holding on to his sidekick. Finally.

"Gotcha," he says, then—with more strain than it should take a man who once threw minivans at giant rampaging mechanical scorpions—the Titan swings me out over the edge of the pit, where I land in a heap. I look up just in time to see him clear the edge himself, landing with a force that causes half the lights in the ceiling to shatter. The ground beneath me shakes, and I find myself suddenly dwarfed by the Titan's enormous shadow.

I hear another scream, not as shrill as my own, and see Jenna curled into a ball by the side of the pit. The Fox is standing over her. I don't know what's just happened, but the Fox has those blue arcs of electricity around her eyes and Jenna is in agony. Something kicks in, some instinct even more powerful than self-preservation. I stand up, fingers in fists, ready to charge, when the Titan steps back in front of me, his massive body eclipsing mine.

The nice lady over the intercom tells us we have nine minutes before we are all incinerated. The Fox turns to face us, determined to finish the job before then.

The Titan tilts his head and says to me in a low rumble that I can feel as well as hear, "Get out of here."

"I'm not leaving," I say. "I'm your sidekick."

And for once, it feels right: to be wearing this mask, to be standing here. It doesn't feel *good*—I am scared to death and my legs threaten to buckle beneath me—but it does feel *right*.

Then the Titan turns around to say something to me, or maybe to just lift me up and toss me out of the room by force, but it's a mistake. In the moment that he turns, the Fox is on him, first hitting him with a shock wave that knocks us both off balance, then driving her foot into his chest, sending him tumbling backward. He falls on top of me, all three hundred pounds, and my legs are trapped beneath his hulking frame. I try to push, but he won't budge. His heart is pounding in his chest, and he's struggling to catch a breath. He doesn't move.

And I realize he can't beat her. Not by himself. Not anymore.

The Fox draws her sword. "The cement would have been so much more poetic," she says. "Preserved for all eternity. But there is something to be said for efficiency." She steps over the Titan, straddling us both. I've seen that sword cut through steel cable. It will go through the Titan like a ripe melon. And I'm underneath him.

"I suppose it's just as easy this way," she says. "To just let you go down in the explosion together. All of you. Supers and sidekicks alike. Leaving me truly the only one. Except you, Titan. I want to finish you myself."

The Fox raises her sword.

And then I hear her, even before the Fox does, moving as fast as I've ever seen her. And I catch that gleam in her eye, her lips curled back, that look of determination engraved on her face, just like the day we met.

The Silver Lynx drives her shoulder into the Fox's back, taking her by surprise and pushing her toward the pit. The Fox twists to attack, swinging hard with her sword, but Jenna ducks just in time, the blade missing her by an inch, the swing knocking the Fox off balance, leaving her teetering on the edge of the pit.

She reaches out with one hand, her eyes wide with terror, but Jenna just stands there, motionless.

Then one foot slips, and the Fox tumbles over. I hear her splash into the wet cement as Jenna scrambles across the stone floor and grabs hold of the control panel, mashing the buttons to close the hatch. The Fox's scream echoes off the walls; lightning bolts shoot out of the pit, striking the ceiling, sending pieces of it crashing around us as the hatch slides into place. Sealing Kyla Kaden, the Fox, the Dealer—the hero and the villain—inside forever.

Jenna kneels beside the hatch, head bowed. I try to catch a breath, which is hard when you have a three-hundred-pound superhero on you.

"You have six minutes to evacuate the building," the intercom reminds us.

"Little help here?" I grunt.

Jenna crawls over to us, then helps pull the Titan up. I manage to scramble to my feet, amazed that nothing's broken. The red lights above the computer console flash the word WARN-ING in big red letters.

"Do you know how to shut that thing off?"

Jenna runs over to the computer console and starts madly pressing buttons. Finally she brings her fist down on top of it, and it shatters in a shower of sparks. Sometimes I forget how strong she is.

"We have to get out of here," I say.

"What about the other Supers?" Jenna shouts. "They're locked away deeper in the building. Some of them can barely move."

"I'll go." The Titan's voice booms from behind me. "You two get out of here."

I turn to protest, to demand that I go with him, but he is already out the door.

"Drew," Jenna starts to say, but I interrupt her.

"Later," I say. I grab Jenna's hand and we take off down the halls, turning one corner and then another, coming to a T junction. Somehow or other I've gotten turned around and can't tell which way to go.

"How the heck do you get out of here?" I scream, but Jenna's just as lost as I am, keeps looking back over her shoulder as if she expects the Fox to be behind us, dripping with wet cement, a sword in her hand and blood in her eyes, like something out of a zombie movie. I start to go right and give Jenna a tug—when suddenly a brown hand shoots out of the wall and grabs hold of my shirt, like something else out of a zombie movie.

I shriek and try to pull away, but then a face appears in the wall as well, surfacing from the stone like a bubble bursting.

The Wisp smiles and steps through the concrete, her eyes wide, pulling Kid Shock behind her. Mike looks completely freaked. His hair is still punked out and his cast is charred black. I can almost see smoke coming out of his ears.

"That was . . . wrong, on, like . . . every level," he says, looking over his body to make sure no parts were left inside the wall.

"Where are the others?" Jenna asks, and I realize Mike and Nikki have no idea what's happened. Who they are really talking to.

"Gavin and Eric are outside, fighting off the rest of those bots, and some lady on the intercom keeps saying this place is going to blow in, like, three minutes," Mike says.

Two, actually, the voice over the intercom tells us. I grab Mike by his cast and pull him along, Jenna and Nikki right behind. "I think it's that way," Jenna says.

We are never going to get out in time.

I look at Nikki. "Can't you just pull us all through?"

"Yeah—maybe—if I knew which way was out!" she says.

"I think at this point any way is out!"

We have one minute.

Then Mike reaches into his pocket with his good hand and pulls out the watch. Mr. Masters's watch. We all take each others' hands as he presses the button.

The next minute is a blur as Nikki pulls us all through one wall after another, hand in hand, headed straight until we suddenly find ourselves in the sunlight near the main entrance. Eric and Gavin are there, a dozen security drones lying in pieces at their feet, and a whole host of officers, agents, and emergency personnel fanned out behind them. From behind me comes the voice counting down from ten, and I yell for everyone to run. Jenna takes my hand and pulls me along as we dive for cover behind the first police car we see. I suddenly feel something very heavy on my shoulders and look up to see Stonewall draping himself over us again, his granite body prepared to shield us from the blast.

I smell something—sulfur, maybe—and look into Jenna's eyes. And then suddenly I am powerless.

I can't see anything but bright light.

I can't smell anything but heat.

I can't hear anything but the explosion. The sound is deafening. Jenna squeezes my hand as the sky falls.

ONE MINUTE MORE

When I can finally open my eyes again, I see the heroes through the smoke. With their badges and their hoses and their bags. Running through the fire and the debris, wearing their thick coats of armor, breathing through their masks, holding their guns down beside them, hoping not to use them. They move without thinking, trusting their instincts, trained, like all heroes, to choke down their fear. The paramedics and firefighters follow behind the police officers, till someone raises his pistol and gives the order to halt.

I'm probably the first to see them clearly and recognize them for who they are. The Titan emerging through the thick black plumes, Kid Caliber draped over his shoulder, just like before. Behind him are Hotshot and Cryos and the Rocket.

At the back of the pack stumbles a man in a blue-and-gray

sweater vest, his glasses busted, his bald head chalked black with smoke. He lets one of the paramedics pull him toward a waiting ambulance, then turns to see us all huddled together.

Mr. Masters just shakes his head, but I can see, even from here, that he's smiling.

I stand up as my own hero limps through the acrid smoke toward me. His shirt and pants are ripped. There are burns on his arms and a cut on his forehead, but he doesn't seem to even notice. Instead he asks me if I'm all right.

I look at my friends, all huddled together. Nikki and Eric and Mike and Gavin, whose skin is back to normal. I nod, then glance at Jenna, but she's not looking at me. She's looking at the Titan. The Titan extends his hand toward her, and I suddenly realize what's going on.

"You understand," he says to her. "I don't have a choice."

"I know," she answers. "Just . . . just give us a minute."

Jenna stands up, but instead of reaching out for the Titan's hand, she leans over Mike and grabs the watch, Mr. Masters's heirloom, which has barely had time to reset. And in that moment before she presses the button, I know I will never see her again. She will escape. A minute will pass, and we will all look around to find her gone. Vanished. Lost in the smoke.

Then she reaches out for me instead.

Suddenly everyone is frozen. The fires and the smoke, the ashes and soot hanging in the air like fat black snowflakes. The sirens silenced. The Titan stands like the statue he almost became, his hand still stretched out to the girl who almost let him die. The members of H.E.R.O. still huddled together. It's just Jenna and me; all the rest is painted backdrop. She lets go of my hand and bites her split bottom lip. I can still catch a faint trace of Purple Passion beneath the layers of smoke and sweat that carpet us. And I don't know what to say. Part of me wants to tell her to go, to run. Part of me wants to scream at her, to ask her what she could possibly have been thinking. Part of me wants to tell her I'm sorry, for not being there sooner. But she doesn't give me the chance.

"I was going to be a hero," she says. "At least that was the idea. But somewhere along the way, it got . . ."

"Complicated," I finish for her.

She nods.

I have so many other questions. I want to know how long she knew about the Fox. If she had helped the Dealer or the Jacks with their crimes. If she was the one who planted the playing card in my locker that day. I want to know if she would have gone through with it if I hadn't been there, if she would have just sat back and watched the Titan die. I want to know if she wanted me to find her all along. But mostly I want to know the answer to that question—the one she asked that day on the bleachers. Because, finally, I think I know what the question is.

"Jenna . . . ," I begin, but she cuts me off.

"Just shut up for a few more seconds, will you?" Jenna pauses,

357

her eyes locked onto mine, and the hand that takes mine is cold and trembling, even with the fire raging behind us.

Then, before I can even catch a breath, she leans in close and kisses me again.

And the world starts to spin.

H.E.R.O.'S RETURN

It's Tuesday, but you probably could have guessed that.

It's Tuesday, and the cafeteria's dalliance with health food is over, which means it's back to sloppy joes—though the salads with eraser ham are still available as an alternative.

It's Tuesday, exactly one week since the explosion that tragically ended the life of one of the finest Supers Justicia has ever known. One week since the rest of the city's Supers were rescued in dramatic fashion by one of their own. One week since the Dealer was at last—and for good this time—defeated.

At least, that's the story. It was the Titan who spun it, in a very rare, on-the-scene interview that was replayed at least two dozen times that night and many nights after. According to him, the Fox was the real hero, swooping in to rescue everyone at the last minute before engaging the Dealer in a fierce final battle that cost both of them their lives.

The story went down easily enough, at least for the masses, who still had something to believe in. As far as the OCs were concerned, that was exactly the way it should have ended, the way it was destined to end—in an epic showdown that claimed the lives of both hero and villain alike. It was sad, yes, but blockbuster. And it made for great TV.

There were other stories, of course, the return of the Titan foremost among them, though quite a lot was also said about the group of sidekicks determined to rescue their Supers as well. Even the Sensationalist received some attention—as much for stealing a police car as anything else. Still, it was generally agreed that the group of mysterious young vigilantes was a promising bunch, and better still, we all managed to stay in character, keeping our identities intact—something Mr. Masters was most proud of.

Mr. Masters, who I was completely wrong about. Not that I was right about a whole lot. Mr. Masters told us that in light of recent events, he saw no reason not to reinstate the H.E.R.O. program. After all, it had been the Fox's idea to shut it down, to keep us out of the way—fat lot of good that did. Besides, Mr. Masters said, we had passed our first real test together, as a team. We were ready to take it to the next level. More field-work. More after-school training sessions. More weekends spent with our mentors, "keeping the trash off the streets."

Yesterday was H.E.R.O.'s first meeting since its brief suspension, though we spent most of it eating the pizza Mr. Masters owed us while he talked on the phone, cleaning up some of the mess and confusion that the Fox left behind. More phone calls to the mayor and the commissioner, making sure everyone had their stories straight, trying to keep as much of H.E.R.O. under wraps as he could. We would have to get back to our training soon, though, he said. The Dealer wasn't Justicia's only threat, and with the Fox gone, ironically, it left a hole in the city's defenses. Until it was filled, we had to be ready to put our masks back on.

Then he told us how we reminded him of another group of Supers from not long ago. How proud he was of all of us.

Though I know he only meant most of us.

It felt strange without her. Sitting together in the circle, I could tell we all felt it, Gavin especially. He barely said a word, just chewed methodically on his crust. We tried not to talk about her, but in doing that we found ourselves not talking about anything. In the halls, the rumor was that she had simply transferred to another school. In the basement, the feeling was that she had been misled or even betrayed by her Super. Everybody believed what they wanted to, I guess.

I didn't say much to the others about what happened. I had already told Mr. Masters everything—or most everything, anyway—and he and I both agreed that it was better to stick to the Titan's version of things. There were lots of questions, of course, but whenever possible I just kept my mouth shut and nodded.

The nod is the easiest lie there is.

When the bell finally rang and everyone trudged back up the stairs to the teachers' lounge, Mr. Masters grabbed me and asked to speak with me for a moment. I still couldn't say no. I followed him back to his office, and he shut the door.

"I know you were in here," he said. I thought about feigning innocence but knew it was pointless. Mr. Masters knew things. That was his job.

He pointed to the broken clock. Turns out he broke it himself, trying to install the video camera secreted behind it. Once he pointed it out, I could see the lens peering through the center. I made a note to be a little more diligent, especially when doing something I shouldn't be.

"It's all right," he said, noticing the look on my face. "I don't blame you. I wasn't completely honest with you before," he began. "With all of you. Though I hope you can understand. I wasn't entirely sure who I could trust. I suspected the Fox had her own agenda, even before the Dealer showed up. That's what the plans were for. I hoped to find some evidence, something definitive to confirm my suspicions. But I needed help."

"The Titan," I said.

Mr. Masters nodded. "We had been working to bring him back for a while. The thought was that if he had a sidekick—especially one who believed in him . . ." I thought about the letter I found in the Titan's folder.

"It didn't work," I told him.

"Oh, I think it did," Mr. Masters replied, then laughed

362

to himself. "It *took* a few tries, but it worked. It's not as if I couldn't have found him if I'd wanted to, of course. But he wouldn't have listened to me. I was right about him, and you, *and* the Fox—it was just . . ."

"Jenna."

Mr. Masters shook his head. "The bond between a Super and a sidekick can be very strong."

"I'll have to take your word for it," I said, forcing a smile.

"Somewhere along the line the Fox convinced her that a world without the Titan, without any superheroes—a world where she and Jenna were the sole arbiters of justice—was a better, safer one. And Jenna believed it. She believed in the Code. Or the parts that suited her, anyway. Unfortunately you can't pick and choose which rules you live by."

I turned and glanced outside the office at the stone engraving on the wall.

"But you saved her, Drew. I know it doesn't seem like it now, but if you hadn't been there, I'm not sure what would have happened. You stopped her."

He means Jenna. Not the Fox. I think about the conversation we had on the bleachers, before she changed everything. In the end, wasn't it all right? Did it really matter how? Kyla's gone. The Jacks are locked away. The Supers were saved. There were no civilian casualties.

"So she was a hero," I said, trying my best to convince both of us.

"The end doesn't always justify the means, Drew. Somehow

or other, Jenna will have to face the consequences of *all* of her actions."

I thought about the Titan leading her away after our minute was over. For a week I'd wondered if I would ever see her again. I told Mr. Masters as much.

"That's actually why I wanted to talk to you," Mr. Masters said. "I'm going to Colton tomorrow. You should come along. Talk to her. You may not have another chance."

So it's Tuesday, and I'm missing school again, supposedly to go to a museum with Mr. Masters and the rest of our science class—at least that's the story. In actuality, we are taking his blue Chevy north to see about a girl. To be honest, I'm not sure my parents believed the whole museum thing anyway, though they did sign the permission slip. Something in the way my mother kept *looking* at me. Mr. Masters says the time will soon come when I'll just have to suck it up and tell them and hope they don't totally freak out and lock me in a closet. He says it's getting too hard to cover our tracks and that constantly lying to your parents isn't good for your karma. I told him I wanted to hold off a little longer. Maybe wait until I get straight As on my report card again, just to soften the blow. But I know he's right. You can only hide who you are for so long.

Colton Maximum Security Prison was completely repaired and refortified after the lone break-in in its forty-year history. A new fence has been added, along with two new watchtowers and an infrared tracking system with an electromagnetic pulse that shocks prisoners who are deemed potential escape threats, such as the three Jacks, who Mr. Masters is here to question. He wants to find out just how much they knew about Kyla Kaden, about her triple identity. If they ever suspected that they were being played, that the cards were stacked against them from the start. They weren't idiots—though you'd have a harder time making that case with the Jack of Spades—but there's a possibility they didn't realize their boss was also their nemesis until they were staring the Fox in the face.

Mr. Masters drops me off at the gate for the juvenile offenders building and says he will be back to pick me up. The guards check me for weapons—I left my belt at home for just that reason—and usher me through a set of steel doors to the visitation area, a large room encased in bullet-proof glass, with several scratched wooden tables and a water cooler. A single row of windows lines one wall, coated in a dingy gray film.

I don't have to see her to know she's there. Even without the Purple Passion. I recognize the pattern of her breathing the moment I walk in the door. The sound she makes when she clears her throat. From across the room she whispers to me.

"Don't look now, but your fly's unzipped."

Of course I look, and of course it's not. But it's good to know she hasn't lost her sense of humor.

I thank the guard and then walk to the back of the room, taking the seat across from her. All part of the code of conduct. I'm not allowed to sit beside her. I'm also not supposed to hug her or hand her anything. There are a dozen other rules, but I don't intend to break any of them. I'm only here to talk.

"Hey," she says.

She looks good in orange, the jumpsuit hanging on her loosely, as if they didn't quite have her size. In here, I can tell, she's just Jenna. Her hair's pulled back, the glasses perched on her nose. When she smiles, my heart hurts.

"Hey," I say back.

"You look . . . um . . . nice," she says. I look down at my jeans and my blue Highview sweatshirt and my holey shoes before I realize she's being sarcastic.

"Yeah, you too."

She looks terrific, as healthy as ever. Still, there's something a little off about her, vagueness in her eyes, as if she's in two places at once.

"So how's life at Highview?" she asks.

"Oh, well, you know. Same as always. Football team still hasn't won a game, and Ms. M. says we have to start reading *Dracula* this week. Oh, and Rebecca Matlin supposedly broke Jon Trotter's nose when she hit him with her backpack last week. Apparently he kissed Rachel Worton. He was gushing like a fountain."

I look at Jenna's nose. It's still slightly bruised around the bridge from where the Fox punched her. I can tell by the look on her face that she doesn't care about anything I'm saying.

"Nikki has a new boyfriend," I add. "Though between you and me, I think maybe she kind of likes Mike. Oh, and Mr. Masters started the program up again."

This grabs her interest a little. Her eyes brighten.

"They miss you," I say.

"So you haven't told them, then? What I did to you?"

I just sit and stare at her. I don't think she has the first clue about all the things she's done to me.

"I told them you saved me."

She laughs. "There's no rule in the Code about lying."

"It's not a lie," I say.

"It's not exactly the truth either," she counters. Behind us, one of the guards ushers in another visitor, who sits at the first table, waiting on someone—maybe her own son or daughter—to be brought in. I wonder how many people my age there are in this place. And whether any of them are really evil, or if they all just lost their way.

"What about you? Are you okay?" It's a stupid question. But she understands what I mean. She plays with a loose string on the edge of her sleeve, wrapping it around one finger, winding and unwinding. "It's just middle school with bars. A bunch of people telling you what you can and can't do," she says. "Though I don't imagine I'll be in here much longer. I've already been approached by some people in the government. They say they can grant me a deal to drop all charges, provided I come to work for them after high school." She leans back in her chair. "They'll ship me off somewhere, some kind of boarding school where they can keep an eye on me, but at least I'll be out of here."

I try to picture Jenna as a government agent, doing covert

ops, slipping past security to disable some nuclear weapon or eliminate some high-profile target or something. She'd be scarily good at it. Still, I'm a little surprised they'd take her. "Aren't there rules?" I say, but she knows what I mean.

"There's an awful lot of gray in the world, Drew," she says.

For some reason this ticks me off. "That's your excuse? There's a lot of gray in the world?" The guard by the door looks at me. I lower my voice.

"I didn't know you wanted an excuse," Jenna says softly, instantly defeated.

"It wouldn't hurt," I say.

"I don't know. I don't know what to tell you that you will understand. It's . . ."

"Complicated," I finish. "I know. Try me."

She turns and looks out the window. "She said we would make the world a better place. That when it was over, we would be unstoppable. The Fox and the Silver Lynx. We would restore the faith, become a power unto ourselves. No more failure. No more one-upmanship. No more epic battles between good and evil. No more lost fathers. No more sidekicks left hanging over the void. We would be above it all. Somehow beyond good and evil. No one would dare stop us once we got started. But we had to prove it. We had to show them."

"And the Titan? And the others?"

"The price we had to pay," Jenna says weakly, looking down at her hands in her lap. "She said we'd be doing the world a favor."

"She was lying," I say. "She was using you."

"Just like Mr. Masters was using you," she counters. "Shaping us all into what *he* thought the world needed in order to save it. That's the way it works, Drew."

"But we were never going to *kill* anyone."

"Neither was the Titan," Jenna says. She looks past me, at the glass all around us. Separating us from the rest of the world. When she turns back, her eyes are scrunched behind her glasses again. "Have you ever wanted to be normal, Drew?"

It's the same question as before. I give pretty much the same answer. "Yeah. Sometimes. Maybe."

"Not me," she says. "Not ever."

Then she reaches over and takes my hand. And in that instant I see her as she might have been five years ago. A confused, powerful, and impressionable little girl, who knows somehow she is special, that she is destined for great things. A little girl so determined to live up to expectations that she doesn't think about the cost.

The guard sees and takes a step toward us. I instinctively try to jerk my hand away, but Jenna flashes the guard a look, almost daring him to take another step. He's armed and backed by another dozen men, and she's only one teenage girl, but there is something in her eyes that freezes him in place. He stops and looks down at his shoes. Jenna turns back to me like nothing happened and smiles.

We sit there for an eternity, holding hands, not saying another word, until our time is finished and she lets go. Only then does the guard come to escort me out.

"Good-bye, Jenna," I say, standing and pushing my chair under the table, looking at her for what might be the last time. And I know I should tell her the thing I've wanted to tell her, the whole reason I even came here.

So I do.

I tell her.

"I forgive you," I say.

And then I turn to leave.

"Drew."

I turn back around. "What?"

"Be good," she tells me.

That night I agree to go bowling with the crew. It will be the first time Eric, Mike, Nikki, Gavin, and I have been together outside of school. Gavin is still a conceited jerk sometimes, and he still acts different when he's around his football buddies, but I have to admit that deep down beneath that hard outer shell of his, he's kind of cool. Besides, he didn't get the girl either, so I guess we have something else in common.

We're walking into the bowling alley, taking bets on whether or not Mike will short-circuit the electronic scoreboard, when I see a figure standing back in the shadows, just visible around the corner. I can smell him too, even now. That same smell that seeps through the cracks of the doors of all the bars he's spent the last few years in. They're inside him, all of those years, and I don't know if he will ever be rid of it, but at least he's fighting.

"Hey, you guys, go on ahead. I'll catch up."

Gavin peers around the corner and nods, then follows the others inside.

He's wearing the outfit. His outfit. Black boots. Torn jeans. Leather jacket. He hasn't shaved, though he has sculpted the mass of hair on his chin into a manageable beard of sorts. He is still wearing sunglasses, though the sun is almost beyond the horizon by now. I wonder if this means something, this outfit, or if he just doesn't have anything else to wear. I picture a closet full of torn jeans and leather jackets.

"Some excitement last week," he says. This is the first time we've had a chance to talk since the incident, just the two of us. Mr. Masters told me to give him some time, that he had a lot to take care of, but that he would come around eventually. I've heard that before too.

"It turned out all right," I say.

"How's your friend? You know, the cute blonde who set me up, knocked you out, and then ended up saving both of us?"

"She's Jenna," I say. "You didn't have to turn her in, you know. You lied about the Fox. You could have lied about her."

"I could have." The Titan sniffs. "Except Kyla Kaden paid for what she did. Jenna hasn't yet. Besides, the Fox was popular. If the OCs were to find out what really happened . . . People need heroes, Drew. Speaking of which," he continues, "I came to tell you that I'm not going to be around much longer."

I resist the urge to ask him how that would be different from before, though I do give him a look that says pretty much the same thing.

"Right. No. I get it. But this isn't like that. I'm retiring. Officially, this time. Red and I are heading west. Conquer the mountains. Do some fishing. I already spoke with Mr. Masters, and he's in the process of getting you reassigned. We both know whoever he finds will be a heap better than I ever was."

"I don't know," I say. "We did all right there at the end."

"You mean the part where I just dangled there next to you, or the part where I fell on top of you and trapped you underneath me?"

"I mean the part in the middle," I say. "When I was falling. And you caught me."

The Titan smiles. It may be the first time I've ever seen the man do that, even in all the photos and news footage, on the posters and trading cards and magazine covers.

"That's the other reason I'm here," he says sheepishly. "I thought I'd see if you wanted to, you know . . . go out with me, just one time."

I look at the Titan, all six feet five of him, hands stuffed in his pockets, nervously shuffling his feet. "The streets are kind of quiet, but we can probably find some robbers to rough up, rescue some old ladies. Maybe try to dig up some drug dealers or something. I figure I owe you that much, for all the other times. So what do you say?"

The Titan offers his hand, the same one that nearly crushed

mine the first time we met.

And I try to imagine myself out there, bounding from rooftop to rooftop, running down alleyways chasing hardened criminals, dodging bullets and leaping over trash bins, standing back-to-back with the Titan, barely up to his chin, confronting wave after wave of sword-swinging assassins or laser-blasting androids, trading quips and catchphrases as we kick and punch our way through the onslaught of evil. That's what the Sensationalist does.

I make a big production of digging in my pockets, coming up empty-handed, and snapping my fingers.

"Didn't bring my mask," I say.

The Titan smiles and nods. He understands. "All right, then. Good-bye, Drew."

"Good-bye, George."

And I watch as my hero walks back across the parking lot of Bob's Bowlarama before vanishing across the street. I'm fairly certain I will never see him again. I doubt anybody will. As he would be the first to tell you, there are plenty of others out there better able to do the job. Who knows, I might even be paired up with one of them someday. But for now, I really don't care. Because it's Tuesday, and I'm hungry, and Bob's has the best greasy breadsticks, absolutely dripping with butter, and my friends are all waiting for me inside.

And I'm feeling normal for a change.

Acknowledgments

Many thanks to all the super people who helped bring *Sidekicked* to the shelf. Thanks to my agent, Quinlan Lee, who works tirelessly on my behalf so I can laze around at home and make believe. Thanks to Debbie Kovacs and Kellie Celia at Walden Pond Press and Renée Cafiero and Amy Ryan at HarperCollins for their tireless efforts and extraordinary publishing, editing, and design powers. Also thanks to Shannon Tindle, who captured Drew's geeky courage on the cover. A big huzzah goes out to my editor, Jordan Brown, who bought me candy, helped build the world beneath Drew's feet, and taught me that "supervillains are people too." Finally, thanks to my own sidekick, my wife Alithea, who *also* works tirelessly so I can laze around at home and make believe. You're all my heroes.

**Turn the page to read
the first chapter of
John David Anderson's
companion book**

MY HERO

When I was twelve years old, give or take, my father strapped a bomb to my chest and drove me to the First National Bank and Trust so we could steal $27,500. I know what you're thinking: if you're going to go through all the trouble of rigging your son with explosives and send him to rob a bank, you should set loftier goals, but my father has a policy that he only steals what he needs at the time, and at the time he needed $27,500 to finish one of his projects and to buy groceries. We were out of frozen waffles.

Dad parked outside the BP across the street to distract himself by playing Angry Birds and eating cashews while I walked through the bulletproof doors of the gray-bricked building. Me, a pale, wispy-banged preteen, green eyed and skinny, wearing a dark-brown overcoat and an impertinent expression, walking into a bank all by myself. There was no guard at the door, but there were plenty of little black globes hanging from the ceiling. Security cameras. My heart caught in my throat, but I forced it down—Dad had told me not to worry about the cameras. They were taken care of. He had my back.

I approached the first teller—a young woman in a navy blazer with her hair pulled into a stern bun and too much makeup masking a potentially pretty face—and opened my jacket, showing her the bomb. I could tell she was impressed by her platter-sized eyes and the choked-down, quietly-pee-your-pants scream, which came out all muffled, like a dog's squeak toy under a couch cushion. I gave her the speech. The one I had recited at least a dozen times the night before and three more on the way over while finishing off a bag of Skittles for breakfast.

"There's a horrible man outside," I said, nodding back toward the glass. "You can't see him, but he can see you, and he says if you don't fill this"—produce Transformers back-pack, old-school cartoon, not those overstuffed Michael Bay movies—"with twenty-seven thousand five hundred dollars, he will hit the detonator and you and me will both be car-ried out of here in Ziploc bags." It was a speech prepared by my father, at least most of it. I added the Ziploc bags part myself.

And it probably would have worked. The bomb. The speech. The Ziploc line. It *would* have, if I had even tried, if I had bothered to get into character. Someone in my posi-tion, a kid picked up off the street, three pounds of explosives taped under his chin, a juvenile IED about to commit his first felony—you'd expect I'd be snot faced and crying, shaking uncontrollably, begging the woman to hurry or to call the police. But I just couldn't make myself do it. I came off flat, I'm sure, as if I couldn't care less.

As if I wasn't worried at all.

Don't get me wrong. I was. A little. I just knew more than I was letting on.

I glanced at the teller standing next to her. A man, mid-forties. Receding hair. Pencil lips. Probably his second job. Or third. Formerly an accountant, or a used-car salesman. I felt sorry for him. Maybe he liked the girl with the bun. Maybe he would try to impress her by leaping over his teller station and tackling me. Maybe he'd always wanted to be a hero when he grew up.

Understandable. But there aren't any heroes left in New Liberty, and I'm pretty sure if Captain Bald Spot had super-powers, he wouldn't be here cashing checks and wearing that stupid-looking paisley tie.

I watched him twitch, his wrinkle-wreathed eyes darting back and forth from me to another man—the bank manager, I figured, a much younger guy, skinny like me and better dressed, cluelessly staring at his computer across the room.

This wasn't going as well as I had hoped.

I turned back to the young woman and whispered, "The bad man outside told me that I only have three minutes."

Actually the last thing my father had *really* said to me was to

3

watch for traffic. "Look both ways." Because *that's* what you worry about when you are going to rob a bank. Still, it's nice that he worries.

The teller blinked at me. Maybe she was in shock. Or maybe somehow she realized that the explosives sitting above my heart were just Lincoln Logs rolled in Reynolds Wrap, with wires and a pulsing LED light attached with electrical tape. Either way, she wasn't moving. The bag sat empty on the counter between us. The accountant/car salesman/bank teller next to her made a little move, a twitch of the arm, no doubt reaching under the counter and triggering the silent alarm.

Now I really did only have three minutes.

"Listen, lady," I said, pushing the bag a little closer to her. "It's okay. No one is going to blame you. You aren't going to get fired over this. Insurance will cover it. And even if not, this job isn't worth it, am I right? You don't really even want to be a bank teller for the rest of your life anyway, and you certainly don't want to explode. So just toss the money in the sack, and I'll go."

I said it in the same even tone I said everything else, except this time I looked square into her eyes, tractor-beam style. Locked on. Sucked in. She looked back into mine, and I saw the little black dots of her pupils blow up big and glassy like a stuffed bear's.

This time I had her. It was a last resort, but I knew when I walked in there that I might have to use the gift God gave me. The bank teller nodded and then knelt down to access the safe

4

under her cash drawer, taking the bag with her.

"You're not going to say anything, are you?" I asked Captain Chrome Dome, giving him the same penetrating stare. It took a moment longer, but eventually he went all glassy-eyed too, and shook his head.

"Come to think of it, you won't really even remember what I look like," I added coolly.

The man put his finger to his lips. Mum's the word. The woman in the blue blazer handed me my bag and smiled too. I zipped it up and slung it over my shoulder.

"You shouldn't wear so much mascara," I said. "Your eyes are pretty enough."

Fifteen seconds later I left the bank with my backpack full of cash and crossed the street to the gas station where our little white Civic was parked, taking care to look both ways. Dad was hunched over his tablet.

"We should go," I said, buckling in.

"Almost finished," he said. His tongue stuck out of his mouth like a curious turtle, and his big orange caterpillar eyebrows were crowding the bridge of his nose. There were cashew crumbles down the front of his Hawaiian shirt. My dad had never been to Hawaii, but he found the shirts cheap at the Goodwill and had a closet full of them. Wore one each day. His green eyes dashed across the screen.

"Seriously, I think it's time to go," I said a little more sternly.

"I've almost got it," he mumbled. I could hear the sirens now. Several blocks away still, but it's not as if we were driving a Lamborghini. The Civic was eight years old and ran mostly on good intentions. It was our only getaway car. I drummed my fingers impatiently on the dash. I could have tried to make eye contact, insisted that we go. But I had a rule against using my power on my own father. Instead I hummed.

"*There* it is!" he said triumphantly. "Take that, you lousy pigs! Hah!" He thrust a fist in the air and then turned the screen so I could see he had three-starred another level.

"I'm proud of you," I said. "Now can we please get a move on?"

"Sure," he said. He started the car and pulled slowly out into the street, headed away from the bank. Away from the sirens. Away from at least thirty years in prison for him and several years of juvie for me, and that was being generous given the things we'd done.

He also pressed a button on a little black box about five inches square that had been sitting in one of the drink holders between us. I instinctively held my breath.

Like all my father's little black boxes, this one had three buttons. Green, white, and red. Green to activate, white to deactivate, and red . . . you never press the red one—I learned that the hard way. Also like all his little black boxes, it had a sticky label telling you what it did. This one was called the Scrambler, and if it worked, it meant Dad had just fried every security camera in a three-block radius. There would be no footage of me entering or leaving the bank. No trace of our white Honda sitting in the gas station. Only the bank employees would be able to offer the cops a lead, and I was confident they wouldn't remember much. The box vibrated a little and then went dead. Exhale.

As we pulled away, I glanced out my window and up at the sky. I'm not sure what I expected to see. A helicopter maybe. Some schmuck in cape and tights. But the sky was crystal blue and beautiful and as empty as the pretty bank teller's safe.

"How'd it go?" Dad asked as we merged onto the interstate.

"Exactly as planned," I said, finally removing the fake explosives from my chest and tossing them in the backseat next to the backpack full of cash. He could have made a real bomb, of course, but we both knew it was only a prop. The hope was for me not to have to use my powers, but if I did, the wires and blinking lights would add to my natural charm, make me even more persuasive. "You should have seen the look on her face when I opened the jacket. She was seriously freaked."

Dad reached over and ruffled my hair. It was a habit, and I didn't have the heart to tell him that it was kind of annoying.

"See?" he said. "People will believe just about anything."

Yes, I thought to myself. They certainly will.